P9-BYK-010

Dear Reader,

Silhouette Books means love stories that touch the heart...but people don't live by romance alone. There's more than just love between a man and a woman throughout our lives. We share love with a complex group of friends and family and explore the many facets that each relationship has to offer us.

We asked reader favorites Diana Palmer, Debbie Macomber and Judith Duncan to write stories celebrating motherhood for this year's *to Mother with Love*. Each award-winning author has come up with her unique vision of what being a mother can mean. A boy, a dog, an apartment, a calamity–all are part of this year's collection.

To everyone who has ever had a mother, we wish you–and her–the very best this Mother's Day.

Enjoy!

Isabel Swift
Editorial Director
Silhouette Books

Mother to with Love '93

Diana Palmer
Debbie Macomber
Judith Duncan

Silhouette® Books

Published by Silhouette Books New York
America's Publisher of Contemporary Romance

If you purchased this book without a cover you should be aware that this book is stolen property. It was reported as "unsold and destroyed" to the publisher, and neither the author nor the publisher has received any payment for this "stripped book."

SILHOUETTE BOOKS
300 East 42nd St., New York, N.Y. 10017

to Mother with Love '93
Copyright © 1993 by Harlequin Enterprises Limited

All rights reserved. Except for use in any review, the reproduction or utilization of this work in whole or in part in any form by any electronic, mechanical or other means, now known or hereafter invented, including xerography, photocopying and recording, or in any information storage or retrieval system, is forbidden without the permission of the publisher, Silhouette Books, 300 E. 42nd St. New York, N.Y. 10017

ISBN 0-373-48254-X

Calamity Mom
Copyright © 1993 by Diana Palmer

The Apartment
Copyright © 1993 by Debbie Macomber

A Special Request
Copyright © 1993 by Judith Mulholland

All the characters in this book have no existence outside the imagination of the author and have no relation whatsoever to anyone bearing the same name or names. They are not even distantly inspired by any individual known or unknown to the author, and all incidents are pure invention.

® and ™ are trademarks used under license. Trademarks indicated with ® are registered in the United States Patent and Trademark Office, the Canadian Trade Marks office and in other countries.

Printed in U.S.A.

Contents

Calamity Mom

DIANA PALMER

A Note from Diana Palmer

When they told me the rabbit had died, all I could think to say was that I didn't have a rabbit in the first place, and were they sure they had the right number? I was thirty-four years old, a full-time newspaper reporter and after eight years of marriage I had no idea that we would ever be blessed with children. What a surprise!

I wasn't the only shocked person. James also mentioned that we didn't have a rabbit and our budget was so small that how could we afford to feed one, anyway? He even smiled. Then it hit him, and we both felt fascination and delight mingle with stark terror as we wondered and worried: 1) How would we stretch our meager budget to include a small naked hungry person? 2) How would we manage to take care of a baby without instruction booklets or self-help guides? and 3) My most important worry, how would I get to the hospital in case of emergency, because at that time James couldn't drive a car!

Number 3 turned out to be the easiest one. I went into labor while covering a fire at a local filling station. After I did the interview–between labor pains–I filed my copy and drove myself to the hospital. Forty-eight grueling hours later, they did a C-section and Blayne Edward joined our family the day before Independance Day. James and I decided that #1 and #2 concerns were also solvable. If Blayne could learn to be a baby, then we could learn to be parents. And our budget didn't have to stretch too far to feed such a small stomach.

Those were magical days. We watched Blayne instead of TV, and it was the happiest time of our marriage.

There were interesting little incidents, too. One still makes me grin. Blayne was two and very imitative. I was watching TV while he stood behind the huge coffee table on which I was sitting with my eternal fresh cup of coffee. The man on TV was dunking a doughnut in *his* coffee. I heard a splash and a giggle and turned around. There stood my son, dunking his dirty little sock in my full coffee cup and laughing! (Note to Blayne: thank your lucky stars, boy, that I didn't tell them the *other* story!)

Diana Palmer

Chapter One

The beach was crowded. A group of college students on spring break were gathered around a ghetto blaster, happily unaware of the vicious looks they were getting from older sunbathers.

"Turn it down," Shelly Astor suggested, grinning as she nodded toward two glowering faces behind them on the beach. "You're creating enemies for us."

"Don't be a wet blanket," the boy chided. "We're young, it's spring break, no more biology and English and algebra for a solid, sweet week!"

"Yeah, right," another student muttered. "I might as well drown myself. I flunked my first exam in prealgebra!"

"Less fun, more pencil-to-paper contact," another suggested.

"Right, Mr. Egghead," came the reply and a glare. "Edwin here blew the curve in biology 101," he added, jerking his thumb at the tall, thin, redheaded boy. "He made 100."

"Dr. Flannery says I'm the best student he's ever had. Can I help it if I'm brilliant?" Edwin sighed.

"You're not brilliant in trig," Pete murmured to him, then said to the others, "I had to tutor him or he'd never have passed Bragg's exam."

"Can't you turn that damned thing down?" An exasperated bellow broke the silence.

"Have a heart, man!" Pete wailed, facing his attacker. "We just survived eight weeks of hell, not to mention trigonometry!"

"And one of us failed it!" Edwin yelled, pointing at Mark.

"We're all on the cutting edge here," Pete agreed, shaking his head. "If we don't get a music fix, God only knows what we might do to the world at large!"

The irate man began to laugh and threw up his hands. He made a dismissive gesture and lay back, closing his eyes in defeat.

Shelly grinned at her friends. "Pete's a sociology major," she whispered to Nan, who was her best friend. "Minoring in psych. Isn't he great?"

"A true credit to his alma mater," Nan agreed. She got up and went to dive into the surf, with Shelly at her side.

"Isn't it wonderful here?" Nan sighed. "And you weren't going to come!"

"I had to fight to get to go to college, much less come to Florida with the group for spring break," Shelly said quietly. She pushed back her windblown blond hair, and her soft blue eyes echoed the smile on her full lips. "My parents wanted me to go to finishing school and then join the young women's social club back home in Washington, D.C. Can you imagine?"

"You haven't told them that you want to become a caseworker for family and children's services, I guess?" Nan fished.

"My father would have a nervous breakdown," she mused. "They're sweet people, my parents, but they want to give me a life of luxury and serenity. I want to change the world." She glanced at dark-eyed Nan with a mischievous smile. "They think I'm demented. They have a nice husband picked out for me: Ivy League school, old family name, plenty of money." She shrugged her slender shoulders. "That's not what I want at all, but they won't take no for an answer. I had to threaten to get a job and go on the work/study program to get my father to pay my tuition."

"I wonder if all parents want to live through their children?" Nan asked. "Honestly my mother has pushed me toward nursing school since I was in grammar school, just because she got married and couldn't finish nurses' training. I get sick at the sight of blood, for Pete's sake!"

"Did someone mention my name?" Pete asked, surfacing beside them with a grin.

Nan sent a spray of water at him with a sweep of her palm, and all the serious discussions were drenched in horseplay.

But later, when they went to the motel to change before supper, Shelly couldn't help wondering if she was ungrateful. Her father, a wealthy investment counselor, had given her every advantage during her youth. Her mother was a socialite and her brother was an eminent scientist. She had an impeccable background. But she had no desire to drift from luncheon to cocktail party, or even to do superficial charity work. She wanted to help people in trouble. She wanted to see the world as it was, out of her protected environment. Her parents couldn't, or wouldn't, understand that she had to feel useful, to know that her life had a purpose of some sort beyond learning the correct social graces.

She enjoyed school. She attended Thorn College, a small community college in Washington, D.C., where she was just one of the student body and accepted without hassle, despite her background. It was the kind of atmosphere that was friendly and warm without being invasive. She loved it.

Living off campus did limit some of her participation in social activities, but she didn't mind that. She'd always thought in her own mind that she was rather a cold woman—at least where men were concerned. She dated, and boys kissed her from time to time, but she felt nothing beyond surface pleasure at the contact of warm lips on her own. She had no desire to risk her life for the sake of curiosity, experimentation or for fear of ridicule. She was strong enough not to flinch at the condescending remarks from one of the more permissive girls. Someday, she thought, she would be glad that she hadn't followed the crowd. She stared at her reflection and smiled. "You-stick-in-the-mud," she told herself.

There was a quick knock on the door followed by Nan's entrance. "Aren't you ready *yet?*" she grumbled. She glared at Shelly's very conservative voile dress, yellow on black, with sandals and her long hair in a French braid. "You're not going like that?" she added, groaning. "Don't you have any idea what the current style is?"

"Sure. Spandex skirts or tights and funny smock blouses. But they're not me. This is."

"Wouldn't catch me dead in that." Nan sighed. Her curly hair sported a yellow-and-white bow, and her white tights were topped off by a multicolored short dress.

"You look super," Shelly said approvingly.

Nan struck a pose. "Call *Ebony* magazine and tell them I'm available for covers." She chuckled.

"You could do covers," came the serious reply. Nan really was lovely. Her skin had a soft café au lait demureness. Combined with her liquid black eyes and jet black hair and elegant facial structure, she would have been a knockout on the cover of any magazine. She looked like an Egyptian wall painting. "I've seen gorgeous movie stars who were uglier than you are," she added.

Nan chuckled. "You devil, you."

"I'm not kidding. Why haven't you ever thought of modeling?"

Nan shrugged. "I have a good brain," she said simply. "I don't want it to get lost in the shuffle. I'm going to be an archaeologist."

Shelly groaned. "Don't remind me that I have two more exams to go in introductory anthropology or I'll scream!"

"I'll coach you. You'll do fine."

"I won't! I barely passed biology! We've still got fossil forms of man and kinship systems and subsistence patterns to go...!"

"Piece of cake." Nan dismissed it. "Besides, you got Dr. Tabitha Harvey, and she's the best. Oops, I mean Dr. Tabitha Reed. Can you imagine her getting married? And to such a dish!" She shook her head. "But to get back to the subject, don't you realize that anthropology is *part* of sociology? How can you understand the way we are as a culture today without understanding how we came to be a culture in the first place?"

"Here you go again."

"I love it. You would, too, if you'd let yourself. I've taken every anthropology course Thorn College offers. I loved them all!"

"This stuff is hard."

"Life," Nan reminded her, "is hard. You can't appreciate a good grade in anthropology until you've had to dig for it." She looked surprised. "I made a funny!"

"On that note, we're leaving," Shelly murmured, dragging her friend out the door.

They had supper in the same restaurant each night. It was their one extravagance, and mainly because Nan had a crush on one of the other diners, a student from Kenya whom she'd met on the beach.

Shelly looked forward to the evening ritual because of another patron who frequented the restaurant. She ran into him everywhere, accidentally. He nodded politely and never stopped to talk, but she watched him with open fascination, to the amusement of her friends. In fact, her fascination was a ruse to keep her friends from trying to pair her off with Pete. She liked Pete, but her attitudes weren't casual enough to suit him. By pretending infatuation for a stranger, she elicited not only sympathy for her unrequited love, but also avoided well-meaning matchmakers among the group she'd accompanied on spring break.

Her unwilling object of affection was beginning to notice, and be irritated by her, though. It had become a challenge to see how far she could push him before he exploded. The thought was oddly exciting for a woman who almost never took chances. In fact, in all her twenty-four years, he was the first man she'd ever pursued, even in fun. It was unlike her, but he wouldn't know that. Her flirting seemed to disturb and irritate him.

To complicate matters, he had a son, about twelve or so, and the son spent considerable time staring at Shelly. She was afraid he was developing a crush on her and she worried about trying to head it off while keeping up her facade of being infatuated with his father. Showing up here for dinner every night wasn't helping her situation, even if it did seem to be doing

wonders for Nan's social life and give Shelly the opportunity to stare longingly at the man she'd singled
out for public adoration.

As if she'd conjured him up in her thoughts, a
movement caught Shelly's eye, and she saw him. He
was tall and elegant, a striking man somewhere in his
middle or late thirties with thick dark hair and pale
silvery eyes. He had his son with him. The boy was a
younger and much more amiable version of him.
Shelly found herself wondering what the man did for
a living. He was very handsome, but he didn't look the
male-model type. He was probably someone who
carried a gun, she thought. Maybe a secret agent, or a
hired assassin. That thought amused her and she
smiled mischievously. Before she could erase the smile,
the man turned his head and saw it, and his glare was
thunderous.

How could someone that handsome look so vicious and unfriendly? she wondered vaguely. And
those silver eyes looked like cold steel in his unsmiling
face. An ugly man might have an excuse for that black
scowl, but this man looked like every hero she'd ever
dreamed of. She put her chin in her hands and stared
at him with a wistful smile. She was always so friendly
that it was hard to accept that anyone could hate her
on sight for no reason.

He looked taken aback by her refusal to be intimidated. But even if the scowl fell away, he didn't smile
back. He turned his attention to a movement of white
silk beside the table and abruptly stood up to seat a

thin brunette. The boy with him glowered and made some reluctant remark, which prompted an angry look from his father. Undercurrents, Shelly thought, and began to analyze them. She felt a wave of sadness. She'd overheard a tidbit of gossip about him in the restaurant the night before—that he was a widower. She'd known that a man so handsome would have women hanging from both arms, but she had hoped he was unattached. It was her fate to be forever getting interested in the wrong man. She sighed wistfully.

"Stop staring at him," Nan chided, hitting her forearm with her napkin as she put it into her lap. "He'll get conceited."

"Sorry. He fascinates me. Isn't he dreamy?"

"He's years too old for you," Nan said firmly. "And that's probably his fiancée. They suit each other. He has a half-grown son, and you are a lowly college student, age notwithstanding. In point of fact, you are barely higher on the food chain than a bottom feeder, since you aren't even a sophomore yet."

"I'll be a sophomore after summer semester."

"Picky, picky. Eat your salad."

"Yes, Mama," she muttered, glaring at the younger woman, who only grinned.

The next day it seemed to Shelly that providence was determined to throw her into the path of trouble. She always got up early in the mornings, before Nan stirred, and went down to the beach to enjoy the brief solitude at the ocean before the tourists obliterated the beach completely. She threw on her one-piece yellow bathing suit with a patterned chiffon shirt over it and laced up her sandals. For once she left her blond hair loose down her back. She liked the feel of the breeze in it.

This morning, she didn't find the beach empty. A lone figure stood looking seaward. He was tall, and had thick black hair. He was wearing white shorts that left his powerful, darkly tanned legs bare and a blue-and-white checked shirt, open over a broad, hair-roughened chest. He was watching the ocean with eyes that didn't seem to see it, a deep scowl carved into his handsome face.

Shelly gave him a wistful glance and took off down the beach in the opposite direction. She didn't want to infringe on his privacy. Since he was obviously attached, it would do her no good to go on mooning over him, for appearances or not. She was giving him up, she thought nobly, for his own good. That being settled, she strolled aimlessly down the beach, drinking in the sea air.

The stillness was seductive. The only sounds to be heard were the cries of the sea gulls and the watery growl of the ocean. Surf curled in foamy patterns up onto the damp beach, and tiny white sand crabs went scurrying for cover. They amused her and she laughed, a soft, breathy sound that seemed to carry.

"What can you find to laugh about at this hour of the morning?" came a rough, half-irritated deep voice from over her shoulder. "The damned coffee shop isn't even open yet. How do they expect people to survive daybreak without a dose of caffeine?"

With the vestiges of her amusement at the crabs still on her face, Shelly turned. And there he was, as handsome as a dark angel, his hands deep in the pockets of his white shorts.

He was devastating enough at long range. Close, like this, he was dynamite. She could hardly get her breath at all. Some sensual aroma exuded from him, like spice. He smelled and looked clean and fastidious, and she had to force herself not to stare at the physical perfection of his body. Hollywood would have loved him.

"I like coffee, too," she murmured shyly. She smiled at him, pushing back her pale, windblown hair. "But the sea air is almost as good."

"What were you laughing at?" he persisted.

"Them." She turned back to the crabs, one of which was busily digging himself a hole. He dived into it like a madman. "Don't they remind you of people running for trains in the subway?" She glanced at him wickedly. "And people who can't get their coffee early enough to suit them?"

He smiled unexpectedly, and her heart fell at his feet. She'd never seen anything so appealing as that handsome face with its chiseled mouth tugged up and those gray eyes that took on the sheen of mercury.

"Are your friends still in bed?"

She nodded. "Most of us have eight o'clock classes during the semester, so there isn't much opportunity to sleep late. Even if it's just for a week, this is a nice change."

She started walking again and he fell into step beside her. He was very tall. The top of her head came just to his shoulder.

"What's your major?" he asked.

"Sociology," she said. She flushed a little. "Sorry I was staring at you last night. I tend to carry people-watching to extremes," she said to excuse her blatant flirting.

He glanced at her cynically, and he didn't smile. "My son finds you fascinating."

"Yes," she said. "I'm afraid so."

"He's almost thirteen and a late bloomer. He hasn't paid much attention to girls until now."

She laughed. "I'm a bit old to be called a girl."

"You're still in college, aren't you?" he mused, obviously mistaking her for someone not much older than his son.

"Well, yes, I suppose I am." She didn't add that she'd only started last year, at the age of twenty-three. She'd always looked young for her age, and it was fun to pretend that she was still a teen. She stopped to pick up a seashell and study it. "I love shells. Nan chides me for it, but you should try to walk across tilled soil with her. She's down on her hands and knees at the first opportunity, wherever she sees disturbed dirt. Once she actually climbed down into a hole where men were digging out a water line! I'm glad they had a sense of humor."

"She's an archaeology student?"

"Other people are merely archaeology students—Nan is a *certifiable* archaeology student!"

He laughed. "Well, that's dedication, I suppose."

She stared out at the ocean. "They say there are probably Paleo-Indian sites out there." She nodded. "Buried when ocean levels rose with the melting of the glaciers in the late Pleistocene."

"I thought your friend was the archaeology student."

"When you spend a lot of time with them, it rubs off," she apologized. "I know more than I want to about fluted points and ancient stone tools."

"I can't say I've ever been exposed to that sort of prehistory. I majored in business and minored in economics."

She glanced up at him. "You're in business, then?"

He nodded. "I'm a banker."

"Does your son want to follow in your footsteps?"

His firm lips tugged down. "He does not. He thinks business is responsible for all the ecological upheaval on the planet. He wants to be an artist."

"You must be proud of him."

"Proud? I graduated from the Harvard school of business," he said, glaring at her. "What's good enough for me is good enough for him. He's being enrolled in a private school with R.O.T.C. When he graduates, he'll go to Harvard, as I did, and my father did.''

She stopped. Here was someone else trying to live his child's life. "Shouldn't that be his decision?" she asked curiously.

He didn't bat an eyelash. "Aren't you young to question your elders?" he taunted.

"Listen, just because you've got a few years on me...!"

"More than fifteen, by the look of you."

She studied his face closely. It had some deep lines, and not many of them were around the corners of his eyes. He wasn't a smiling man. But perhaps he wasn't quite as young as she'd suspected, either. Then she realized that he was counting from what he thought her age was.

"I'm thirty-four. But that still makes me an old man compared to you," he murmured. "You don't look much older than Ben."

Her heart leaped. He was closer to her age than she'd realized, and much closer than he knew. "You seem very mature."

"Do I?" His eyes glittered as he studied her. "You're a beauty," he said unexpectedly, his silver gaze lingering on her flawless complexion and big pale blue eyes and wavy, long blond hair. "I was attracted to you the first time I saw you. But," he added with world-weary cynicism, "I was tired of buying sex with expensive gifts."

She felt her face go hot. He had entirely the wrong idea. "I'm . . ." she began, wanting to explain.

He held up a lean hand. "I'm still tired of it," he said. He studied her without smiling, and the look he gave her made her knees go weak, despite its faint arrogance. "Do your parents know that you're making blatant passes at total strangers? Do you really think they'd approve of your behavior?"

She almost gasped. "What my parents think is none of your business!"

"It certainly is, when I'm the man you're trying to seduce." He glared at her. "So let me set you straight. I don't take college girls to bed, and I don't appreciate being stalked by one. Play with children your own age from now on."

His statement left her blustering. "My goodness, just because I smiled at you a time or two . . . !"

"You did more than smile. You positively leered," he corrected.

"Will you stop saying that?" she cried. "For heaven's sake, I was only looking at you! And even if I was after that kind of . . . of thing, why would I pick a man with a son? Some father you are! Does he know that his father wanders all over the beach accusing people of propositioning him? And you must be attached—"

He was oddly watchful, not at all angry. He was studying her face with keen, faintly amused interest. "My, my, and you're not even redheaded," he murmured, watching the color come and go on that exquisite complexion. "My son is too smitten with you to consider my place in your thoughts, and I don't have a wife. She died some years ago. I do have a fiancée—almost," he added half under his breath.

"The poor woman!"

"She's quite well-to-do, in fact," he said, deliberately misunderstanding her. "So am I. Another reason to avoid college students, who are notoriously without means."

She wanted to tell him what her means were, but she was too angry to get the words out. She flushed furiously at being misjudged and insulted. She decided then and there not to tell him about her background. He'd have to get to know her for herself, not her "means."

"Thinking up appropriate replies?" he asked helpfully. "Something along the lines of feeding me to the sharks?"

"They'd have to draw straws so the loser could eat you!" she blurted out.

She turned and set off back down the beach, hot all over from her surge of fury.

She ran along the beach in her haste to get away from him. She'd been playing mind games with herself. She hadn't realized that he mistook her rapt regard for serious flirting. She'd certainly be more careful in future to keep her fantasies to herself! Never again would she so much as glance at that man!

It was a pity she didn't look back. He was standing where she left him with a peculiarly predatory look in his pale eyes, and he was laughing.

Shelly and Nan stuck to the beach and the shops for the rest of the day, and that evening she persuaded Nan to go to a fast-food joint with some of the other students instead of the restaurant. She didn't dare tell anyone why, or confess the result of her stupid behavior. If Nan suspected, she was kind enough not to say anything.

Two good things had come out of the experience, Shelly thought as she now walked by herself along the beach. It had been two days since she'd run into the man. She'd managed to avoid the worshipful glances of Mr. Sexy's son, and she'd learned a painful lesson about obvious flirting. He was a banker. Wasn't he supposed to be dignified and faintly reticent and withdrawn? Her father was an investment counselor, and he was like that. Of course, he had inherited wealth, too, and that made him faintly arrogant. Mr. Sexy almost cornered the market on arrogance, of course, and conceit. She had to add conceit to the list, since he thought she couldn't wait to jump into bed with him!

I might have known, she told herself, *that no man could be that perfect to look at without having a few buried ugly flaws. Conceit, stupidity, arrogance...*

As she thought, she walked. There was a long pier that ran down from the hotel, and usually at the end of it were fishermen. But this particular day the pier was deserted. A sound was coming from it. A series of sharp cries.

Curious, Shelly walked onto it and started out toward the bay. The sounds grew louder. As she quickened her pace to reach the end of the pier, she heard splashing.

She stopped and peered over the edge.

"Help!" a young voice sputtered, and long, thin arms splashed for dear life. She knew that voice, and that face. It was the teenage son of Mr. Sexy, the one she'd been dodging for two days. Talk about fate!

She didn't stop to think. She tugged off her sandals and dived in after him, shoes, cutoffs, sleeveless white blouse and all. She'd taken a Red Cross lifesaving course and she knew what to do.

"Don't panic," she cautioned as she got behind him and caught him under the chin to protect herself. Drowning swimmers very often pulled their rescuers down with them, causing two deaths instead of one. "Stop flailing around and listen to me!" she said, moving her legs to keep afloat. "That's better. I'm going to tow you to shore. Try to relax. Let your body relax."

"I'll drown!" came the choking reply.

"No, you won't. Trust me."

There was a pause and a very exaggerated bout of breathing. "Okay."

"Good fellow. Here we go."

She struck out for shore, carrying the victim she'd appropriated along with her.

It wasn't that far to shore, but she was out of practice towing another person. By the time they reached shallow water, she was panting for breath along with the boy.

They flopped onto the beach and he coughed up water for several seconds.

"I thought I was a goner." He choked. "If you hadn't come along, I'd have drowned!" He looked at her and then grinned. "I'm sure you've heard the old axiom about saving a life."

She frowned. Her brain wasn't working. "What axiom?"

His grin grew even wider. "Why, that when you save a life, you're responsible for it as long as you live!" He threw his arms wide. "I'm yours!"

Chapter Two

"Thanks," she said. "But you can have your life back."

"Sorry, it doesn't work that way. You're stuck with me. Where are we going to live?"

She knew her expression was as perplexed as her thoughts. "Look, you're a nice boy..."

"I'm twelve and a half," he said. "I have all my own teeth, I'm in good health, I can do dishes and make beds. I don't mind cooking occasionally. You can trust me to feed and water whatever pets you possess," he concluded. "Oh, and I'm an Eagle Scout." He raised three fingers.

She glared at him. "Two fingers, not three fingers! Three fingers mean you're a Girl Scout!"

He snapped his fingers. "Darn." He looked at her. "Does that mean I have to give back the green dress?"

She burst into laughter. After the shock of seeing him almost drown, and the strain of rescue, her sense of humor came back in full force. She fell back onto the beach and laughed until her stomach hurt.

"I can't stand it," she choked.

He grinned down at her. "Great. Let's go and feed me. I do eat a lot, but I can get a part-time job to help out with groceries."

"Your father is not going to give you to me," she told him somberly, and flushed when she remembered what his father had said to her two days ago, and what she'd said back. She'd been lucky, because she'd managed to avoid him ever since.

"Why not? He doesn't want me. He's trying to give me to a school with an R.O.T.C. and after I get out of there, he's going to sell my soul to Harvard."

"Don't knock college fees," she told him firmly. "I've had to fight every step of the way for mine."

"Yeah, Dad and I saw you with the other college students," he agreed. "Dad was right. You really *are* pretty," he added critically, watching her look of surprise. "Do you like chess and can you play computer games? Oh, you have to like dogs, because I've got one."

She looked around to make sure he was talking to her.

"Well?" he persisted.

"I can play chess," she said. "I like cats, but my dad has two golden retrievers and I get along with them. I don't know about computer games . . ."

"That's okay. I can teach you."

"What am I auditioning for?"

"My mother, of course," he said. "Dad's business partner has this daughter, and she's done everything but move in with us trying to get Dad to marry her! She looks like two-day-old whitefish, she eats carrot sticks and health food and she takes aerobics. She hates me," he added curtly. "She's the one who thinks I belong in a school—a faraway school."

"And you don't want to go."

"I hate guns and stuff," he said heavily. They were both beginning to dry out in the sun. His hair was dark brown, a little lighter than his father's. He had those same silver-gray eyes.

"I know what you mean. My parents didn't want me to go to college." She leaned toward him. "My dad's an investment counselor. All he knows are numbers and accounting."

"Sounds just like my dad." He scowled. "Listen, you won't hold that against him? I mean, he's real handsome and he has good manners. He's a little bad-tempered," he confessed, "and he leaves his clothes laying all over the bedroom so that Jennie—she's our maid—fusses. But he's got a kind heart."

"That makes up for a lot," she said, thinking privately that his father hadn't been particularly kind to her.

"He likes animals, too."

"You're very nice to offer me your life, and your father, to boot," she said pleasantly, "but I've got at least three more years of college to go, and I can't think about a family for a long time. I want to be a social worker."

"My dad's real social," he remarked. "You can work on him."

"God forbid," she said under her breath.

"He'll grow on you," he persisted. "He's rich."

She knew about being rich. She came from old money herself. His father seemed to think that she was after his. That was almost laughable.

"Money can't buy a lot of things," she reminded him.

"Name three."

"Love. Happiness. Peace of mind."

He threw up his hands. "I give up!"

"Try to give up swimming alone," she advised. "It's dangerous."

"Actually," he confessed, "I didn't just jump in on purpose as much as I tripped over a bucket and fell in. But I would have been just as dead."

"Indeed you would. Keep your mind on what you are doing," she admonished.

He saluted her. "Roger, wilco."

"You might like R.O.T.C.," she said.

He shrugged. "I like to paint birds."

"Oh, boy."

"See what I mean? My dad hunts ducks. He wants me to. I hate it!"

This boy had a real problem. She didn't know what to tell him. His father was obviously rock-headed and intractable.

"Have you been without your mother for a long time?" she asked gently.

"All my life. She died just after I was born. Dad and I get along all right, but we aren't close. He spends so much time at work, and out of the country on business, that I almost never see him. It's just Jennie and Mrs. Brady and me most of the time. They're good to me. We had a wonderful Christmas together...."

"Where was your father?" she exclaimed.

"He had to fly to Paris. *She* found out and got on the plane when he wasn't looking. Since he couldn't send her home, she went with him," he muttered.

"She?"

"Marie Dumaris," he said curtly.

"Maybe he loves her," she suggested.

"Ha! She comes from an uptown family and he's known her since Mom died. She was a cousin or something. She's always around. I guess he was too busy to notice other women, and she decided to acquire him. From the way she acts lately, she has."

Shelly could have debated that, about his father being too busy to notice women. From what little he'd said to her, she gathered that he was no stranger to brief liaisons. He'd even thought she was angling for one. The brunette's skinny form flashed into her mind and she wondered absently how a man could find pleasure in caressing ribs and bones with skin stretched over them.

"If he marries her, I'll run away," the boy said quietly. "It's bad enough that I don't get to say what I want to do with my life, or where I want to go to school. I can't stand having her for a stepmother as well." He looked up at Shelly. "We'll have to work fast, since you're only here for a week."

"I'm sorry to disappoint you, but I really don't want your father," she said.

"That leaves me," he said worriedly. "Look, I'm only twelve. I can't get married for years yet, and I'm too short for you. My dad's a much better bet."

"I don't want to get married," she said kindly. "Couldn't you settle for being friends?"

"That won't save me," he moaned. "What am I going to do? My whole life's an ongoing calamity!"

She knew how it felt to be young and helpless. She still had to fight her own well-meaning father to live her own life.

"Have you talked to your father? I mean, have you really talked to him, told him how you felt?"

He shrugged. "He thinks I'm just a kid. He doesn't talk *to* me, he talks *at* me. He tells me what I'm going to do and then he walks out."

"Just like my dad," she mused.

"Aren't fathers the pits?"

She chuckled. "Well, from time to time they are." She studied his wet profile. "Are you sure you're all right?"

"I'm fine. Are you?"

She nodded. "Just wet. And I think it would be a good idea if we both went and got dried off."

"Okay. I'll be back to see you later," he promised. "My name's Ben. Ben Scott. My dad's first name is Faulkner."

She shook the hand he offered. "I'm Shelly Astor."

"Nice to meet you. Shelly Scott would have a nice ring to it, don't you think?"

"Listen . . ."

"A life for a life," he reminded her. "Mine belongs to you, and you're responsible for it."

"I didn't do anything except pull you out of the ocean!"

"No. You saved me from a calamity," he said. "But we have several calamities to go. Calamity Mom—that's *you*," he added with a grin.

She glared at him. "I'm not a mother."

"Yes, you are."

"No!"

"Are so, are so, are so!" he called, and ran away, laughing.

She threw up her hands in frustrated impotence. Now what was she going to do? And how was she going to explain what had happened if his father came gunning for her after he was told that his son now had a mother? She didn't know where they came from, or anything about them.

She almost wished she'd never agreed to come with the other students on the trip. But it was too late now. She'd jumped into the ocean, and into the frying pan—so to speak.

That evening, she and Nan walked through the lobby of their motel and came face-to-face with a haughty Marie Dumaris, with Faulkner Scott at her side, and a subdued Ben trailing behind.

The boy brightened at the sight of Shelly. "Hi, Mom!" he said brightly. Faulkner's eyebrows shot up and Marie bristled.

"She is *not* your mother!" Marie snapped.

"She is so," Ben told her belligerently.

Shelly colored, and Nan patted her on the shoulder. "I'll meet you at John's Burger Stand, okay?" she asked quickly, and retreated.

Shelly would have a few things to tell her later about desertion under fire, she thought wickedly. She didn't look at Faulkner. She was barely composed and painfully aware of her shabby attire. She and Nan had decided to have a casual supper, so she hadn't bothered over her appearance. She wasn't even wearing makeup. Marie had on a green silk pantsuit with designer shoes and bag. Last year's style, Shelly thought with gentle spite, but trendy enough. Shelly herself was wearing faded jeans and a worn blue-striped top with a button missing at the top.

"She says you shouldn't send me to military school." Ben set the cat among the pigeons, grinning as he retreated toward the television on one wall.

"I did not!" Shelly gasped.

"You have no right to comment on Faulkner's decisions about his son," Marie said with cool hauteur and a speaking look at Shelly's attire. "Really, I can't imagine that Ben's education is of any concern to a tacky little college girl." Her cold green eyes measured Shelly and found her lacking in every respect.

Shelly's eyebrows rose. Tacky college student? This social climbing carrot-eater was looking down her nose at Shelly? She could have burst out laughing, but it was hardly a matter for amusement.

Faulkner wasn't saying anything. He was watching Shelly with those devil's eyes, smiling faintly.

Shelly glared at him with bitter memories on her face. "Ben is my friend," she said, turning her eyes to Marie. "I have a vested interest in his future. Or so he says," she added under her breath. "He hates military school and he doesn't want to shoot things."

"Don't be absurd, they don't have to shoot anything! Besides," Marie added, "people have hunted since time began."

"They hunted when they had to eat," Shelly agreed. "That was before supermarkets and meat lockers."

"Faulkner enjoys hunting," Marie countered, smiling up at him. "He's very good at it."

Shelly nodded, staring at him. "Oh, I don't doubt it for a second," she agreed readily. "Drawing blood seems to be a specialty of his. You don't have any vampires in your family lineage...?"

Faulkner was trying not to smile, and Marie was about to explode, when Ben came running back up blowing a huge bubble.

"Throw that stupid bubble gum away," Marie told him icily. "And stop slouching. Must you dress and act like a street person?" She glanced haughtily at Shelly, beside whom Ben was standing. "It must be the influence."

How dare that woman talk about Ben that way, and in public! The youngster went scarlet and looked as if he wanted to go through the floor. That was the last straw. Shelly glared at her, her eyes deliberately noting Marie's silk jacket. "That particular jacket was on sale last fall, wasn't it? You do know that it's out of style this season?" She smiled deliberately, having delivered an insult calculated to turn the other woman's face white. It did, too.

Marie took an indignant breath. "My wardrobe is no concern of yours. Speaking of which...!"

"Ben, I want to know what's going on between you and Ms. Astor," Faulkner drawled, leaving Shelly stunned because she hadn't realized he knew her name.

"Nothing is going on. Ben and I are friends," Shelly said firmly.

"I don't want Ben associating with her," Marie said coldly.

"I hardly think that's your decision to make, Marie," Faulkner interrupted. "Ben told me what you did this afternoon," he added quietly, searching Shelly's eyes. "I'm in your debt. You're no shrinking violet when the chips are down, are you?"

"No guts, no glory," she quipped. He was making her nervous. The way he was watching her made her knees week. She had to get away. "Sorry, but I have friends waiting. See you, Ben."

Ben waved, but he looked miserable. And that haughty brunette treating him like a pet animal...! Shelly's blood boiled.

Ben ground his teeth together. He'd wanted to drag Shelly into his family circle, but Marie was spoiling everything!

"That was terrible of you, to involve your father with a haughty, ill-bred little tramp like that," Marie scolded Ben. "How could you...?"

"She saved my life," Ben told her curtly, his voice firm and authoritative, amazingly similar to his father's.

"She did what?" Marie asked, taken aback. They hadn't told her.

Ben sighed. "I fell off the pier. She jumped in and pulled me out."

Faulkner studied his son with new eyes. He'd done a lot of thinking since Shelly had exploded into their lives. Now he was regretting what he'd said to her. Her comments the other day had helped him to realize that he had a son he didn't even know. He'd spent years making money, traveling, letting business occupy every waking hour of his life. And in the process, Ben had become a stranger.

"Can we go and eat now?" Marie asked petulantly. "I'm hungry. We can have salads and spring water."

"I'm not having a salad and spring water," Ben told her belligerently. "I'm having a steak and a soda."

"Don't you talk that way to me!" Marie shot back. "And you're not having red meat . . . !"

"He can have a steak if he wants one," Faulkner told her coldly. "In fact, I'm having one myself. Let's go."

Ben and Marie wore equally shocked looks. Faulkner moved ahead of them toward the restaurant. He spared a sad, regretful glance toward the door where Shelly had vanished. He supposed he was going to have to apologize to her. He wasn't looking forward to it.

A little while later, Shelly had worn out her meager supply of bad language on Marie's behavior and was catching her breath when Pete came up to join the two women at the burger place.

"There's a beach party tonight, dancing and beer. You two coming?" he asked.

"Sure," Nan said. "How can we resist dancing?"

Pete glared at her. "Well, there's me, too."

"I can resist you," Nan said, smiling.

"I can't," Shelly said with a theatrical sigh. "You make me swoon!"

Pete grinned. "Do I, really? What a treat! That's radical!"

"She's acting," Nan whispered loudly. "She's already promised to an investment broker back home."

Pete stared at Shelly blankly. "Are you?"

"My father keeps trying," Shelly said ruefully. "He wants to see me settled and secure." She laughed.

"Well, I've got long legs and I can run fast. Not to worry. I'll escape."

"Make sure you escape by way of the beach," Pete made her promise. "We're going to have a ball."

"The last time he said that, six of us spent the night in the holding tank down at Fort Lauderdale."

"I gave you an intimate look at life in the raw," Pete said, wounded. "You learned incredible things about people."

"Three hookers, two drunks and a man accused of murder were in there with us," Nan translated. "The drunks were sick at the time," she added pointedly. "One threw up on me."

"Oh, my," Shelly mused.

"No police this time," Pete promised. "No drugs, no trouble. Drugs are stupid, anyway. We'll just drink beer and eat pizza and dance. Okay?"

"In that case, I'll come," Nan said.

"Me, too, I guess," Shelly said. "I don't have much of a social life these days."

Nan was looking past Shelly's shoulder. "I wouldn't say that."

Shelly followed the wide-eyed stare. Mr. Sexy was walking toward her, resplendent in his white slacks and electric blue silk shirt and white jacket. He looked very sophisticated, and women up and down the strip of developments were openly staring at him.

"Wow," Nan sighed softly.

Shelly had time to wonder what he'd done with Marie and Ben before he stopped in front of her.

"I'd like to speak to you. Alone," he added with a meaningful stare toward Nan and Pete.

"I'm a memory already," Pete said quickly.

"Same here." Nan followed him, leaving Shelly alone at the table with Faulkner.

He sat down, giving his surroundings a cold appraisal. His silver eyes settled on Shelly's face in its frame of windblown, wavy blond hair. Her complexion was perfect, softly pink, and her blue eyes were like pools at midnight. He studied her in reluctant silence, drinking in her beauty.

"Ben told me that you saved his life. I want to apologize for the things I said to you."

"Don't apologize for your bad manners, Mr. Scott," she said gently. "It would ruin your image."

He grimaced. "Is that how I sounded?"

"Despite what your woman friend thinks, I am neither a street person nor a lady of the evening," she said quietly. "As for Ben, I pulled him out of the water and we talked for a few minutes. That is the extent of our acquaintance. I have no desire to become his mother, despite the impression he may have given you."

"I appreciate what you did for Ben," he said quietly. "You may not think so, but he's very important to me."

"Is he?" she asked with faint sarcasm, and a ruddy flush ran over his high cheekbones.

"Yes, he is," he returned curtly. "I can do without any more insults from you."

"Isn't turnabout fair play? You've done nothing but insult me since the first time you spoke to me. All right, I shouldn't have flirted with you. I made eyes at you and pretended unrequited love to get my friends off my back, and it was wrong. But you had no right whatsoever to assume that because I smiled at you, I was eager and willing to warm your bed!"

"No, I didn't," he agreed surprisingly. "Perhaps I'm more jaded than I realized. You're very lovely. It's been my experience that most women with looks find a market for them."

"Perhaps you've known the wrong kind of women," she said. "And while we're on the subject, whether or not she's your fiancée, that woman has no right to talk to Ben as if he's a pet dog!"

His dark eyebrows arched and he smiled. "My, my."

"He's a fine boy. Better than you deserve, and a walking miracle considering the lack of guidance he's had."

He sighed slowly, watching her through narrowed eyes. He toyed with a plastic fork on the table and muscles rippled in his broad chest, dark hair visible through the thinness of his shirt as they moved.

"I've been busy supporting us," he said.

"Your son will be away from home for good in about six years," she reminded him. "Will he want to come back for visits then?"

He scowled. "What do you mean?"

"Ben doesn't want to be a military man. He doesn't want to go to a school with rigid discipline or become a hunter. He wants to be an artist. Is it really fair of you to try to relive your life through him?"

He looked shocked. "I wasn't."

"Ben doesn't see it that way." She grimaced. "Neither do I," she said honestly. "My father is just like you. I've had to fight him constantly to get to do anything my own way. He's got a husband all picked out for me. College, you see, is a waste of time for a woman."

He lifted an eyebrow and didn't reply.

"You think that way, too, I gather. A woman's place is in the bedroom and the kitchen—"

"I wouldn't know," he said curtly. "My mother was a corporate executive. She was never home."

She stared at him warily.

"Surprised?" he asked mockingly. "My father worked himself to death before he was fifty. Mother inherited the company. In order to keep it going, she decided that I was expendable. She stuck me in a private school and devoted the rest of her short life to high finance. She died when I was in my final year of college. She dropped dead of a heart attack in the middle of a heated board meeting."

She was shocked. "I see."

"No, you don't see anything. My father thought my mother was a home-loving woman who would want to give him children and love and care for them until they were old enough to live alone. But she never wanted children in the first place. God knows, she said so often enough when I was growing up!''

"Oh, you poor man,'' she said softly, and with genuine sympathy. ''I'm so sorry!''

He glowered at her. ''I don't need pity!''

"Some women aren't suited to domestic life,'' she said gently. ''Surely you know that by now?''

"Then they shouldn't marry.''

She searched his hard face. A lot of things were clearing up in her mind. He was raising his son as he'd been raised, in the only way he knew.

"There are other ways to make a boy self-sufficient and independent,'' she said. ''You don't have to banish him to make him strong. He thinks you don't want him.''

He got to his feet, towering over her. ''I can manage my own private life.''

"Heavens, what kind of life is it?'' she asked, searching his silver eyes. ''You aren't happy. Neither is Ben. Haven't you learned that business isn't enough?''

Her assessment of his life hurt. He'd already had enough of Marie's criticism that he was too soft with Ben, and here was Shelly telling him he was too hard. He reacted more violently than he meant to. ''What is enough?'' he asked abruptly. ''To turn out a penniless, scruffy little college student like you?''

Probably if his assumption about her had been right, his attitude would have hurt. But it didn't. She smiled mockingly. ''I wouldn't presume to think so,'' she said. "Marie's just your style. But I feel sorry for Ben. He's sensitive, despite his brashness. She'll destroy him if you let her."

He gave her a speaking glare and strode off with anger evident in every line of his hard body.

She drank too much that night. She hadn't eaten right, she'd been too annoyed at Mr. Sexy, and before she knew it, she'd had much too much beer. Three cans of it, when she hardly ever had more than a sip of white wine. If Nan hadn't been there to look after her, her carelessness could have had terrible repercussions. Pete, who'd had four cans of beer on his own, was more than willing to take advantage of her condition. But Nan warded him off, parceled up Shelly and herded her back to the motel.

"Idiot," she muttered as she helped a swaying Shelly into the lobby. "What on earth would you do without me?"

"I'm not drunk, Nan," Shelly said, and smiled vacantly.

"Of course not! Come on, hang on to me."

She got into the elevator with her heavy burden and was about to select the proper floor number when Faulkner and his ladylove joined them.

"Of all the disgusting things I've ever seen," Marie said with a haughty glare. "You college girls have no morals at all, have you?"

Nan stared at the other woman without speaking, her liquid black eyes full of muffled insults. Marie flushed and looked away, but Nan didn't stop staring.

"Hello, Miss Ribs," Shelly said, smiling at the thin brunette. "If you had a little meat on those bird bones, you'd be much more attractive. I expect Mr. Sexy over there bruises his fingers every time he touches you."

"How dare you!" Marie exploded.

"Here's our floor. Out you go, my dear," Nan mumbled, helping Shelly out of the elevator.

"I'll see you tomorrow, Marie. Go on up." Faulkner got off the elevator and, without breaking stride, lifted Shelly in his arms. "Lead the way."

The elevator closed on Marie's startled gasp, and Nan hesitated only a minute before she started off down the hall toward their ocean-facing room.

Shelly looked into Faulkner's hard, dark face with dazed curiosity. "I'm sorry you don't like me."

He smiled gently. "Don't I?" he asked. "Hold tight, little one. I wouldn't want to drop you."

He pulled her very close and eased her hot face into the curve of his neck, enveloping her in his warm strength and the seductive scent of his cologne. She felt like heaven in his arms. He had to stifle a groan.

Shelly was barely aware of his reaction, but she was feeling something similar. Smiling, she sighed and drifted into a warm, wonderful sleep.

Chapter Three

Shelly woke the next morning with a frightful headache and vague memories of being carried to bed in a man's hard arms.

Nan held out a bottle of aspirin and a cup of black coffee the minute Shelly walked into the living room. "Here," she said curtly. "And next time you pull a silly stunt like that, you'll be sharing a single room at this motel, all alone, by yourself."

"Don't yell," Shelly groaned.

"I'm whispering, *can't you tell?*"

"Oh!" Shelly put her hands over her ears. "You're horrible!"

"One of us is, that's for sure."

"I dreamed that I was being carried," she murmured, holding her aching head.

"That wasn't a dream."

She stared blankly at Nan. "Oh, no."

"Oh, yes. Your nemesis carried you in here and put you to bed. He was pretty nice, considering what you said to his fiancée."

Shelly groaned aloud. "I don't want to know, but what did I say?"

"You're right. You don't want to know. Sit down and drink your coffee."

Shelly sat down and held out her cup. "Have you got any hemlock?"

Nan only shook her head.

Ben was lying in wait for Shelly when she came out onto the beach much later, wearing dark glasses and feeling vaguely sick. Nan had promised her that some sea air would cure her. So while Nan was having a shower, Shelly slipped into her yellow one-piece bathing suit and her terry cover-up and oozed down to the beach.

"Marie's really mad at you," Ben said, and grinned. "I knew you'd make a great mother!" He scowled. "You look terrible. What's the matter with you?"

"Excess," she said.

"Excess what?"

"Beer." She found a single bare spot between tourists and sat down gently on the sand. She groaned at the blazing sunlight, which hurt her eyes even through the dark glasses. "It's your father's fault."

"My dad made you drink beer?" he asked hesitantly.

"He drove me to it. He's a terrible man!"

"Well, he isn't, really. I exaggerated a little because I was mad at him," Ben said pleasantly. "But he's re-thinking sending me to that school. Thanks, Mom!" He grinned at her.

"Think nothing of it. Is there a facility near here? I think I have to throw up."

"Why don't you lie down?" Ben suggested. "It might help. Where did your friends go?"

"They are going sailing." She took off the robe and stretched out on a towel, grimacing as her head contacted the ground. "I feel awful."

"I can imagine. I'm glad I don't drink," he observed. "Neither does Dad, except for a glass of wine occasionally."

"Delighted to hear it. I'm sure your future stepmother doesn't approve of wine."

"She only hates things that taste good," he agreed. "I hate wine."

"Haven't you got something to do?"

"Sure. I have to look after you. Poor old Mom."

"I'm not your mother," she croaked.

"Yet."

"Ever!" She let out a pained sigh.

"How about something cold to drink?"

"Anything, as long as it isn't beer!" She dug into her pocket for change and handed him some.

"That's too much."

"Get yourself something, too."

"Gee, thanks!"

He darted off. She lay quietly on the sand, trying to breathe, and a dark shadow loomed over her.

"Nan?" Shelly said.

"Not Nan," came a familiar deep voice. He dropped beside her on the sand. "How do you feel?"

"Sick."

"Serves you right. If you can't hold your liquor, don't drink. You could have ended up in severe circumstances last night, except for Nan."

"Rub it in," she muttered.

"I intend to. Nan's had a go at you already, I'm sure."

"Several. My head hurts."

"No wonder." He smoothed back her windblown hair. His hand was big and warm and surprisingly gentle. She opened her eyes and looked up. She wished she hadn't. He was wearing white swimming trunks and nothing else, and he looked better than the sexiest suntan commercial she'd ever seen. He was beautiful, just beautiful, and she was glad she had on dark glasses so that he couldn't see her appreciation.

"Where's your shadow?" she muttered, closing her eyes again. "Or does she sunbathe? It must be disconcerting to have men screaming 'put your clothes back on!'"

"Not nice," he said firmly. "Being thin is fashionable in our circles."

"It is not," she said, forgetting that he didn't know she frequented the same circles he did. "Thin is fashionable only with models and—" she sat up, taking off her sunglasses to glare at him "—your ladylove."

He shrugged, powerful muscles rippling in his chest and arms. "Some men like well-endowed women, I suppose. I never have."

She was too aware of her full hips and generous bosom. She glared at him. "Then don't waste your time sitting here talking to me."

He laughed mirthlessly. "I have a vested interest in you, and kindly don't take this as a sign of sexual intent. Even if you appealed to me, which you do not physically," he added pointedly, "the fact is, you're still in school."

She started once again to correct his assumption about her age, and stopped. Plenty of time for confidences later, if he stuck around. Otherwise, pretending a lesser age than she owned might not be a bad form of protection. He was obviously pretty experienced, if the look he was giving her body was any indication. He wasn't blatant, but he had seductive eyes and a voice that was more than a little persuasive. His words denied any interest or intent, but his eyes belied that. She wondered if he even realized it.

"I'm back...!" Ben hesitated before he sat down beside his father and Shelly. "Oh. Hi, Dad. Where's Marie?"

"Sleeping late, I suppose." He watched as Ben handed Shelly a soft drink.

"Delicious," she whispered, holding the icy can to her temples.

"Are you assimilating it through osmosis?" Ben asked. "We studied that in biology."

"You don't know what biology is until you've had to study DNA, enzymes, proteins and genetics in college."

Ben blinked. "What happened to animals?"

"You study them in zoology."

"You study enzymes in biology?" Ben muttered.

"That's right. And if you really want to understand biology, taking chemistry helps. I haven't yet." She grinned. "I'm a sociology major. I only have to take biology. Since I passed it, I don't have to take chemistry."

"How far along are you?" Faulkner asked.

"Oh, I'm still a freshman."

He didn't reply. His face grew thoughtful, and he turned his attention seaward.

"Where are you from?" Ben asked her suddenly.

"Washington."

"State?" he persisted.

"D.C."

"So are we!" Ben said excitedly, and Shelly was aware of his father's interested gaze. "Where do you go to school?"

"Thorn College," she replied. "It's very small, but nice."

Faulkner knew the college and the area in which it was located. A nice, middle-class community. Nothing fancy. Older homes on small lots near the interchange.

"Oh," Ben said. "We live several miles away from there. Some of our neighbors are senators."

"Are you on vacation?" she asked hesitantly.

"No," Faulkner replied. "There's a convention here this week—bankers."

"Dad's the keynote speaker," Ben said proudly. "Shelly, didn't you say your dad was good at numbers and accounting?"

He certainly was. He was on the board of directors of two banks. She hoped Faulkner's wasn't one of them. "Sort of," she said.

"What does he do?" Ben persisted.

"Actually very little," she said, feeling her way.

"I see," Faulkner said quietly, and his tone indicated that he was developing an impression of Shelly's father that classed Mr. Astor as a street person. Shelly had to bite her lip to keep from laughing at the picture that came to mind. Her father contributed to several charities that helped street people, but he was far from being homeless.

"What are you going to do with your degree when you get it?" Faulkner asked with genuine curiosity.

"I'd like to be a social worker," she said. "There are plenty of people in the world who could use a helping hand."

"No doubt about that," he replied.

"Well, I want to be a wildlife illustrator," Ben said firmly.

"He wants to do his duck shooting with a camera," Faulkner said with a sigh.

"Good for him. I think it's atrocious the way people treat our living natural resources."

Ben grinned from ear to ear. "You tell him, Mom!"

"I am *not* your mother," she said shortly, and then groaned and held her head.

"She's much too young to be anyone's mother," Faulkner agreed, and there was, just briefly, a wistful look about him. He quickly erased it and got to his feet. "I've got to go and collect Marie. We have a luncheon engagement. Ben..."

"I can stay with Mom. Can't I?"

"I'm not—!"

"—your mother! I know, I know!" Ben said chuckling. "Can I stay with you?"

"She's not able to look after you," Faulkner said.

"I want to look after her," Ben replied solemnly. "She certainly needs looking after, and her friends are going sailing. I don't think she can go sailing, do you?"

Shelly swallowed and made a moaning sound.

"Good point. Is it all right?" Faulkner asked Shelly.

"Just as long as he doesn't talk too loud," she agreed.

"Don't give her any trouble," Faulkner cautioned the boy.

"Isn't Marie going back home today?" Ben asked with glee.

"She's leaving with her father. If he goes today, so will she, I imagine."

So they weren't sharing a room, Shelly thought. She was surprised that a woman of Marie's age would travel with her father, especially when she was apparently all but engaged to Faulkner.

"Marie's father is one of the bankers at the convention," Ben explained. "We flew down together."

"None of that is of any interest to Ms. Astor, I'm sure," Faulkner said. "Stay out of trouble. We should be back around three o'clock."

"Okay, Dad."

Faulkner wandered off, absently thinking that he'd much rather be on the beach with Ben and Shelly than sitting around talking business. But that was part of his job.

Shelly and Ben left the beach half an hour later and after two pain tablets and another icy drink, Shelly felt well enough to go fishing off the pier with Ben.

"Isn't this fun?" she asked on a sigh, lying back on the boards with her eyes closed and the fishing pole held loosely in her hand. "I'll bet that fishing concession makes a fortune without selling a single worm."

"Your hook isn't baited," Ben muttered. "That's not fair."

"I don't want to catch a fish, for heaven's sake! I just want to lie here and drink in the smell of sea air."

"Well, I want to catch something. Not that I expect to," he said miserably when he pulled up his hook and it was bare, again. The minnows under the pier kept taking the bait in tiny nibbles and missing the hook.

"Don't fall in," she said firmly.

"Okay."

The sound of footsteps didn't bother her, because there were plenty of other tourists dropping lines off the pier. But these came close. She looked up and there was Ben's father, in jeans, a gray knit designer shirt and sneakers. He didn't even look like the same man.

"Catch anything?" he asked.

"Some sleep," Shelly remarked.

"I'm catching cold," Ben grumbled as he baited his hook for the fourth time.

Faulkner's narrow silver eyes slid over Shelly's trim figure in tight white jeans and a pink sleeveless blouse tied at the midriff. Her glorious hair was tamed into a French braid and even without makeup, her face was lovely. He couldn't stop looking at her.

She flushed a little and sat up. That level stare was making her self-conscious. "Since you're back, I'll leave Ben with you. I have to try to find Nan and the others."

"I thought they went sailing."

"They did," she agreed. "But Nan's a much worse sailor than I am. I expect she's lost breakfast and lunch by now, and is praying for land."

He reached down a big, strong hand and helped her up. Oddly his fingers were callused; her fingers lingered against the tough pads on his and she looked up at him with kindled interest.

"Your hands are callused," she remarked.

He smiled slowly, closing his fingers around her own. "I have a sailboat," he remarked. "I love sailing."

"Oh."

"And you don't like the sea," he murmured dryly.

"My stomach doesn't like the sea," she corrected.

He searched her soft eyes and she didn't look away. Currents of electricity seemed to run into her body from the intensity of that stare, until her breathing changed and her heartbeat doubled. He still had her hand in his and unexpectedly, he brought the soft palm up to his lips and pressed them hard into its moist warmth.

She felt the color run into her face. "I, uh, really have to go." She laughed nervously and extracted her hand from his.

He smiled at her, without rancor or mockery. "Thanks for taking care of Ben."

"He sort of took care of me," she replied. Her eyes searched his, and there was a little fear in them.

His smile was indulgent, faintly surprised. "It's all right," he said softly, his voice deeper than ever, his eyes narrowed and intent.

She gnawed on her lower lip, understanding his response in her subconscious even if it sounded odd to her conscious mind. She turned away. "See you, Ben!"

"Sure. Thanks!"

She almost ran the length of the pier. She dated, and boys liked her. But she'd never liked them. Now, in the space of a few days, a man who thought she was much too young for him had blazed a path to her most secret self, and she didn't know how to chase him out

again. There were plenty of reasons she should keep
her distance from him, and she wanted to. But Ben
was making it impossible.

She walked into the motel, almost colliding with a
very irritated Marie Dumaris.

"You again," the older woman said curtly. "Stay
away from Faulkner. I don't know what you think
he'd see in a ragamuffin like you, but I don't like the
way you've attached yourself to him and Ben."

The attack was staggering. Shelly stared at her
blankly. "I beg your pardon?"

"If you don't leave Faulkner alone, I'll make you
sorry. My people are well-to-do and I have influence.
I can have you kicked out of school if I feel like it."
She smiled haughtily at Shelly's expression. "Faulkner told me that you go to Thorn College. So watch
your step. You don't know who you're dealing with."

Shelly looked her in the eye, and she didn't smile.
"Neither do you," she said with quiet dignity.

Marie started to say something else, but Shelly
turned and kept walking. She couldn't imagine why
Marie would warn her away from Faulkner, who
wasn't interested in her that way at all. Besides, she
was only going to be here for four more days. That was
hardly enough time to capture a man's heart. She
overlooked the fact that hers was slowly being chained
already....

That evening, after they'd eaten fish and chips, she
and Nan were startled by a knock at the door.

Shelly went to open the door and found Faulkner. He smiled gently at her surprise. She was still wearing her jeans and pink blouse, but he'd changed into white slacks and a patterned shirt.

"Do you like Latin music?" he asked.

She was flustered, and looked it. "Yes."

"Come on. There's a live band down the way. Nan?" he added, looking past Shelly. "Want to come with us?"

"I'd love to, but there's a PBS special on about a dig in Egypt," Nan said apologetically. "I *love* classical archaeology."

"Indulge yourself, you stick-in-the-mud," Shelly grumbled.

"I will. Have fun!"

Faulkner waited while Shelly tied a pink knit sweater loosely around her neck in case it got cooler, and found her purse.

She waited until they were in the elevator headed down to the ground floor before she spoke. "Isn't this sudden?" she queried. "And where's Ben?"

"He's staying with some friends of mine for a few hours."

She lifted both eyebrows.

He chuckled. "You know how I feel about May-December relationships. I've already said so. I don't have anything indiscreet in mind. I thought you might like the impromptu Latin concert on the beach, so I came to get you."

"Am I substituting?"

He tilted her face up to his and shook his head, holding her eyes. "Oh, no," he said quietly. "Not you."

She smiled gently. "That was nice."

"I am nice," he replied, letting go of her chin. "It takes some people longer than others to notice it, of course."

She laughed. "Conceit, yet."

"I am not conceited. In fact, my modesty often shocks people."

"I'll let you know if I feel in danger of being shocked."

His silver eyes twinkled. "You do that."

"You aren't what you seem," she said with faint curiosity. "I thought bankers were staid and businesslike."

His powerful shoulders rose and fell. "I am, when I'm in the office." He glanced down at her. "I'm not in the office tonight, so look out."

She chuckled. "I can hardly wait."

The music got louder the closer they got to the beach. A boom box was blasting Latin rhythms and food and beer were being passed around while couples danced in the sand. A crowd of merrymakers had gathered to watch, including some of the students Shelly was travelling with. One of them, unfortunately, was Pete.

"So this is where you went to!" he said impatiently, glancing warily at Faulkner. "Want to join us?"

Faulkner slid a possessive arm around her waist, and smiled at Pete. It wasn't a pleasant smile. "She's with me," he said quietly.

"Yes, I am," Shelly added. "Thanks for the invitation anyway."

Pete didn't say another word. He stalked back off to the other group.

"He's been drinking again," she said. "Ordinarily he's very nice."

"Nan told me that she was barely able to peel him off you last night," he said curtly. "I don't like that. A man who'll take advantage of an intoxicated woman is no man at all."

She stared at him. "Which means that you wouldn't seduce me if I got drunk?"

"Of course not. Besides, even cold sober, a college freshman is a little green on the tree for a man my age," he added, and his voice was unusually soft.

She should have been glad that her subterfuge had been successful. But instead, she was miserable that he thought she was too young for him.

"Will you relax and enjoy the music?" he chided.

"Sorry." She smiled. "I'm glad you asked me. I love music."

"So do I."

"Elevator music and classic rock and roll?" she teased.

He cocked a thick eyebrow. "Axl Rose and Aerosmith," he shot back.

She chuckled. "Mr. Scott, you are nothing like your image."

"Thank God for that."

The music got louder and couples moved into the circle to dance. Because her parents were ballroom dancing fans, she'd grown up knowing how to dance the mambo and tango. Faulkner seemed surprised that someone of her tender years would know how to do a sophisticated tango, but after he gauged her style, they seemed to flow together to the passionate refrain.

The music was wild. What she felt with every sensual brush of his body against hers was wilder. Her heart ran away with her. There was no tomorrow—only tonight. She began to act as if the moment was all that existed, deliberately tempting him with the brush of her breasts against his broad chest, the soft glide of her thighs beside his, the intoxicating fencing of her steps with his.

She hung beneath his narrowing gaze, feeling the effect she was having on him in his quickened breath, the tightening of his hands on her waist and then, sliding lower, on her hips as he brushed her body against him.

It was arousing and she was too hungry to hide her reaction to him. As the music built to a climax, her eyes found his and held them. By the time it wound down, she was clinging to him, like a life preserver.

They finished the dance with a trembling Shelly draped over one powerful arm. Faulkner's mouth poised scant inches above her own. The whole crowd applauded, but they were so lost in each other, in the intoxicating magic of aroused awareness, that they barely noticed.

"Oh, for a few seconds of privacy," he murmured huskily, searching her eyes as he slowly drew her back up again, the sensual brush of his hard body against her soft one arousing her suddenly and violently.

The dance had been sensual. She could feel her heart, and his, pounding in rhythm. "What would you do?" she challenged.

"I think that you're not quite that naive," he said, and his silver eyes fell to her soft mouth, lingering there until her lips parted and a tiny, frustrated moan escaped them.

His breathing was suddenly audible. "Shelly, stop it!"

She wanted to, she really did. But for the first time in her life, she wasn't quite in control. The feel of his chest against her soft breasts made them swell and she felt a sweet trembling all through her body. She was young and untried and hungry for her first taste of physical ravishment. All that was in the eyes she lifted bravely to his.

His jaw clenched. He swallowed. "All right. But not here," he said roughly.

He took her hand in his and drew her along with him. Her head was spinning; he'd read her thoughts as surely as if she'd spoken them. She'd never before experienced that kind of communication. It was frightening, similar to the headlong rush into passion that made her legs tremble.

"People. Damn people!" he muttered under his breath as he searched for a single uncrowded place. There wasn't one. He looked toward the beach, where the sea oats and sand dunes gave at least the illusion of privacy.

If he'd been thinking rationally, he'd have taken her straight back to the hotel and left her with Nan while there was still time. But she was wearing some sort of tangy perfume that made his senses whirl, and the thought of her softly rounded body in his arms made him reckless.

He led her along the dunes and then helped her down to the level of the beach with him, holding her so that, for an instant, her eyes were even with the aroused glitter of his.

He let her slide gently against his muscular body until her feet touched the sand. Behind him was the roar of the surf with moonlight glistening like diamonds along the waves that ran into the beach. But louder even than that was the frantic beat of her heart as he drew her to him with a self-mocking smile and bent his head.

"Every man is entitled to make a fool of himself once," he whispered into her mouth as he took it.

Chapter Four

Shelly wasn't model-lovely, but her wealth had guaranteed that she'd had suitors in the past. None of them, not one, had made her mouth ache for his kisses, her body plead to be touched and caressed. But Faulkner did. Her response to him was instant and alarming.

Once, she tried to draw back, but his big hands slid to her hips and pushed them hard into the changing contours of his body while his lips teased around her trembling mouth.

He felt her instinctive withdrawal and checked it expertly. His nose brushed against hers and there was no urgency, no brutality in the touch of his mouth on her face. He was remarkably tender for the level of arousal he'd already reached.

"Don't be afraid of me," he whispered, his voice gentle, indulgent. "You can stop me whenever you like. Force is for bullies."

The calm tone pacified her. For just an instant she'd counted her folly in coming out alone with him, when she hardly knew him. There was a very real danger in being secluded with a strange man. The papers were full of tragedies that a little common sense, caution and wise counsel could have prevented.

"I read too many newspapers, I guess," she said unsteadily.

"Some women should read more," he replied flatly. He pushed the hair back from her flushed cheeks and stared down at her in the faint light. "You're quite safe with me. I wouldn't advise you to come out here with your friend Pete, though."

She smiled at the dry tone. "I know that already, thanks." The smile faded as she studied his broad, rugged face. It had lines that an artist would have loved. She reached up hesitantly, and stroked his thick eyebrows. He had big, deep-set eyes that seemed to see right through people. His nose was a little large, not oversize, and very straight. She traced it down to the wide, sexy line of his mouth, to the chiseled lips that had teased her into reckless response.

"This isn't wise," he said quietly, a little regretful. "You taste of green apples, young Shelly."

She reached up and caught his full lower lip gently in her teeth, acting on pure instinct. His big frame shuddered a little. "Teach me," she whispered unsteadily.

His hand tightened on her waist. "Teach you what?" he asked roughly.

Her lips opened and brushed against his. "How to...make love."

"That would be dangerous," was all he could get out. His body was burning; his heartbeat shook him.

"Yes." Her hands went to the front of his shirt. Holding his eyes, she gently undid the top button. He didn't say a word. Encouraged, she opened the next, and the next, and the next, until she'd bared his hair-covered chest to her fascinated gaze.

"Oh, my!" she whispered. She pressed both hands into the thickness of the hair and felt the hard, warm muscle through it. He was strong. She could feel it. He indulged her, letting her explore him, until the needs she kindled became unmanageable.

"That's enough," he said softly, stilling her hands against him.

"Why?"

"Because I'll want equal time."

Her eyes met his; her gaze was curious, a little shy. "I haven't let anyone see me like that. Not yet."

His eyes fell to her pink blouse and he saw the hardness of her nipples through it.

"I didn't have time to put on anything under it," she whispered softly.

"Oh, my God!" He ground out the words.

That deep groan, she decided, was pure frustration. As she thought it, he looked around to make sure they were still isolated. Then, with a total disregard for sanity, he dropped her sweater to the beach and began to unfasten her blouse.

His lips parted, as if he was finding it hard to breathe while he worked the tiny pearl buttons. So was she. But she wanted his gaze on her so badly that she banished common sense. When he pulled the edges of the blouse apart and looked at her, it seemed that she wasn't the only one with that terrible need. His eyes were narrow and hot with admiration as he savored the firm, beautiful curve of her pink breasts.

"You said you liked . . . small women," she whispered unsteadily.

"Did I? I must have been out of my mind! Shelly," he whispered. "Oh, Shelly . . . !"

She didn't know what she'd expected, but it wasn't the sudden descent of his dark head and the warm moistness of his open mouth on her breast. His tongue pressed against her while she cried out in a strangled voice and clutched his head closer. Her whole body throbbed, ached, shook with an avalanche of uncontrollable need. She whispered to him, pleaded with him for more, more, her eyes closed, her body in anguish.

Vaguely she felt the cool sand at her back and the weight of Faulkner's body as he lifted his head to find her mouth. He kissed her with open passion, his tongue pushing deep inside her mouth while his hair-roughened chest rubbed over her bare breasts and made the ache intolerable.

Her hands found his hips and pulled him to her, trembling as she pleaded for something she'd never experienced. As far gone as she, he indulged her for one brief ecstatic second, levering down between her soft thighs to press himself hard against the very core of her hunger. She cried out and shifted to accommodate him, and the stars seemed to crash down on her.

But he groaned and threw himself over onto his back, shuddering, openly vulnerable to her hungry, fascinated eyes.

She looked at him as if he belonged to her already, sketching him with eyes that adored the power and sensuality of his aroused body. He seemed to be in agony and she wished she were more sophisticated, that she knew what to do for him.

She sat up, hugging her knees to her bare breasts. Probably she should fasten her blouse, she thought dazedly, but everything seemed a bit unreal now.

He sat up beside her and glanced sideways, noticing the open blouse. "Put your knees down," he said quietly. "I want to look at you."

She obeyed him, watching his eyes stroke her with pure pleasure, feeling sensations that made her tingle.

"You make my head spin," he said, leaning close to put his lips softly over her breast. "Do you like this?" he whispered, teasing the nipple with his tongue. "Or is it better for you...like this?" His mouth opened and suckled her with tender ferocity.

"Faulkner." She lay back on the sand, her arms spread, her eyes welcoming, her body completely open to him. She wanted him so badly that nothing else mattered for the moment.

He studied her with banked-down hunger for a long time while he fought his better judgment and lost. "It would be the first time, wouldn't it, Shelly?"

"Yes."

"If you've said no to men before—and I must assume that you have—why are you saying yes to me?"

She didn't want to think about that. She felt uncertain, when she'd been out of her mind with need of him only seconds before. Embarrassed now, she sat up and tugged the edges of her blouse together, buttoning them up in an excruciating silence.

She had to say something. Words were difficult in the cold sanity of the aftermath. "Listen, I want you to know... I don't go around doing things like this..." She faltered. "I'm sorry. I feel ... rather ashamed."

He turned her face toward his and searched her eyes with a somber, intense scrutiny. "You did nothing to make either of us ashamed or embarrassed. We both know I'm too old for you. That doesn't make me regret what happened just now." He traced her lips slowly with his hand, and there was a faint unsteadiness in his fingers. "I'll dream of you as you were tonight for the rest of my life," he said through his teeth. "God, Shelly, why do you have to be so young...?" He caught her to him and his mouth burned into hers for endless moments while he fed an impossible hunger. He forced himself to lift his head. She lay against him, her lips swollen, her eyes wide and soft and willing. He groaned audibly. "You'd let me, wouldn't you?" he asked in a hoarse, agonized tone. "You'd lie here in the moonlight and let me undress you. You'd open your arms and lie under my body and envelop me in your softness ..."

She blushed at the images he was creating in her mind, shivering as she pictured his muscular, hair-roughened body pushing hers into the sand while he possessed her. She moaned.

"Shelly!" His cheek lay against her soft breasts and he shivered in her arms. "Shelly, I want you so badly, honey!"

"I would let you," she whispered brokenly. "I would, I would . . . !"

His arm contracted and he rocked her against him with rough compassion, his face lifting to nestle against her throat, in the scented softness of her hair, while the wind blew around them and the surf crashed.

"I'm years too old for you," he said quietly, looking past her at the ocean. "And while my son wants a mother, I do not want another wife."

"Then why are you marrying *her?*" she asked.

"I'm not. And she knows it. She likes to pretend that things will change, and so does her father, who owes me money and thinks that my marriage to his daughter would negate his debt."

"I see."

His cheek nuzzled her hair. "I'm in my middle thirties and you're a college freshman. We're a generation apart. I come from a social set that you couldn't begin to cope with," he added when she was tempted to speak and deny what he was saying. "I come from money. Plenty of it." He laughed bitterly. "You'd have to organize and plan luncheons, dinner, business gatherings. You'd have to know how to dress, how to defend yourself at social functions, because I have enemies and former lovers who would savage you." His chest rose and fell heavily. "Marriage is out of the question, and I can't offer you an affair because my conscience would beat me to death."

"I see."

"Will you stop saying that?" He lifted his head and searched her eyes, looking for secrets that they wouldn't yield. She looked odd. Faintly amused and bitter, all at once.

"You want to make love to me, but that's all it is." She summed up what he'd told her.

"Basically that's about it." He couldn't tell her what he was beginning to feel for her. The cost was too dear. She'd forget him and he'd forget her, because they had no future together. Let her think it was only physical with him. It might make it easier for her to get over him.

She smiled with controlled dignity. "In that case, we'd better break this up and go back to the motel, hadn't we?" She got up, brushing off her jeans. She retrieved her sweater, shook the sand out of it and slipped it on. She was suddenly chilled.

He got up, too. "I'll walk you back to your room," he said formally.

"Thank you."

They didn't touch. She felt betrayed. He thought she was several years younger than she really was, and that she was beneath him socially. She could have told him the truth, but if he couldn't accept her as he thought she was, then he obviously didn't care about anything except her body. In fact, he'd said so. Thank God he was too much a gentleman to take advantage. She'd been crazy for him. It was embarrassing to remember how wanton she'd been. The memory was going to hurt for a long time.

She couldn't love him, of course. It was impossible to think that when she'd only been around him briefly. It was physical infatuation, surely, and she'd get over it.

They were at her door all too soon. "Thanks for the music," she said, without quite meeting his eyes. She even smiled. "Tell Ben good-night for me. Nan and I have plans, so I don't imagine I'll see much of him until we leave for home."

He frowned. Until now, he hadn't remembered how close Ben was getting to her. "You don't have to jettison Ben because of what happened tonight," he said curtly.

"I'm not."

He tipped her face up to his, scowling at the way she avoided his eyes. "Look at me, damn you!" he said sharply.

The anger shocked her into meeting his eyes, and she wished she hadn't. They were blazing.

"I didn't want to hurt you," he said shortly. "I never meant to do more than kiss you. You deliberately baited me until I made love to you, so don't put all the blame on me!"

She went scarlet. She was too sick with embarrassment and too flustered to even answer him. Jerking away from him, she fumbled the door open and went through it, locking it nervously behind her.

Faulkner stood staring at the closed door with shocked self-contempt. He couldn't believe he'd made a remark like that to her, when she'd been so generous and uninhibited with him. He hadn't meant to make her ashamed of such a sweet giving, but the look on her face had hurt him. He cared deeply for her, even if he didn't want to. He had no right to wound her, to scar her young emotions by taunting her with her responsiveness.

"Shelly," he said quietly, one big hand against the door. "I'm sorry."

He didn't know if she'd heard him, but he hoped she had. He turned and walked away, aching with regrets.

Shelly went to bed, pleading a headache from the music. She figured that Nan wasn't fooled, but she couldn't face questions now. She'd moved away from the door so quickly that she hadn't heard Faulkner's apology. She climbed under the covers, and her pillow was wet when she finally slept.

She meant to avoid Ben, so that she could avoid his father, but the boy was waiting for her in the restaurant the next morning. He stood up, beaming, when she and Nan came in.

"I've already ordered coffee for both of you," he said with a flourish. "Do sit down."

Shelly and Nan chuckled involuntarily as they took their seats.

"What am I going to do with you?" Shelly asked softly.

"Adopt me," he said. "She saved my life," he told Nan. "Now she has to take care of me for as long as I live." He frowned. "She's sort of reluctant, but I'm working on her. I really do need a mother, you know. And don't say I'll have one when Dad marries Marie," he added gruffly when Shelly started to speak.

"Where's your dad?" Nan asked, because she knew Shelly wouldn't. Something had happened the night before, and it must have been something major for Shelly to be so tight-lipped about it.

"Dad's gone to a meeting," Ben said. "He sure was upset. He didn't even want breakfast. I guess he's missing *her*," he added miserably. "He said something about us going home earlier than expected."

Shelly felt her pulse leap. So he was that anxious to be rid of her. Did he think she'd make trouble? Embarrass him with confessions of undying love? He needn't have worried. She wasn't that sort.

"I'll miss you, Ben," she replied, smiling. "But life goes on."

"You look sick," Ben remarked. "Are you okay?"

"I'm just fine. No more hangovers," she promised.

But she wasn't fine. She went through the motions of having a good time, joining in a volleyball game on the beach and sunbathing and swimming. But her heart wasn't in it. Nan had paired off with a nice student from New York she'd met on the sailing trip, and Shelly wished she had someone, if only to keep Pete at bay.

"We could go back to my room and have a drink or two," he suggested. "Come on, Shelly, loosen up!"

She looked straight at him. Courtesy wasn't working. Perhaps stark honesty would. "I don't want to have sex with you."

He actually flushed. "Shelly!"

"That's what you're after," she said flatly. "Well, it isn't what I'm after. I came down here to have a good time. I'm managing it, barely, *in spite of you!*"

He got up, looking embarrassed, and shrugged. "Okay. You don't have to get upset. No hard feelings." He walked off, and very soon he was talking up another girl. Thank goodness, she thought. One complication resolved.

She felt tired and drowsy, and she began to doze. A sudden sharp movement brought her awake.

"This is stupid," Faulkner said roughly. "You're baking yourself. Haven't you put on any sunscreen at all?"

"Of course I have."

"Not on your back."

"Well, I can't reach it, can I?" she asked angrily. She sat up. "And don't offer to do it for me, because I don't want you touching me. Go away."

He searched her eyes slowly. "I apologized, but you didn't hear me, did you?"

Her eyes dropped. She didn't like looking at him in swimming trunks. He was disturbing enough fully clothed.

"I have to go back to the room," she said stiffly. "Nan and I are going shopping with some other— Faulkner!"

He had her up in his big arms and he was carrying her lazily down the beach to the water.

"Listen, you . . . !"

He put his mouth softly over hers, closing the words inside it, while he waded far out into the ocean until they were up to their shoulders in it. Only then did he release her, just enough so that he could bring her body completely against his and deepen the long, slow kiss that locked them into intimacy.

"Oh, don't," she pleaded, but her arms were already holding him, her mouth searching for his.

He gave it to her. His big hands slid down to her hips and his fingers teased under the brief yellow bikini bottom as he pulled her to the hard outline of his body and moved her against him.

He nibbled her lower lip while he positioned her in an intimacy that made her gasp and shiver.

"I can't get you out of my mind," he whispered into her mouth, groaning. "You torment me."

"Faulkner...!"

"I want you so, Shelly!" He kissed her hungrily. His hands released her hips and slid up to untie her top. It fell to her waist and his hands caressed her while his mouth teased and tormented hers. She felt his fingers teasing her nipples into even harder arousal, and she moaned sharply.

"Come here."

He caught her against him, rubbing his chest against her breasts in a soft, sweet abrasion that made her cry out. His arms enfolded her and he buried his face in her wet neck, holding her, rocking her in an intimacy she'd shared with no one else.

"You feel of silk and it excites me when I touch you and you make those sharp little noises deep in your throat. Shelly, you want my mouth on your breasts, don't you?" he whispered, letting his cheek slide down hers until he could reach her mouth.

The thought of it made her body ache. "Yes," she moaned. "But we can't!"

"I know. I'd have to lift you out of the water to get to you, and we'd be seen. Shelly...!"

His mouth fastened onto hers and his hands slid down her back, under the bikini briefs. He touched her with slow, deft intimacy. He held her like that, feeling her shiver and moan against his mouth as the intimacy took away all her inhibitions.

But he was too hungry for her. He had to pull back while he still could. An unwanted pregnancy was a terrible cost for a few minutes of pleasure.

For her, he thought as he restored her bathing suit to belated decency, it probably wouldn't be very pleasant at all, after the foreplay. Because she was virginal. Virginal. His head spun wildly at the thought of initiating her into sex, teaching her how to feel and give the ultimate sensual pleasure. But she was young. Too young, and too far away socially and economically.

"Why did you do that?" she asked miserably when he was holding her, soothing her in the heated aftermath.

"For the same reason you didn't stop me," he replied quietly. "Because I needed to touch you. Just as you needed to be touched by me."

"I'm too young and I don't know anything and there's Marie...!"

He bent and brushed his mouth softly, softly, over hers. "Open your mouth," he whispered tenderly. "You know already that I like to touch the inside of it with my tongue while we kiss."

She moaned. He could have thrown her down on the beach and made love to her in full view of the population and she didn't think she'd have a protest in her.

He drew back with evident difficulty. His face was drawn and wan as he looked down at her. "There are just too many obstacles," he said, thinking aloud.

She knew it. Standing in his arms, with her whole body screaming to belong to him, she realized that after the pleasure would come regret, shame, hurt. "Far too many," she agreed sadly.

He sighed heavily. "You deserve more than a man's lust."

She swallowed. "Are you...sure...that's all it is, Faulkner?" she asked miserably.

His face closed up. He let go of her. "Yes," he said flatly, ignoring the denial building deep inside him. "An uncontrollable, feverish lust that makes me ashamed. I'm sorry. I genuinely meant to apologize, not to compound the problem."

"I know."

"I go mad the instant I touch you." He laughed coldly. "It's a quirk of nature. Fate mocking both of us." He grimaced. "This can't happen again."

"I know. It won't. I was trying to avoid you," she confessed.

"So was I," he agreed ruefully. "And you can see where it got us both."

She flushed, averting her eyes as she remembered with unwanted vividness exactly how intimate they'd become in the water.

"I'll try to think of it as a reality-based exercise in sex education," she said bitterly.

He turned her face up with a long sigh. "Oh, no," he said. "It wasn't that." His eyes dropped to her soft lips. "It's been years since I've enjoyed a woman's body, since I've indulged the need to touch and stroke and arouse. You make me want to find out how gentle I could be, Shelly." He stopped, looking puzzled and irritated and even a little vulnerable.

Shelly searched his face with sad, quiet eyes. "Do I?"

He touched her face with something like wonder. "In the very beginning, I loved Ben's mother. I felt such tenderness for her, such aching need. But she wanted what I could give her in a material sense. For her it was a business deal, and Ben was my price." He winced. "She never loved me. She died in the arms of another man, and I hated her and loved her and mourned her for years afterward. Since then, women have been nothing more than an amusement. I've used them," he confessed, lifting his eyes to hers. He searched her face slowly. "But, I couldn't use you. And that being the case, I think it's better for both of us if we forget everything that's happened."

Chapter Five

Shelly lowered her eyes to his chest and tried not to appear as devastated as she felt. She was already looking ahead to a time when she wouldn't see him again. He wanted her, but wanting was not going to be enough. She knew that and so did he. His mind was clouded by the desire he felt. Once he satisfied it, the clouds would vanish and he'd hate them both. Even if she were tempted, and she was, it wouldn't be wise to let things go any further.

"You mean we shouldn't see each other again," she said miserably.

"That's about it." He moved away from her, pushing the wet hair from his damp face. "We won't be here much longer," he added. "We'll muddle through." He searched her face quietly. "Somehow."

She forced a smile. "What about Ben?" she asked.

"He's crazy about you. Don't deny him your company."

"I hadn't planned to."

He touched her soft cheek gently. "Shelly," he said huskily, "you know it wouldn't work. Even if I took a chance on your age, our social backgrounds are too far apart."

"And that would never do," she agreed, averting her eyes.

"I'm a banker. I have a position that requires discretion." He shrugged. "I've never cared much for convention, but when the jobs of other people depend on it, I can give the image I need to give. Besides," he added bitterly, "it isn't as if marriage would ever enter into any relationship I had. Do you understand?"

She lifted her eyes to his hard face, seeing the resignation and stubborn determination there. "You don't trust women. Is that why you let Marie get such a hold on you? She was safe?"

"I know all about Marie," he said, without taking offense. "She's devious and snappy, and selfish to a fault. She has grown up around wealth. She enjoys throwing her weight around."

"So I noticed," Shelly said.

"Ben thinks you're very special," he said, his voice deep and soft. "So do I, Shelly. I'm sorry. I wish . . . I really wish things had been different. We seem to have a lot in common. We might discover even more."

"So we might. But taking risks isn't your specialty, is it?"

He shook his head. "I only bet on a sure thing. This isn't." He touched her mouth and slowly drew back. "I'm sorry."

"So am I. But," she added, drawing in a steady breath as she struggled for something light, "whatever happens, we'll always have Paris."

It took a minute for that to sink in. By the time he started to laugh, she was already halfway to the beach.

Faulkner, true to his word, didn't come near her again. Ben did. He haunted her.

"Can't you find something else to do?" she wailed.

He grinned and shook his head, because he knew she liked him. Her face was an open book. "You can't banish your only child."

"But you're not!" she cried.

"How do you know?" He looked very serious. "I mean, you could have had me and forgotten about it. You might have advanced amnesia."

"I couldn't have become a mother when I was twelve," she muttered. "And besides that, I'd remember having had a child. It isn't something anybody forgets."

Ben didn't say a word, but he could add. His father thought Shelly was in her teens, but she'd just subtracted his age from hers and come up with twelve. That made her twenty-four. He pursed his lips.

"How old are you?" he persisted.

"How old do you think I am?" she asked foxily.

"Twenty-four."

She glared at him. "How in the world..."

He told her how in the world, and she let out a long, slow breath.

"I won't tell Dad. But why don't you want him to know?" he asked.

She couldn't explain that without giving herself away. "I have my reasons," she said. "So it's our secret. Okay?"

"Okay. After all, a boy can't afford to argue with his own little mother."

She opened her mouth to protest, groaned and closed it again. Arguing did no good.

The night before they were to leave for home, Ben maneuvered Nan and Shelly into a leisurely supper with him and his father. It was a less than sparkling evening, with Shelly and Faulkner trying to ignore each other and act normally. They failed miserably. Finally Nan and Ben went in search of souvenirs at the shop next door to the motel office, leaving them alone.

"This wasn't my idea," he said gruffly.

"I know." She stared into her coffee cup with eyes that barely saw it. She was leaving and so was he. They'd never see each other again.

"Damn it, you know it's for the best," he said through his teeth. "Will you look at me?"

She lifted her eyes and winced at the temper in his. "Yes, I know it's for the best!" she muttered.

His lips parted on a rough breath. His silver eyes searched hers until she flushed. "I want you," he said unsteadily.

She glared at him. "That's it, reduce it to the most common terms you can!"

"What else is there besides lust?" he demanded. "That's all we really have in common. And we wouldn't have that if you hadn't spent your entire holiday here coming on to me!"

"That's right, blame it on me," she raged. "Tell the world I tried to seduce you!"

"Tell me you didn't," he shot right back. His hand curled around his wineglass and tightened until the stem threatened to snap. "Every time I turned around you were making eyes at me."

"I told you why..."

"You lied," he said flatly, his smile world-weary and full of cynicism. "Don't you think I know when a woman finds me attractive? I'm rich. I've spent my adult life fending off willing women."

"Including Marie?" she asked sweetly, with blazing pale eyes.

"I don't need to fend off Marie," he returned. "She has status of her own."

"You mean, her parents do," she shot back.

"It's the same thing."

"No, it isn't," she replied seriously. "Life is about making choices on your own, taking your own chances, making your own way. A life-style should be earned, not inherited."

"Ahhh," he murmured sarcastically. "A budding socialist."

"Hardly." She glared at him. "Haven't you been listening? I think people should earn what they get."

"Marie earns it," he said, his tone faintly suggestive.

She remembered how it felt to be in his arms, and she flushed, averting her eyes.

"I keep forgetting how young you are when you bait me," he said angrily. He drained his wineglass.

"I'm not so young that I don't know what you were insinuating about your relationship with Marie," she said shortly. "If she's what you really want, why were you kissing me on the beach?"

He searched her eyes. The memories were darkening his. "Maybe I wanted to see how far you'd go."

She felt her cheeks becoming even ruddier. "As you said, I'm young," she muttered. "A pushover for any experienced man," she added pointedly.

He wanted to believe that, but he couldn't. He toyed with the empty wineglass, watching the light from the chandelier reflected in the faceted crystal. "No," he replied. "It was much more than that, for both of us." He lifted his eyes back to hers and felt the heat shoot through him like fire as he saw his own hunger reflected in her soft, sad eyes.

His breathing roughened; quickened. "I want to make love to you, one last time."

Her lips parted. "Faulkner..."

He signaled the waiter and paid the bill. Scant minutes later, he'd asked Nan to take a delighted Ben back to the girls' motel room, and he and Shelly were walking down the dark, deserted beach.

Shelly was much too aware of the brevity of the strappy little green sundress she was wearing with high-heeled sandals. She felt vulnerable as she thought about his strong, callused hands on her bare skin. But she had no pride left and she couldn't pretend that she didn't want this. It would be their last time together.

He turned to her when they were along a sheltered bit of beach, elegant in his white dinner jacket and dark slacks. He seemed bigger somehow, towering over her, unsmiling.

"You came with me," he reminded her. "I didn't drag you here by the hand."

"I know." Her voice was almost drowned out by the crashing of the surf. She searched his dark eyes in the faint light. "I'm not taking anything," she said abruptly.

He drew in a long breath. "Shelly, we can't make love to each other here. And I can't take you to my room because Ben might decide to come back on his own, without Nan." He caught her shoulders in his lean, warm hands and drew her to him. "You're a virgin," he whispered softly, drowning her in his strength and the drugging, delicious scent of masculine cologne as he moved closer. "I'm not quite that much of a rogue..."

His mouth opened as it touched hers, teasing her lips apart. He felt them tremble softly as he began to increase the pressure of his mouth. She moaned, pressing against him, and he felt his body react sharply to her proximity.

She tensed and started to draw back, but his hand swept down to the base of her spine, gently preventing the withdrawal.

"You're safe," he whispered into her mouth. "This feels good. Don't ask me to stop."

It felt good to her, too, but it was embarrassing. She tried to tell him, but his mouth became slowly invasive, and she clung to him as the intimacy of the kiss grew suddenly and exploded into something approximating possession.

He felt her nails through the thick fabric of his jacket. He wanted to feel them on his skin.

With a rough sound, his hand moved between them, his knuckles brushing over the tops of her breasts as he worked at fastenings. Seconds later, he coaxed her hands into the thick mat of hair that covered him and let her caress him.

"Oh, God, it isn't enough," he whispered shakily, his mouth harder now, hungrier. "Shelly!"

His mouth covered hers again. He moved the thin straps of her dress away from her shoulders and abruptly stripped her to the waist with deft, economic movements of his hands. Before she could utter a protest, he had her against him, inside the folds of his shirt and jacket, her breasts rubbing with exciting abrasion against his bare skin.

His thumbs caressed her breasts while he kissed her, his teeth nibbling, his tongue probing deeply. She was trembling and so was he, and the surf was hardly louder than their erratic heartbeats.

"Please!" she sobbed against his mouth.

He barely heard her. His body throbbed where hers touched it. His hands were possessing her, exploring her exquisite softness in a silence that was total and overwhelming. None of the differences between them mattered when they were this close. He'd never felt this way. Not even with his late wife when he was in the throes of first love.

He lifted his head a few inches and looked into her rapt, vulnerable face.

"If you were on the pill," he said roughly. "Would you let me?"

"I don't know." She rested her forehead on his chest, shivering with reaction. "It's a big step. I've always believed that it belongs in marriage, between two people who are committed to each other for life." She lifted her eyes to his. "Is that unrealistic, in a world where love is nothing more than a euphemism for sex?"

"What a profound question." He smiled, but a little bleakly. "I'm not the one to ask. Anyway," he added with a forced note of humor, "where would we make love? This is hardly a deserted place, and Nan and my son are in your room. If we went to mine..." He sighed heavily. "I couldn't. I want to, and if you were even faintly experienced, I would. But this isn't for you, Shelly. As I've already told you, I have nothing else to offer."

She pressed her cheek against the warm, heavily throbbing flesh of his chest. The thick hairs tickled her nose as they stood together in the semidarkness, unspeaking.

"If I were older," she began. "Richer..."

"You'd still be a virgin," he replied simply. "And I've had all I want of marriage." He tilted her chin up to his eyes. "I'll regret this night until I die."

"That you kissed me?"

He shook his head. "Oh, no. That I couldn't strip you down to your silky skin and ease you under me, here in the sand," he whispered, tracing her soft, swollen lips. "As intensely as we want each other, I don't think I'd ever hurt you."

She nibbled on his thin upper lip, her fingers stabbing into the hair that covered him. "It would take a long time, wouldn't it?" she whispered. "For me, I mean."

"Yes." He kissed her back, lazily, tenderly. His hands found her soft breasts and caressed them in a warm silence.

"They feel good."

"What?"

"Your hands on my skin," she said at his lips. "Do it . . . harder."

"I can't."

"Why?"

He teased around her mouth with the tip of his tongue. "You know why. Your breasts are very delicate, and I'm no sadist. I don't want to hurt you."

She smiled. "It wouldn't hurt. I meant like this."

She guided his thumb and forefinger to the hard, dusky tip and showed him what she wanted. She gasped as it sent a wave of heat through her body.

"Shelly," he whispered roughly, "does it make you hot all over when I do that?" he asked at her lips. He asked something else, something very intimate and explicit. "Does it?" he persisted huskily.

"Yes," she confessed shyly.

It wasn't wise. He knew it, even as he bent his head and took the nipple between his teeth. But the sensations she was describing very closely resembled those of fulfillment. It excited him to think he could give her complete ecstasy with such a small demonstration of love play. He had to know...

When he felt her convulse and cry out in his arms, he groaned and kissed her with slow anguish. He'd never been able to do that to another woman. Was it because she was a virgin that she reacted so violently to his ardor? Or was it something more?

He lifted his head and she hung in his arms, her body trembling, her face flushed with embarrassed shame.

He held her up, slowly replacing her bodice and refastening the soft straps. His hands were a little unsteady. He was still blatantly aroused.

"You shouldn't have...!" she managed to say, flustered.

"I think I should." He tilted her eyes up to his quiet, wise ones. "You do understand what happened?"

She flushed and averted her eyes. "Well, yes..."

"It's nothing to be ashamed of. You're one in a million," he said, his voice deep and slow and tender.

"Most men would kill for a woman as passionate as you."

"It's embarrassing!" she groaned.

"That you should reach fulfillment because I suckled your breast?" he asked, his voice explicit but somehow comforting. "Shelly, I feel ten feet tall. I've never felt so much a man."

She looked up, slowly. "You don't think I'm odd?"

"I think you're dynamite." He smoothed back her disheveled hair with hands that weren't quite steady even now, although he was less tormented. "I'm flattered that you want me that much."

She lowered her eyes to his chest. "But this is all there is."

"That's right." He held her close for a long time, savoring the scent and feel of her in his arms. "Shelly?"

"Yes?"

He kissed her hair. "We'll always have Paris."

Despite her sorrow, she smiled.

They went home the next day. Shelly hadn't seen Faulkner again, and she hadn't tried to. She'd said her goodbyes to Ben when they'd returned to her motel room, a little tearfully. Ben had wanted to keep in touch, but Shelly didn't dare do that. She couldn't risk having them find out the truth about her background, about her parents. Washington was a big city, and despite her father's wealth and influence, he was one of many wealthy investment bankers in the city.

She didn't remember her father ever mentioning Faulkner Scott, so it was unlikely that they knew each other. For the sake of her sanity, she had to keep it that way. After all, Faulkner had admitted that the main problem was his inability to make a commitment. He wanted an affair and she wanted forever. It wasn't easy to compromise on two such wide viewpoints.

She was going to miss him. And Ben. She'd lived her whole life without knowing either one of the Scotts, but she knew she'd live the rest of it without forgetting them.

Nan had noticed her friend's pallor and unusual quietness, but she hadn't remarked on it.

They boarded the plane and with adjoining seats, had time to talk, away from the rest of the students they traveled with.

"I'm sorry it didn't work out for you," Nan told her. "Really sorry. He was a dish, and the boy was special."

"Thanks. I'm sorry, too." She leaned back, closing her eyes. "Nan, if only I were liberated."

"You are."

"You know what I mean."

"Liberated as in sharing one night of explosive passion and spending the rest of your life living on it?"

Shelly glared at her. "Stop confusing me."

"You don't live the rest of your life on one night, no matter how explosive it is," Nan said firmly. "And in that one night, you could catch a disease that would kill you or make you untouchable. You could sacrifice all your principles and have nothing left except the certainty that the man you worshiped felt justified to treat you like a fast-food plate."

"A fast-food plate?"

"Something you use to feed yourself from and then throw away."

"Nan!"

"Well, it's true," the black girl said firmly. "You won't catch me risking my life or my health for the sake of a romantic one-night stand. Not me. I'm saving it all up for one lucky man who's going to thank God daily, on his knees, that I waited just for him." She leaned close. "*That's* romantic."

Shelly grimaced. "You have this nasty way of making me feel like pond scum."

Nan frowned. "Speaking of pond scum, where's Pete?"

"He got on the plane just behind you," Shelly said, chuckling. "Shame on you for calling him that."

"But he is pond scum," the other woman said seriously. "He seduced one of the freshman girls and then wouldn't have a thing to do with her the next day."

"You're right. He is pond scum!" Shelly exclaimed.

"So are a lot of other men, whispering sweet nothings so that they can have their way."

"Not all of them," Shelly said miserably. "There are men who feel protective toward women with no sense of self-preservation."

"So that's why he looked like that last night," Nan mused dryly.

"How did he look?"

"Frustrated. Confused. Puzzled. Delighted," she added softly. "The way he looked at you when you didn't see him!" She sighed. "Oh, Shelly. If you'd had another week together, there would have been wedding bells."

"I'm afraid not. He doesn't want to get married."

"What man does?"

Shelly closed her eyes. "Well, it doesn't matter, does it? Spring break is over and I'll never see him again."

"He knows that you go to Thorn College," Nan remarked. "And he lives in D.C., too."

"It won't matter." Shelly said it with conviction, but deep inside, she hoped she was wrong....

The semester was finally over, and Shelly went home to sweat out her grades until the registrar notified her on what they were. She felt pretty confident about her subjects, but she always worried.

"Darling, must you wear *that* dress?" her mother muttered.

"It's perfectly respectable..."

"It's so old-fashioned, Shelly," Mrs. Astor replied, glaring at the deep blue velvet gown that covered Shelly from neck to toes, except where it dipped seductively in the back.

Tonia Astor wore a black silk dress that flattered her still-youthful body, helping the contrast between her naturally black hair and its streak of pure silver. She looked elegant and chic, which she was. Shelly despaired of ever having her mother's unshakable poise at society gatherings.

The Astors were giving a gala party tonight in honor of a new president at one of the banks where Bart Astor was a member of the board of directors. Shelly had been persuaded into helping her mother hostess. She had no excuse, because she wasn't going to attend summer semester at the school.

"You've just been on holiday," her mother reminded her. "This is just a small get-together, darling. You'll enjoy yourself. It's time you stopped this silly college idea and got married. Charles is a delightful man, very settled and influential."

"Charles is a bore. He likes to quote stock averages to me."

"He's settled," her mother repeated.

"He should be, he lives with his mother."

"Shelly, really! Oh, there's Ted."

Her mother moved away, dragging Shelly with her across the crowded room where a full orchestra was playing. With her upswept salon coiffure and discreet but expensive sapphire choker and matching bracelet, Shelly's subdued elegance matched the tone of the party.

"Ted Dumaris," Tonia exclaimed, taking both his hands in hers. "So nice to see you again!" she added, totally unaware of Shelly's shocked expression and sudden panic as a tall, dark-haired man with a familiar thin brunette in tow made their way through the crowd to Antonia Astor and Shelly. "And is this the daughter you were telling me about?" she exclaimed with enthusiasm.

"Yes, this is my Marie and her...*our*...friend, Faulkner Scott. This is Antonia Astor."

Faulkner's expression was faintly curious. He hadn't seen Shelly, standing just to the side and behind her mother. He was obviously connecting the name.

"How lovely of you to have invited us," Marie was gushing to Antonia. "I adore your home. *So* impressive!"

Shelly wasn't impressed. Marie's fawning made her nauseous. And seeing Faulkner again wasn't helping.

"Where's Shelly? Oh, there you are, darling, do come and be introduced. She's a college freshman, you know, at twenty-four! We were absolutely horrified...!"

Her mother rambled on, but Shelly wasn't listening to the explanations or introductions. She was lost in Faulkner's glittering silver eyes. He stared at her with shock and dawning realization, barely aware of her mother or his surroundings.

"Twenty-four?" he asked gruffly.

"Yes, isn't she ancient to be starting college?" Tonia laughed. "But she has a high grade point average and we're very proud. What do you do, Ms. Dumaris?" she asked Marie.

"When she isn't looking down her nose at other people, I expect she goes to parties, don't you, Ms. Dumaris?" Shelly, diverted, fixed her cold blue gaze on the shaken older woman. "Ms. Dumaris mentioned just recently that she could use her influence to have me booted out of college."

"Shelly," Tonia began uncertainly, because she'd never seen her daughter lose her temper.

Marie swallowed, blushing and back-stepping. "I never meant it that way!" She laughed nervously, chattering. "I'm sure you must have misunderstood me!"

"I didn't misunderstand a single word, unfortunately for you."

She turned her back on Marie and her eyes found Charles. She motioned to him, ignoring Faulkner and Marie's almost pitiable attempts to smooth over her vicious attitude in Daytona Beach with Shelly's mother.

Shelly caught tall blond Charles by the hand and turned to face the others. Her face was pale but she was as composed as she'd ever been.

"I'd like you all to meet Charles Barington," she said with a forced, dazzling smile. "He's my fiancé!"

Chapter Six

"I can't believe you're finally willing to marry me," Charles blurted out when they were out of earshot of the others. "Shelly, what a surprise!"

"I hope you aren't going to be upset, Charles, but I really didn't mean it," she said gently. "I'm sorry, but I was in a very tight spot. I'll explain later."

He looked torn between disappointment and relief. His eyes glanced toward a young woman named Betsy, for whom he was slowly developing deep feelings. "What will everyone say?" he asked.

"Nothing at all," she assured him. "And I'll simply say that I wasn't quite enough for you, if anyone asks why we got unengaged."

"That's very nice of you," he said, surprised.

"Not really, and I'm sorry I had to involve you. But we've been friends for a long time, and I hoped you wouldn't mind."

"Of course I don't."

"I'm glad." She smiled, watching him blush. He was a sweet man, in his way, but he had no imagination and no stomach for a fight. Shelly knew instinctively that she'd spend her life walking on him if they got married. And that wouldn't suit either of them, especially Charles. She noticed a familiar younger woman watching him with covetous eyes and an idea was born. "Do go and have something to drink, Charles, and we'll talk later. Oh, there's Betsy, remember her? She's looking very lonely. Wouldn't it be nice if you asked her to dance?"

"Yes, of course," he said eagerly.

"Why don't you, then? She's a dear girl."

Charles nodded. He'd never understand Shelly. But Betsy was sweet, and she seemed to like him very much. She only danced with him at parties. He smiled as he approached her and she blushed. He wondered if he hadn't been turning his interest in the wrong direction all along as he took a radiant Betsy into his arms on the dance floor.

Shelly, meanwhile, went to the drinks table and poured herself a large brandy. She made a face as she sipped it.

A big, lean hand shot past her, took the glass and put it down on the table. "You can't hold your liquor. Leave it alone."

She whirled, her eyes angry. "Don't tell me what to do. I don't like it."

His eyebrows arched. "My, how you've changed. A young, virginal, college freshman with no money—isn't that how the story went?"

"All lies," she said, smiling up at him. "I had fun. Didn't you?"

"Not all lies," he replied, reading fear through the bravado. Her eyelids fell quickly. "I may not be able to tell a poor student from a socialite, but I damned sure know a virgin when I make love to one."

"We didn't," she said sharply.

"Make love? No, we didn't," he replied quietly. "You're twenty-four and wealthy. There are no barriers, isn't that what you expect me to say?"

She lifted her eyes. "I still believe in forever after, and you don't want to get married." He looked stunned. She laughed coldly. "I don't believe in fairy tales. You told me yourself that commitment was the real obstacle, not my background. Or, rather, what you thought was my background." She smiled cynically. "I'm much sought after, you know. Men love my father's money."

"So that's why."

"Why what?"

"Why you went back to school without letting anyone know who you were."

"It beats being on the appetizer list."

He searched her flushed face. "Your fiancé is dancing with another woman. Much too close," he added with a glance at Charles and Betsy. "Don't you mind?"

"I would if I planned to marry him. He thinks I do. So does my father, who arranged it. My father wants me to be Mrs. Charles Barington. With all due respect," she added softly, "I hardly think a banker would be high on his list of son-in-law prospects. Unless, of course, you owned all the assets in your bank."

He glared down at her. "You know nothing about me, financially or otherwise. And if I wanted to marry you, the only opinion I'd give a damn about would be yours."

"My father has taken down bigger men than you. I fought him to get to go to college." She glanced towards Charles with sad resignation. "I don't feel like fighting him anymore. You were right. There's no such thing as love and happily ever after. I've been dreaming."

He caught her arm. It hurt to find her like this, so cynical and self-effacing and sad. He'd been lonely, but she looked as if the weeks they'd been apart had hurt her even more.

"Shelly," he said softly.

She pushed his hand away and smiled that social smile that never reached her eyes. "So nice that you could come tonight, Mr. Scott," she said. "If you'll excuse me, I have to circulate."

She took Charles away from Betsy with a murmured apology. "Do you mind being engaged to me for the rest of the evening? I'll square it with Betsy."

"No, of—of course not," he faltered.

She laid her cheek on his chest and closed her eyes. "Then dance, Charles. Just dance."

The next day, she went to Nassau and checked into a hotel and casino complex overlooking Cable Beach, with its blistering white sand and incredibly clear turquoise waters. She'd told Betsy about the masquerade before she left and hoped that Charles would have enough sense to notice that the young woman was crazy about him.

Shelly herself had no interest in Charles or marriage. Seeing Faulkner again had destroyed her serenity. Now she had to find it again, and she didn't know how she was going to manage. What she'd felt for him hadn't vanished. It had grown stronger.

The yellow bikini was all too brief, but everyone else was wearing things just as skimpy. She closed her eyes with a sigh and let the sun warm her back.

The sudden sprinkle of icy water on her spine made her lift up. "Hey!" she said angrily.

A pair of gray eyes in a young face met hers—laughing eyes. "Hi, Mom!" Ben said chuckling. His hair, and the rest of him, were wet. He was wearing bathing trunks and carrying a towel. "Fancy meeting you here!"

"Oh, God," she groaned, laying her head on her forearms.

"Not quite," came a deep, gravelly voice from overhead.

She didn't look up. She didn't have to. She knew who it was. "What are you doing here?"

"Taking a vacation. Marie and her father have flown to England on business and I had some time off due. Ben's just out of school. We like the Bahamas, don't we, son?"

"There are seven hundred islands down here in the Bahamas chain," she mentioned. "Couldn't you like another one?"

"This is great," he said. "There's even a casino. Do you gamble?"

"I don't gamble. I lose. That's all I do." She lifted her head and glared at him. "Lately it's getting to be an affliction!"

"Not nice," he chided, sliding closer to her. He looked as relaxed as his son. He was wearing dark bathing trunks with white stripes down the side, his magnificent chest bare and rippling with muscle and thick black hair. He watched her watching him and chuckled. "Throw me that towel, Ben," he said, and sat down beside her. "Nice hotel. I'm glad you picked one close to the water."

"All of them are close to the water."

"Not really. Ben and I once stayed in a hotel high on a hill overlooking the bay. Very nice. Swimming pool and five-star food. But no ocean."

"That's right. This is a nice hotel, Mom. Dad had to call half the hotels in Nassau to find you...."

"Don't you want to go and swim, Ben?" he was asked.

"Oh. Oh, sure!" He chuckled. "See you later, Mom!"

Shelly groaned, giving up all hope of denying that she was. Nobody listened anyway.

Faulkner lay back and stretched hugely, his powerful legs crossing. "Your mother said to tell you that Charles has asked Betsy for a date. Your father is livid."

"Poor old Daddy," she said unenthusiastically.

"He only wants you to be happy."

"If he did, he'd let me live my own life."

"Parents sometimes take a little convincing that children are capable of making their own decisions. I did," he reminded her. "You'll be glad to know that Ben and I are getting along very well these days. He's hardly the same boy he used to be."

"I hope he gets to stay that way," she said stiffly. "Your Marie strikes me as a woman who wants to reshape everyone around her in her own image."

"She didn't used to be quite so bad," he replied. "You set her on her heels. It did her good. She'll think twice before she acts in an offensive way to strangers again."

"When's the wedding?" she asked, trying to sound casual when her heart was breaking.

"I don't know." He rolled over onto his stomach and looked down at her. "When do you want it to be?"

She swallowed. "Don't make jokes."

"I'm not." He lifted his hand and just the tip of his forefinger began to work its way slowly down the strap of her bikini, teasing the soft bare skin of her shoulder down to the slope of her breast.

"Don't!" she whispered.

"Why not, little one?" He caught her eyes and held them, and still that maddening finger moved, traced, teased. The nipple beyond it grew visibly hard and she bit her lip to keep from crying out as he increased her sensual anguish.

"Faulkner, don't," she pleaded brokenly.

"I wouldn't if you didn't enjoy it so much." He smiled, spreading the radius of his touch until she flinched. "That's nice," he murmured huskily. "I like the way you look when I touch you."

"There are people everywhere, didn't you notice?" Her voice sounded high-pitched, squeaky.

"Yes, but they're sunbathing and swimming. No one's watching us. Not even Ben." He moved, shifting just slightly so that his body was between her and the other sunbathers. "Which means," he breathed, "that I can do this..."

His whole hand slid gently beneath the yellow triangle and over her soft breast. He watched her shiver, felt her nails biting into his arm. He smiled through his own excitement. She was very sensual, and he loved the way she felt under his hand.

"Faulkner, no!" she whispered.

His thumb and forefinger gently caressed the taut nipple and she pushed at him, frightened of the sensations slicing through her body.

She wasn't the only one who was becoming aroused. As he watched her reactions, he felt his own body growing tense.

With a groan, he moved away from her and lay on his belly, trying to breathe normally.

"Are you all right?" she asked when she could speak again.

"Isn't that my line?" He took a slow breath and glanced at her with a rueful, self-mocking smile.

"Would you like to make a guess at why I'm lying on my stomach instead of my back right now?"

"Not really," she murmured, averting her eyes.

"Coward."

"You should be ashamed of yourself, trying to seduce innocent women on crowded beaches," she muttered.

"Not women. *Woman*. Only you."

"Still..."

"But the first time should be on a beach, don't you think?" he mused, lifting his head to watch her. "In the moonlight. Just the two of us, our bodies fitting together as perfectly as two puzzle pieces."

"You're driving me crazy!" she said through her teeth.

"I ache in very unpleasant ways," he remarked. "There's a Jacuzzi in my room. Ben has a room of his own. You could come upstairs with me while he's swimming and we could make love in the whirlpool bath."

"Faulkner!"

"It was just a desperate thought." He shifted his attention to the sand. "A white wedding is going to be horrific. I dread the thought of it. Between us, we know far too many people. That will mean just the right clothes, the right caterer, reception at the country club..."

"Then why don't you and Marie elope?" she asked, trying to hide her misery.

"I'm not marrying Marie and you know it. You knew the night we almost went too far on the beach," he said quietly. "I think I knew, too, but I couldn't quite accept it then. I've had time to get my priorities straight. You and Ben come first with me."

The earth was spinning around her. She was sure of it. She forced her gaze up to his and her eyes widened. "What are you saying?" she whispered.

"Don't you know?" He moved closer and kissed her. His lips were soft, and slow, and tender. "I love you," he whispered. "Say yes and put me out of my misery."

"But...but Marie, and Charles...!"

"Shut up!" he breathed into her mouth, and dragged her close while he deepened the kiss to madness.

Something wet was dripping on them. She opened her eyes and looked up a little blankly.

"Well?" Ben asked impatiently.

"She said yes," Faulkner managed huskily, pulling her back to him.

"Whoopee!" Ben yelled. He turned around and told everyone on the beach that he was going to have a brand-new mother. Everyone laughed and cheered him on. Everyone, that was, except the couple on the beach, who were oblivious to everything except each other.

The wedding was held a month later in the big Presbyterian Church near where Shelly and her parents lived. Her family had belonged to this church for three generations, so it was like home. The minister who'd baptized Shelly at the age of three months officiated at the ceremony, and Ben was his father's best man. Nan, of course, was maid of honor.

It had been the longest four weeks of Shelly's life, and she was certain that Faulkner felt the same way. They'd been incredibly circumspect during the strained engagement. It wasn't Shelly's idea. She'd tried repeatedly to tempt him into her bed, going so far as to remind him that even the Puritans didn't condemn premarital sex between engaged couples. But it didn't work. He was determined that they were going to have a white wedding and a wedding night.

The big day had arrived. Shelly was almost shaking with nerves, and her new husband didn't seem much calmer. They were off to Jamaica on their honeymoon, and Shelly thought to herself that it was going to feel like years before they finally had any time to themselves.

"Take deep breaths," he whispered when they were halfway through the reception. "We'll get through it."

"I hope so." She glanced at him. "You didn't kiss me at the altar."

He searched her soft eyes. He'd lifted her veil, but he hadn't kissed her. He'd kissed the palms of both her hands and given her a look that would have fried tomatoes.

"The way I want to kiss you would be almost indecent in a church," he said quietly. "That's why I'm saving it."

Her lips parted. She searched his hard, lean face hungrily. "I want you," she said unsteadily.

"I want you, too." He traced her mouth with a long finger. "It won't be much longer."

"I know."

Her parents came up to congratulate them again. Her father was more enthusiastic about the match than she'd imagined he would be. Even her mother raved about Faulkner and young Ben. There had been nothing but congratulations and praise from the morning they announced the engagement. It was a little surprising, but Shelly hadn't questioned it.

They were wished well by the others when they drove away in the nicely decorated car, courtesy of a beaming Ben, who was to stay with his new mother's parents for the duration of the honeymoon, and then Nan and some other college classmates. As they were driven to the airport by Faulkner's chauffeur, Shelly kept staring with wonder in her whole expression at the wide gold band Faulkner had slid onto her finger.

It was a long, tiring trip. By the time they got to their hotel in Montego Bay and got checked in, it was time to eat something. Shelly had little appetite, but she sat with her new husband in the dining room and nibbled on seafood while he ate a rare steak.

They walked along the beach on the way back, staring out over the ocean as the sun set. Then he turned her and led her back into their room.

There was a balcony overlooking the bay—a very private balcony, high up and concealed. Faulkner led her onto it, where a big chaise longue was already spread with a beach towel.

Gently he undressed her and laid her on it, standing over her to savor every soft line of her with eyes that shone like beacons with love.

"Do you want me to make you pregnant, or do you want to wait a few months?"

Her lips parted on a shocked breath. This was something they hadn't discussed. She was embarrassed by the heat that accompanied the softly spoken words, by the thought of allowing him to give her a child. She shivered, her eyes lost in his.

"You want it, don't you?" he asked huskily.

"I'm sorry," she whispered. "Yes . . . I do!"

"There's nothing to be sorry about," he said, his voice deep and slow. "I want it as much as you do."

"Will Ben mind?"

He smiled. "No. He won't mind."

His hand went to his shirt. He stripped very slowly, letting her watch him. His breathing changed when the last of the fabric came off and she could see the altered contours of his powerful body. Her eyes lingered there, fascinated.

"How does it feel to look at me like this?"

She caught her breath. "Intimate," she whispered, forcing her eyes up to his. "Very, very intimate. And very exciting. I feel hot all over."

"I can take care of that," he said, smiling gently.

He eased down onto the chaise with her, and began to kiss her. At first the kisses were lazy and soft and undemanding. But then he touched her, and with each soft exploration of his fingers, her body shivered even more, until she sought the full length of him with a need as violent as a summer storm.

He indulged her, his mouth as slowly invasive as the fingers that traced her and teased her and discovered her most intimate secrets. When she was ready, he slid her over onto her back and moved his body gently to fit hers.

He kissed her tenderly while he moved between her soft thighs and eased down. She jerked a little, but a few seconds later, she relaxed and shifted to make it easier for him.

"You flinched then," he whispered, lifting his dark head to look directly into her eyes. "Do you want me to arouse you a little more before I take you?"

She flushed at the explicit question. "But you already are...!"

"No." He kissed her eyelids closed and moved forward. As he did, she felt the sting and began to stiffen. "It's going to be difficult," he whispered at her lips. "You need more time. It's all right," he added when she looked set to protest, because he was shivering with a need of his own. "I can wait. Here, Shelly..."

True to his word, he started all over again, his mouth and his hands so tender, so thorough, that he very quickly brought her to a stormy peak of tension. Far from trying to push him away, she went crazy with the need for him. She sobbed against his mouth and pushed up with her hips, completing his possession even before he realized what she meant to do.

He shuddered and suddenly there was a rhythm, a fierce urgency that blotted out the sea and the sky and the night. She heard his voice against her mouth, but she was climbing, climbing, climbing...

There was a sharp explosion of heat that caught her unawares. She clung and stiffened, aware of desperate motion, a harsh cry and the convulsive shuddering of the body so intimately joined to her own. And then, slowly, the world came back into focus.

She lay beneath him, exhausted with pleasure, too shaken to move, fighting to get her breath.

"As first times go," she managed to say unsteadily, "and on a scale of ten, that was at least a twenty."

"Even as experience goes, that was a twenty," he breathed at her ear. "Are you all right? It isn't too bad?"

"It isn't bad at all." She moved against him, glorying in his nudity and her own, at the feel of him so close. "Are you going to roll over and go to sleep now?"

"Yes, and so are you." He chuckled.

He got up, lifting her, and carried her to bed. He slid her under the covers, pulled her gently into his arms and turned off the light. "Try to get some rest," he whispered. "You're going to need it in the morning."

She laughed delightedly, resting her cheek on his chest with exquisite delight.

"Shelly."

"Hmmmm?"

"You haven't said you love me."

"Yes, I have," she murmured drowsily. "I've said it a hundred times, but you haven't heard it. I love you madly. I always will."

He smiled and brushed his lips against her forehead.

"I'm glad. Because you're my life now."

She sighed, stretching as she snuggled closer. "Faulkner."

"Hmmmm?"

"We'll always have Paris."

He chuckled. Just before he closed his eyes, he felt a twinge of sorrow for that fictional character who'd walked away with only a gendarme for consolation. He had something much, much sweeter. He had Shelly... and Ben... and a future full of love.

* * * * *

Diana Palmer

Diana Palmer is the pseudonym of author Susan Kyle. Born in Cuthbert, Georgia, she now lives in the northeast Georgia mountains with her husband of over twenty years, James, and her son, Blayne Edward, who is in middle school.

After graduating from high school in Chamblee, Georgia, Susan moved to the north Georgia mountains with her parents and sister and began working for various newspapers when she was eighteen. She spent sixteen years as a journalist on the staff of both weekly and daily papers and for a time was a columnist. When Blayne Edward was born, she gave up the pressure of newspaper work and "retired" to write novels full-time.

Her career as a novelist began in 1979 when an editor named Anne Gisonny bought her first book, *Now and Forever.* Susan started writing for Silhouette Books in 1980, and now produces novels for both the Romance and Desire lines.

In 1991, she went back to college as a full-time student, and she is currently a history major with a minor in anthropology and holds a 4.0 average for four semesters of work!

Her busy life makes replies to fan mail very slow. But she loves her readers and enjoys hearing from them as often as they care to write!

The Apartment

DEBBIE MACOMBER

A Note from Debbie Macomber

Like most women, I went into this motherhood business with my head in the clouds and my heart filled with grand visions. My first clue that I might have been led astray came during my labor with our firstborn daughter, Jody. My mother, not wanting to frighten me, assured me labor was a lot like premenstrual cramps. I thought I'd take two aspirin before heading for the hospital and relax until the baby came. About two hours into my labor I knew something was terribly wrong.

It's been like that from the beginning. I assumed that being a mother was instinctive and I'd immediately *know* all the answers when it came to molding these young lives God had placed in my hands. Wrong again. Worse, the answers became all the more vague as Jody, Jenny, Ted and Dale entered their teen years.

Ah, those wonderful teen years. At one point, I had four teenagers living under one roof. There's a special place in heaven for those of us who've ever had to deal with more than one at a time. Can you imagine four? Against overwhelming odds we've all managed to survive.

By the time you read this, Jenny, who's twenty-one, will be married. Jody, a year older, is convinced, for the moment, no man will ever want her. She's happy with her job in downtown Seattle. Ted, my nineteen-year-old, is a Ranger in the U.S. Army and looking forward to being an attorney. (I'm not sure I understand how being a paratrooper leads to law school, but Ted's got that covered.) Dale, seventeen, my athlete, is a high school junior, and continues to break track records. His goal is to participate in the Olympics.

Once again I find myself in a new stage of motherhood, and I recognize my babies have become adults in their own right. Now more than ever I've come to realize that mothering is tricky business, this holding on and letting go. The holding on part comes naturally; it's the letting go that gives me so much trouble. That's why I chose the story line I did for "*The Apartment*." Hilary's mother is facing the difficult task of releasing her daughter. It isn't as easy as it seems. Trust me, I know.

Debbie Macomber

Chapter One

Freedom. Hilary Wadsworth savored the sweetest of nectars. She was becoming fanciful, she decided, giddy with exhilaration.

"Frankly, my dear, I don't give a damn," she shouted into the wind as she traveled across the Golden Gate Bridge, laughing without reason. The top was down on her red GEO convertible, her hair was whipping across her face, and she wasn't the least bit concerned what the wild breeze was doing to her hair, her skin, her eyes and every other concern her mother had listed.

Louise Wadsworth, her devoted, sweet mother, had been shocked when Hilary had purchased her first car. It was unsafe, a death trap. The damning rays of the sun would destroy her peaches-and-cream complexion. People would stare at her. The list seemed endless. Hilary had listened with the patience of Job, then promptly explained she'd accepted a position with the Portland Symphony and packed her bags.

She was on her own. For the first time in her twenty-three years she was out of her mother's clutches. For once, there wouldn't be someone looking over her shoulder, commenting on everything she said and did. For once, Hilary could see who she wanted, when she wanted, without censure or disapproval. She could

wear white shoes after Labor Day and black ones after Easter. No longer would she be constrained by
convention and her mother's outlandish, outdated
rules.

Hilary had her own apartment, her own job, and
neither was connected to her domineering mother.

By the time Hilary arrived in Portland, Oregon, a
day later, she experienced the first twinge of conscience. Her mother meant well. Her concerns had
been prompted by a deep, bonding love.

Hilary hesitated as she unloaded the car, knowing
Louise was waiting to hear from her, but she refused
to give in easily. Louise Wadsworth would make a
nuisance of herself if Hilary permitted it.

She hesitated. It wasn't as though she could completely ignore her own mother from here on out.
Feeling a little foolish that such a small decision
should be so difficult, she carted the last of the bags
into the duplex and reached for the telephone.

"I've arrived safe and sound," she announced into
the receiver.

"Oh, Hilary, darling, I was so worried about you.
Did Mr. and Mrs. Greer—"

"Mother, I've already explained that the Greers will
be gone for six weeks." Apparently her mother assumed the owner of the duplex would be baby-sitting
her.

"But, Hilary..."

"Mother, please, I'm completely and totally on my
own."

"Why couldn't you have found employment closer to home? Is that so much to ask?"

"Mother..." Hilary expelled a small, but not discourteous sigh. "I don't mean to hurt you, but it's time I left home. It's better for us both." Portland was perfect. Just far enough from San Francisco to prevent her mother from popping in unexpectedly and smothering her with gifts and advice. But close enough to plan occasional visits.

"It's just that I'm going to miss you so much." Resignation echoed in the elder Wadsworth's voice. "You'll call home often, won't you?"

"Of course..." Hilary found herself agreeing without thinking. "Once a week."

Louise's hesitation made her disappointment obvious. Hilary was certain her mother expected her to phone at least once a day. "I...love you, Hilary."

"I know, Mom. I love you, too."

They spoke for a few minutes longer before Hilary ended the call. She stood in the middle of her new kitchen and breathed in the magical feeling of independence. It was all she could do not to spread her arms out at her sides, whirl around and break into the chorus from "The Sound of Music."

Everything had fallen into place for her like marching tin soldiers. After several fruitless months of waiting for a flute position with the San Francisco Symphony Orchestra, Hilary had heard of an opening in Portland. It seemed like a lark to apply, but encouraged by friends and her own growing sense of discontent, she'd flown north for the audition. From the first, her mother had a list of objections which Hilary ignored.

The tryout had gone exceptionally well. Hilary had played a selection from Mozart's Concerto in G Major in the first round with other flutists. Later she'd been called back and asked to perform several sections of Debussy's *Prelude to the Afternoon of a Faun*. After what seemed like an interminable wait, she'd been offered the position.

With the help of the orchestra director, Hilary was able to find part-time employment at a music store to supplement the meager income she'd collect from the symphony. Although she received an adequate income from a trust account, she felt it was important to live entirely on what she earned herself. It was a matter of pride. A trait—she hated to admit this—that she'd learned from her mother. One that had been drilled into her since birth.

By the time she arrived back in San Francisco, Hilary had already made arrangements for the interest on her trust fund to be reinvested. She would burn her bridges behind her when she moved. The only way to travel was forward. Her goal, her purpose, was to become totally independent of her family, to support herself.

Being accepted with the Portland Symphony had been the first step in this bid for freedom. If she was going to be completely on her own, then she would need to make her own decisions. Within a few hours of accepting the job, she rented a small two-bedroom apartment. The owner, a retired couple, lived in one half of the duplex and rented out the second half.

Hilary had expected a full-fledged battle with her mother over the impending move. She'd gotten one, which had ended with her mother in tears and Hilary more determined than ever to move away. Her mother was suffocating her. Louise was ruling Hilary's life, and if Hilary didn't leave soon, she was convinced she was going to shrivel up and die.

It wouldn't have been so bad if her father were still alive. Hilary had been thirteen when her wonderful, fun-loving father had been killed in a car crash. The freak accident had sent Hilary and her mother's comfortable world into chaos.

Her mother had never been the same and neither had Hilary. Louise seemed to live in constant fear that something would happen to Hilary, too. For years, Hilary had tolerated her mother's protectiveness. She'd always been a quiet, unassuming daughter. The good daughter. Introspective, intelligent and talented. It had taken her years to come up with enough courage to break free. She was free now—and the air had never smelled sweeter.

It took several hours to unpack. The apartment was ideal, and she loved it more now than when she'd first seen it. She took the larger bedroom as her own, grateful for the second room, which she intended to set up for practice.

As third-chair flutist she'd need to rehearse for two to five hours a day. Not that she begrudged the time. Music was the one true love of her life. Her means of escape.

Hilary had dated over the years, but had never been involved in a serious relationship. Unless she counted William, which she refused to do. There was only herself to blame for the lack of romantic interests in her life. Hilary didn't understand men. She'd lived so long without one that she felt awkward and ill at ease with them.

She was attractive enough, she supposed, both slender and delicate. She'd inherited her father's dark good looks, his coloring and her mother's beautiful gray-blue eyes. In the last few months she'd turned down several dates because she strongly suspected her mother had arranged them. If and when she found a man, she preferred to do so on her own.

Although Hilary was exhausted by the time she finished unpacking, she cooked herself dinner, a small spinach quiche which she had with a glass of white wine and fresh slices of pear.

Then she lingered for a full forty minutes in a tub of hot water while her cassette player sounded the strains of Rimsky-Korsakov's *Scheherazade*. This was heaven, she decided.

She'd best relax now, since the following day would be exceptionally full. In the morning she started her job at the music shop and later that afternoon she was scheduled to meet with the full symphony for practice.

If she anticipated trouble sleeping, Hilary was wrong. Her eyes drifted shut the moment her head hit the pillow, and dreams weren't far behind. She was about to begin the grandest adventure of her life.

She was on her own. In her own home. Out from under the thumb of her loving, domineering mother.

An odd sound drifted toward Hilary. It came from the living room, or it seemed to. It was as if someone had dropped something heavy, which of course was ridiculous, since she was alone.

She wasn't concerned, especially when she didn't hear anything else. Sounds carried easily in the still of the night. Half listening, she decided it was either her imagination or the apartment settling, welcoming her to her new home. . . .

Sean Cochran stood in the living room of the duplex, his camouflage duffel bag on the floor before him. He was exhausted to the bone. The flight out of Boston had been delayed by nearly two hours, which meant he'd missed his connecting flight in Chicago. All in all, he'd had a long day.

Luckily Dave, a buddy from Operation Desert Storm, had been able to pick him up at the airport. He was sorry to have missed meeting Allen Greer. The man he'd rented the duplex from had been both friendly and helpful.

It was going to be a hassle to be without wheels, but the army would deliver his own car within the next week. Sean didn't know who was parking in his space now, but he'd make sure whoever it was didn't do it again anytime soon. Not that it was likely anyone would argue with him. At six-three and a solid two hundred pounds, his brawn intimidated most.

The army was behind him now, Sean mused, experiencing a brief sense of loss. Out of habit he walked to the refrigerator.

He was hungry and tired, a nasty combination. He'd intended to pick up something to eat at the airport before Dave arrived, but there hadn't been time. He didn't know what he was hoping to find in the refrigerator. A miracle?

That was exactly what happened. The refrigerator was stocked with several items, including a slice of quiche, a small bottle of French wine and a carton of milk.

Before the landlords left, the landlady must have brought him over something to eat. It was certainly patriotic of her. Unnecessary, but kind, and he appreciated it.

Had Mrs. Greer ever met him, she'd have known a slice of quiche wouldn't come anywhere close to filling him. Nor did he enjoy delicately flavored French wines. If he was going to drink anything alcoholic, it'd be a beer. Preferably dark ale.

Standing in front of the open refrigerator, Sean reached for the thin slice of pie and ate it in four bites.

He toyed with the idea of drinking the wine, then decided against it and downed the milk directly out of the carton.

He had to hand it to the landlady, she was one hell of a cook. The quiche was excellent. He'd gladly have eaten more.

The kitchen clock told Sean it was nearly eleven, which was two East Coast time. He was exhausted. Too exhausted to hassle whoever had taken his parking space. Too exhausted to worry about scrounging up anything to eat. All he wanted was a bed.

Without bothering to take his duffel bag with him, he wandered down the hall and took the first bedroom on the left. He didn't even bother to turn on the light.

He undressed and turned back the covers, grateful to find the bed made. In the morning there'd be plenty of time to sort out the changes in his life. He'd come two thousand miles for a fresh start. He wasn't in the Special Forces, wasn't one of the army's elite Green Berets anymore. Nor would he continue in his role as a well-trained advisor.

The army was making deep cuts these days. He'd once thought the military would be his career, but when the opportunity came for him to reenlist, Sean declined. The way things looked, there would be little room for advancement.

Dave Krier had assured Sean there was ample opportunity for a helicopter pilot in the Portland area.

It was the most promising offer Sean had, so he'd decided to accept his friend's proposition.

Dave had helped him make the arrangements on the West Coast. He'd found the apartment and given Sean's deposit to Allen Greer. The setup sounded ideal. An elderly couple who often traveled in their motor home and rented out one half of their duplex. Sean liked the idea of his landlords being away a good portion of the time. He liked his privacy.

Sleep came to him as a welcome friend. He had a good feeling about all this. Leaving the army could well have been the best move he'd made in several years.

Like most everything else in life, time would tell.

Hilary woke early, stirring just after dawn. The days were growing longer, Portland's famous roses were budding, and the warm scent of spring perfumed the air.

Dressed in her thin robe, she wandered into the kitchen to brew herself a cup of *latte*. The espresso machine had been a going-away present from her mother. Hilary couldn't help but feel a small stab of guilt at the thought, then resolutely turned her mind to heating the milk for her *latte*.

Once the drink was complete, she took a tentative sip and placed the milk carton back inside the refrigerator. It was then that she noticed the empty plate. She hesitated. Now that she thought about it, the milk was half-gone, too.

What in heaven's name happened to her leftover quiche? Who'd drunk her milk?

Frowning and confused, she closed the door and turned around. The noise. She remembered hearing something odd the night before, but had been too exhausted to get up and investigate.

Obviously some . . . cat burglar had broken into her home and eaten her quiche and drunk her milk.

Her heart started to pound heavily against her ribs as she glanced about the room, seeking out evidence. Nothing else seemed to be amiss.

Walking into the living room, she stopped abruptly at the sight of a large . . . sandbag. At least, it looked like a sandbag, although she'd always thought they were made of burlap. This one seemed to be constructed out of some jungle fabric.

In his haste to escape, the cat burglar had apparently left it behind.

Although she was more than a little frightened, she refused to phone the police the first full day she was on her own. It made sense for her to check out the bag first before leaping to conclusions.

"Come on," she said aloud, groping for the necessary fortitude. "It can't be that bad. What's there to scare you?"

With slow, easy steps, she walked around the counter and into the living room. The bag rested just inside the door. On closer examination, Hilary realized this wasn't a sandbag after all. More than likely, whoever had broken into her home had left behind a bag of stolen goods.

Something or someone had frightened him off and he'd dropped the goods. There was no help for it now. The choice had been taken away from her. She had to phone the police and turn it in. Her only prayer was that her mother wouldn't hear about this. It was just the type of thing that would send Louise into a tizzy.

Her decision made, Hilary turned and came within two feet of the biggest man she'd ever seen in her life. He loomed over her like the World Trade Center, menacing and angry.

Hilary's heart went into a panic.

"Who the hell are you?" he boomed in a voice that echoed like a Chinese gong.

Chapter Two

"Who am I?" Hilary cried indignantly. "The question here is who are you!" It was a wonder she hadn't fainted from sheer terror. How dare this...this bully break into her home—her very first home—and make demands of her. "Furthermore, what are you doing in my apartment?"

"You've got this all wrong, lady. I'm the one who lives here."

Hilary folded her arms and gave him a look that suggested she wasn't stupid, nor would she let him intimidate her. If she could deal with her mother, then she was capable of handling King Kong.

"I happen to live here," she told him as forcefully as she could. He might outweigh her by a hundred pounds and tower a good ten inches above her, but she refused to be browbeaten. "Now I'd like to suggest you leave. Otherwise I'll be forced to contact the authorities."

The intruder's eyes narrowed as he took in her best finishing-school voice. A slow, deliberate smile appeared. "Dave Krier put you up to this, didn't he?"

"I assure you I don't know anyone named Dave," she informed him stiffly. "Now kindly leave and take that...that sandbag with you, before I call the police."

"Be my guest." He crossed his massive arms, his dark eyes cold and arrogant. "It should be interesting, since I have a lease on this apartment."

"You couldn't possibly have a lease," Hilary responded tartly, "because *I* have a lease."

"Prove it."

"You prove it!" she demanded, refusing to be cowed. It was only too clear the man was lying, but for what purpose, she could only speculate.

"Fine, I will." He stalked over to the bag that had been the cause of her curiosity earlier. He opened it, reached inside and withdrew a thick envelope. He shuffled through some papers, then peeled one away and examined it.

"I signed a six-month lease," he said. "Allen Greer's signature confirms it."

"Allen Greer," Hilary repeated slowly as she read over the agreement. "I . . . rented this place from his wife more than a week ago." She had the papers with her as well, but they were in her room.

"Mrs. Greer rented you the apartment?"

"Apparently there's been some misunderstanding," Hilary said slowly, collecting her thoughts. She read over the paper and noted his name, neatly typed, on the top of the lease agreement.

"Then we should allow the Greers to settle this," Sean suggested. "It's apparent each of them rented out the unit without the other knowing."

"Yes, but I'm afraid the Greers aren't going to be much help."

Sean frowned fiercely. "Why not? Once we contact them, we can settle this thing once and for all."

"Because," Hilary said, growing impatient, "the Greers aren't here. When I last spoke to Mrs. Greer, she told me they would be gone for the next six weeks."

"Six weeks!" Sean exploded, and Hilary swore his voice boomed like thunder through the living room.

"There's no reason to yell."

"Listen, lady, I've got every reason to be upset. I have no intention of moving."

"But you'll have to—you don't have any choice," Hilary said, as calmly as she could under the circumstances. "I moved in here first and possession is nine-tenths of the law. The least you can do is the gentlemanly thing and—"

"Forget that. You can do the honorable thing and move. By the way, who's to say which one of us was here first?"

"Well, I was, of course," Hilary claimed indignantly, "because you ate my leftover dinner." He was frowning again, realizing, she hoped, that she was unquestionably right.

"Possession isn't the only means to judge who's entitled to the apartment. Get your lease and check the date of your receipt. It makes sense that whoever paid the deposit first should have it. The other will have to move. Agreed?"

"All right," she said hesitantly. She brushed the long strands of dark hair from her face, a nervous trait that angered her. Sean would look upon it as a display of weakness, and she refused to give him a single foothold.

It only took her a moment to find the signed lease. When she returned, Sean was standing next to the stove. A pan of water was boiling away. He added coffee grounds to the water and then strained it into a cup. Hilary had never seen anyone brew coffee using such primitive methods, but she was forced to admit he was resourceful. She only hoped he'd be equally so when it came to his locating other accommodations.

"My agreement was signed the tenth of the month," she said, handing him the proof.

Sean took the paper from her hand and carefully read it over while she reached for his lease. A deep sigh of gratitude went through her as she realized she had signed the agreement a day before Sean had.

"I'm sorry, I really am," she said, having a difficult time disguising her relief. "But I have to tell you the apartment is perfect for me. My job's less than a mile away." He glared at her, suggesting the apartment was equally convenient for him. "I'll be happy to do what I can to help you find someplace else," Hilary offered weakly.

His frown darkened and deepened.

"Is there someplace else you can live?" Hilary asked, feeling mildly contrite. She wanted to be gracious about the whole thing, since it was clear neither of them was at fault. She was just grateful that she wasn't the one who had to move.

"No," he said thoughtfully after a moment. "I flew out from Fort Deavon yesterday. My friend Dave met me at the airport."

"What about this Dave? Surely you could move in with him on a temporary basis?"

"That's not likely. He's living with his in-laws as it is. If you'll just write me out a check for the deposit and the first month's rent, I'll be out of your hair as soon as I can."

"Your deposit?" Hilary repeated. "First month's rent..."

"Three hundred and fifty dollars, plus the six hundred, equals—"

"I don't have nine hundred and fifty dollars." Hilary's heart sank all the way to her ankles. She couldn't get into her trust fund and she absolutely refused to ask her mother for the money.

"I'd say we have a problem, then, don't you?" Sean growled. "Because I'm not budging until I get my money back."

"You're being unreasonable," Hilary said, swallowing down a sense of dread. "The Greers have your money, not me."

"How do you expect me to rent someplace else without the cash to do it?" he barked impatiently.

Hilary blinked at the abruptness of his tone, then stiffened with righteous indignation. "I don't know... and I don't have the time to argue with you now. I've got to be at the music store in less than an hour. I'll try to think of something while I'm there."

"I suggest you do that."

"And I suggest *you* do some thinking, too."

This was one hell of a mess, Sean mused as he stood beneath the pelting shower. For weeks he'd been looking forward to the time he could be on his own again. He knew his family was disappointed that he'd opted to head west instead of returning to the Chicago area. His younger half brother had offered him a job, but Sean didn't think there was much call for a helicopter pilot in the furnace business.

For the first time, he wondered if he'd made the right decision. His mother had died long before he could remember her and his father had remarried when he was five. Sean had felt oddly out of place within his own family.

He'd enlisted in the army as soon as he finished high school and had been in the Special Forces for the last nine years. One of those years had been spent in Saudi Arabia. He now spoke Arabic well enough to pass as a national.

Dave phoned around ten that morning. Sean didn't mention the mix-up with the apartment. No need to, since it was fairly obvious to him what was going to happen.

Hilary didn't want to move. He didn't, either. And it wasn't likely she was going to be able to come up with nine hundred and fifty dollars.

They had no choice.

Hilary had rarely had a more unnerving morning Now her afternoon wasn't going much better. Just when she was beginning to understand what Mr. Murphy expected of her, Sean Cochran casually strolled into the store.

Talk about a bull in a china shop! The man couldn't have been more out of place.

With Mr. Murphy smiling serenely toward her, indicating she should assist this newest customer, Hilary walked purposefully toward Sean, doing her best to disguise her irritation. This entire situation irked her. It seemed that she was never going to be free. First her mother, and now...Rambo.

"How may I help you?" she asked calmly, although her eyes were spitting fire.

"Do you have my nine hundred and fifty dollars?" he asked.

Hilary briefly closed her eyes, calling upon every ounce of composure her mother had so laboriously drilled into her. "I've already explained that I don't."

"Any chance of getting it?"

Hilary had spent the majority of the morning pondering that same question. She couldn't very well ask for an advance on her salary since she'd only been employed for three hours.

She'd debated approaching her mother for the money and decided it was out of the question. The bank wasn't likely to give her a loan, either, since she was from out of state and had only recently established credit.

Hilary didn't know what to do.

"Well?" he pressed. "Do you have a way of getting it or not?"

"Not on such short notice," she admitted reluctantly.

"That's what I thought."

"I'm doing the best I can," she said between gritted teeth.

"Is there a problem?" Mr. Murphy inquired.

"None at all,' Sean assured the music-store owner with a satisfied smile.

"Are you trying to get me fired?"

"Not when you owe me a thousand dollars."

"I don't owe you any money, the Greers do." The man was becoming increasingly unreasonable. He looked even more intimidating now than he had earlier.

"But the Greers aren't here. You are," Sean reminded her casually.

"I'd give it to you if I had it." Hilary knew that was little consolation, but it was all she could offer.

"Listen," he said, rubbing his hand along the back of his neck. "I've come up with a tentative solution. For now it's the best I can do."

"All right," she said, hoping he had more ideas than she did. As far as Hilary could see, they were deadlocked. She didn't have the money and he wasn't going to budge until he got it.

"We share the apartment," he said, "just until the Greers are back."

Share the apartment! So much for being independent. So much for freedom. She'd leapt from the frying pan into the fire. "But that's six weeks," she said, tasting defeat.

"I know how long the Greers are going to be gone," Sean returned testily. "I'll stay out of your way and you stay out of mine. It isn't like I plan on sticking around there much. I haven't got a job yet, otherwise I wouldn't be so concerned about the cash."

"I'm going to be busy, as well," Hilary added, realizing they had no choice and might as well make the best of a difficult situation.

"Do you agree to sharing the apartment, then?"

Hilary hesitated. Things were not going as she'd planned.

"Well?" he demanded.

Feeling frustrated and miserable, she nodded. Glaring at him, she added, "But only on one condition."

His jaw tightened. "Name it."

Hilary glanced over her shoulder to be sure Mr. Murphy wasn't listening. "Under no circumstances are you to answer the phone. My mother can't find out about this.... Is that understood?"

Chapter Three

Hilary woke to the rhythmic sound of clapping. She didn't know what Sean was up to now, but she guessed it was something unpleasant. Something specifically designed to irritate her. Heaven help her, she didn't know why she'd ever agreed to this arrangement.

Struggling out of bed, she reached for her robe and traipsed into the middle of the living room. Sean was dressed in gray sweats and was down on the floor doing push-ups. Just when he'd levered himself off the carpet, he slapped his hands together and caught himself in time to keep from crashing into the floor. It was an ego thing, she guessed, to prove how strong he was.

Before she could comment, he twisted around and started doing sit-ups, moving so fast his upper body seemed to blur.

"Is this really necessary?" she asked, walking into the kitchen and brewing herself a *latte*.

He ignored her, which was fine. She'd spent much of the previous day pretending he wasn't there. Not that her game had helped any. Sean had assured her he'd stay out of her way, and naively she'd believed that meant they wouldn't be seeing much of each other. They didn't really spend long stretches of time together, but even thirty minutes was more than she could take. His presence in her home had quickly become a constant source of irritation. He apparently felt the same way about her.

"You left the radio on your country-and-western station again," she remarked, not bothering to disguise her resentment. "In case you've forgotten, and apparently you have, I prefer classical music. Since it's *my* radio, I'd appreciate it if you'd kindly change it back to my station once you've finished."

"Yes, Your Highness."

"Stop calling me that." Hilary hated the tag he'd given her. He seemed to delight in calling her names of royalty. If she wasn't Fergie or Diana, she was Princess Grace. Hilary normally didn't give him the satisfaction of knowing how his name-calling annoyed her, but she couldn't stop herself now. What troubled her most was that her mother's pet name for her was Princess. She didn't like the tag any better from her parent than she did from Sean, but at least when her mother called her Princess it was done with genuine affection. Sean did it to get her goat, inferring that she put on airs when all she was doing was protecting her own space.

"I'm only asking that you... Oh, never mind." Talking to him was next to impossible.

"You left three pairs of panty hose hanging over the shower stall," he said indifferently. "How am I supposed to close the shower curtain with a bunch of nylons dangling in my face?"

"You might have moved them."

"As I recall, you asked me not to touch anything that belongs to you."

"You ate my dinner." She'd been furious with him and rightly so. After a grueling three-hour rehearsal with the symphony, she'd arrived home, hungry and exhausted, to discover Sean had eaten her shrimp salad. He claimed it was an honest mistake, but she didn't believe him.

Somehow, someway, she suspected her mother had brought this man into her life to torment her. Since she couldn't convince Hilary to move back home, she'd hired a Rambo to make her life miserable.

"You've got a memory like an elephant, haven't you?" Sean asked, continuing his sit-ups with an intensity that irritated her even more.

"Okay," Hilary said, inhaling a deep, calming breath and briefly closing her eyes. "As I see it, we've got a choice here. We can continue to insult one another all morning or we can call a truce. Thus far, all we've managed to do is make one another miserable."

"You can say that again."

Hilary shivered, then realized it was more than his continuous insults, more than the fact they couldn't be civil with each other. The apartment was freezing—literally. Her teeth were starting to chatter.

Fuming, Hilary walked over to the thermostat, then whirled to confront Sean with this latest atrocity. "You turned down the heat!"

"I couldn't stand it. You had it set hot enough to grow orchids in here."

"You have it set so low I could store ice cream in the living room," she bellowed, losing all control. Before she had met Sean Cochran, she'd barely raised her voice. Now, inside of a week, she was a shrew. "Don't you dare touch this thermostat again." Ignoring his glare, she readjusted the temperature. No wonder she was shivering.

Adroitly Sean stood, reached from behind her and set the thermostat back to where he'd placed it earlier.

Hilary wanted to scream, but she realized it would do no good. "This isn't working," she said, close to breaking into tears of frustration and anger. They'd tried. They'd both given it their best shot, but they were never going to make this arrangement work.

"You're telling me," Sean said, his teeth clenched. "Living with you is like walking on eggshells. You have more rules than the Pentagon. We might have made a go of this if you weren't so damn unreasonable."

"Me? I'll have you know, buster, I'm one of the most even-tempered, good-natured women you're likely to meet. At least, I used to be until I met up with a bullheaded, illogical exercise freak."

"You want to talk about excesses—fine," he shouted, crossing his arms over his massive chest. "I've never known anyone in my life who's as compulsively neat as you are. I don't dare leave a magazine open because you'll close it and stack it under the coffee table.''

"I happen to like my home tidy. Is that such a sin?''

"Yes,'' he returned heatedly. "Furthermore, you're Mommy's little girl. You're so afraid of doing anything that will displease her.''

"You don't know anything about my mother and me!''

"I know you're so afraid of her finding out about me that I dare not answer the phone.''

"I'm not afraid of my mother.''

"Heaven forbid she learns her sweet little girl is living with a man.'' His voice raised in a strained falsetto.

"Leave my mother out of this,'' Hilary cried, stamping her slipper-covered foot.

"Gladly. If she's anything like you, I'd prefer not knowing anything about her.''

Hilary wrapped her hands around her middle to ward off the chill his words produced. He was right. As much as she wanted to be on her own, live her life as she chose, she remained tied to the apron strings.

She *was* worried about her mother finding out about Sean. It shouldn't matter what Louise thought. But why was Hilary so concerned? There certainly wasn't anything romantic going on between Sean and her.

What troubled her more was what Sean said about her being a neat-freak. Her mother was like that. All her life, Hilary had hated being constantly followed around and picked up after. Now she found herself doing the very same thing. It boggled her mind.

"You keep me up half the night practicing that flute of yours, then complain if I so much as turn on the television," Sean continued.

"All right, then let's end it right now," Hilary stormed, slicing the air with a karate-chop motion that was so full of anger she nearly lost her balance. "I'll move. Gladly. If you wanted me out of here, then congratulate yourself, because you've succeeded. Write me out a check for the deposit and my fair share of the rent—then I'll be more than happy to make other arrangements."

Sean went silent. He lifted the towel dangling from his neck and wiped the perspiration from his face. "I don't have it."

"You don't have it," Hilary echoed, and to her horror her voice cracked. "Then what am I supposed to do now?"

"I don't know."

"You're making it impossible to live here."

"Living with you hasn't exactly been a bowl of cherries, either," he growled.

"But I don't fiddle around with your radio station."

"I didn't use your shaver on my legs," he snapped.

"I didn't do it on purpose—I thought it was my own."

"How was I supposed to know three tiny shrimp on a bed of lettuce was your entire dinner?" Sean asked, his voice growing less irritated. "Admit it, there've been sins committed on both sides. What you said earlier makes a lot of sense."

"About me moving?"

"No," he said reluctantly. "That we call a truce. We're both mature adults—at least, I'd like to think we are."

"So would I," she murmured, surprised to realize her hands were trembling. She hid them behind her back, not wanting Sean to notice.

"We can make this work if we're both willing to put forth the effort," he said after an elongated sigh. "Are you willing to give this another try?"

Hilary nodded slowly, hesitantly. "All right."

"Good, then I will, too. It won't be for much longer—just how long can five weeks last?"

"I don't think I want to know," she muttered under her breath. There wasn't time to discuss this armistice, since she had to be at work within the hour. Twice a week she went directly from work at the music shop to the symphony. She wasn't sure if Sean had figured out her schedule yet. On her way out the door, she hesitated.

Sean was seated at the table, eating a gigantic breakfast of eggs, toast, fruit and cereal. In one meal he consumed more food than she downed in a week.

"I'll...be late tonight," she said, hoping she didn't sound defensive. "I have practice with the symphony after work.... I thought it might work better if we let each other know our schedules."

"Good idea. So, you won't be home until late, then?"

Hilary nodded. "Sometime around eleven."

He nodded. "It makes for a long day, doesn't it?"

Hilary smiled. "I don't mind. I really love what I do."

Sean set aside his fork and dabbed his mouth with a napkin. "You're good at it, too. I don't have much of an ear for music, but I can't help hearing you practice nights. It's really beautiful."

Hilary couldn't keep from smiling. "A compliment, Sean?"

He looked mildly surprised at himself. "Yeah. You're one hell of a musician."

"Thank you. And you're one heck of a...a muscle man."

He grinned almost boyishly. "In other words, if I don't find a job soon, I could always get hired as a bouncer."

Hilary laughed. "Sure, why not?"

Sean returned her laugh with a wide smile, and Hilary couldn't help responding with one of her own.

"That wasn't so bad now, was it?" he asked gently.

"No." Hilary didn't have a clue how Sean kept himself occupied. It was one reason she'd volunteered the information about her work schedule. She'd never asked what he did and he'd never volunteered the information. If they were ever going to form a bridge of trust with one another, it would be now. She hesitated, not wanting to ask, yet yearning to know.

"I've got a job interview at one o'clock," he said, his gaze linking with hers. "It looks promising."

Hilary felt a load lift from her heart. With effort they could learn to be friends. "Good luck."

"Thanks."

Hilary was reluctant to leave. It was the first cordial conversation they'd had in a week. Sean had never smiled at her before, as best as she could remember. He had a nice smile. Very nice. His dark eyes had sparkled, and Hilary swore it was like seeing lightning cut through a thundercloud.

She wasn't so bad, Sean mused after Hilary had left the apartment. Ironically, the things that had irritated him most about her were the same ones that intrigued him. True, she practiced the flute until all hours of the night, but he admired her dedication and her discipline. Those were qualities he'd cultivated himself and admired in others.

From the first, he'd viewed Hilary as a prig, but he might have misjudged her. Until this morning at breakfast, he couldn't remember them sharing a single conversation where the main objective wasn't to point out each other's faults.

Although she tried not to show it, Sean knew calling Hilary Her Highness made her furious. He had to admire the way she held her temper. She rarely raised her voice, rarely let on that she was upset. If it weren't for the way she tucked a strand of hair around her ear, he might have had some trouble reading her. Naw, he corrected: She was Dick and Jane and Spot all over again.

Hilary was also lovely, in a delicate sort of way. She was a fragile beauty, the kind of woman men liked to pamper. He'd never been interested in that sort himself. He liked his women with a little more flesh on their bones, the ones who were a little less demanding.

Nor was he keen on her penchant for neatness. He'd lived the last ten years of his life under military rule. If he wanted to keep his shoes in the living room, that was his right. He hadn't been amused when she'd picked up his dirty socks with a pair of kitchen tongs and carried them into the laundry room. Okay, so they smelled a bit, but she had clearly overreacted. It wasn't as though they were a cesspool holding a live cancer virus.

He liked her. Or he'd come close to it for the first time. True, living in such close proximity was going to take effort on both their parts, but they could make this work, and be better for the experience.

Hilary Wadsworth had taught him a good deal about the opposite sex that he'd been ignorant of before meeting her. It was better to have learned these lessons with a woman he wasn't emotionally involved with than someone he cared about.

When the time came, he'd find an apartment of his own, but he hoped that when he left he'd still be on friendly terms with Hilary. For the first time there was a chance.

A good chance.

Hilary was anxious to arrive home. Her schedule on Tuesdays and Thursdays was the most demanding. Her days were long, and she generally didn't take time to eat dinner before rehearsal, so she was ravenous by the time she arrived back at the apartment. Which meant her mood was a cross between that of a bobcat and a porcupine.

This evening, however, she'd taken time for soup and a small salad before hurrying to the music hall. She wasn't entirely sure why she was so anxious to get home.

That morning had been a turning point for her and Sean. They'd both felt it. Hilary hoped they could continue in this vein. It'd help matters tremendously if they could be civil with one another.

When she neared the apartment, she noted several vehicles parked out front. She saw Sean's Blazer, which had arrived the day before, but there were two other cars she didn't readily recognize.

Not sure what to expect, she let herself into the house. Sean was sitting at the kitchen table with three other men, all about the same age. They were playing cards. Several open bottles of beer were on the tabletop, along with uneven stacks of red, blue and white chips.

No one was aware of her presence.

"Sean, I'd like to talk to you," she said quietly, walking into the kitchen. Her heart was pounding like a giant turbine. So much for their new start! So much for the new communication between them. She was furious.

He looked up from his cards and a shocked look came over his face. "Hilary...what are you doing home?"

"I happen to live here, remember?"

Her announcement was followed by a couple of whistles and catcalls. "She lives here?"

"Leave it to Cochran to get himself a woman."

"Not bad, buddy, not bad at all."

"Sean, can we talk...privately?" she asked, ignoring his friends' comments.

He followed her into the laundry room. "I thought you said you were going to be late tonight."

"I *am* late. In case you haven't noticed, it's nearly ten."

"But...what about dinner out with your friends?"

"I ate earlier. Who are those men?" she demanded, pointing toward the kitchen. "And what are they doing here?"

"I should think that much is obvious. We're playing poker. Now, listen, I know you're upset—"

"You might have checked with me first. It would have been the courteous thing to do."

Sean sucked in a deep breath. "You're right, but I didn't expect you'd be back for another hour."

"So you think it's fine to bring strangers into my apartment without letting me know?" she asked primly.

"It's my apartment, too."

"I'd never pull this kind of stunt without checking with you."

"Stunt," he flared. "Come on, Hilary, you're overreacting again."

"Again?"

One of his beer-drinking, card-playing, T-shirt-clad buddies called from the kitchen, "Hey, Sean, the phone's ringing, you want me to catch it?"

"No," Sean shouted impatiently.

His friend had the receiver to his ear before Hilary or Sean could stop him. "Joe's Massage Parlor," he joked. "Women are our specialty."

Hilary closed her eyes and leaned against the washing machine.

"Joe," Sean barked, "give me the receiver."

"No," Hilary cried, springing to life.

Before either of them reached Joe, he replaced the phone. "Not to worry," he said with a saucy grin. "It was a wrong number. Some old lady from Frisco looking for her daughter. Your name doesn't happen to be Hilary, does it?"

Chapter Four

"Hello, Mom," Hilary said when the phone promptly rang a second time. "This is an unexpected surprise...especially so late."

"A young man answered this number only a moment ago. Who was that?"

"Young man...oh, you mean...Sean," she said, glaring at her roommate. It would be impossible to explain Joe to her mother. Besides, it was Sean's fault, anyway. Naturally her mother had her phone on automatic dial so there wasn't any chance of convincing her she'd gotten the wrong number. "He's my... neighbor." Hilary turned her back on Sean and his friends. She could hear them quietly picking up their things and shuffling toward the door, guided, no doubt, by her black-hearted roommate.

"Neighbor, you say," her mother repeated slowly. "Is he handsome?"

"Mother, please. We were talking, and when the phone rang I asked Sean if he'd mind getting it for me. He's something of a clown."

"So I gathered." Her mother's voice dipped softly. "I'm beginning to think your move to Portland might have been a good idea after all."

"I'm sure it was," Hilary said tightly, realizing her mother was using reverse psychology. If Louise could convince Hilary moving to Portland was such a good idea, then her daughter might have a change of heart and return home. It was a ploy Louise had used all too often.

"Don't you miss me even a little?" Louise pleaded.

"Of course, but..."

"Remember the good times we had sitting up and chatting while we watched the eleven-o'clock news? You used to like those tiny marshmallows in your hot chocolate?"

"Mother, I was ten years old!"

"I know... it's just that I can't sit through the newscast anymore without getting teary eyed. I worry about you living all alone."

If only her mother knew.

"We used to be so close."

Hilary missed those times with her mother as well, but not enough to consider returning to San Francisco. She was adjusting to her new life, a new schedule. She was adjusting to a man!

"I'm getting along just fine. There's no need to worry about me," Hilary said, hoping to reassure her mother and at the same time terminate the conversation before it dragged on.

"I've only phoned once since you moved out. I got your letter this afternoon, but somehow it's not the same."

"I've been busy, Mother. Time got away from me."

"You're working too hard, aren't you, Princess? I bet you're not eating properly, either."

"Mom," Hilary said shortly, "could you stop being a mother, just for once?"

"Stop being a mother," Louise repeated in a low, pain-filled voice. "I . . . don't know that I can."

"I'm not a little girl anymore. I'm a woman and I'd appreciate being treated like one." The time away from home gave her the courage to speak boldly.

"I see." Her mother's voice dipped softly.

Hilary resisted a sigh of regret. She didn't mean to be so abrupt, but it seemed the only way to reach her parent. "It isn't like I need to be tucked into bed every night."

"I know, it's just that I miss you so much."

Hilary was growing tired of the argument. "If you're phoning past ten, I assume you must have a good reason."

"Well, yes . . . I've got a small surprise for you. I thought I'd fly up to Portland to be with you on Mother's Day. That is, if you don't mind."

"Of course I don't," Hilary said, feeling increasingly guilty over her outburst.

"I realize you can't be with me because the symphony's performing, so it makes sense for me to come to you. I've already booked my flight, but I realize now that was a bit presumptuous of me."

"Not in the least. I'll look forward to your visit."

"I'm so pleased," Louise went on to say. "I got your letter this afternoon and felt just terrible that we'd be apart on Mother's Day. It wasn't until later that I realized if you couldn't come to me, then I could visit you. I booked my flight and then waited until I thought you'd be home this evening.''

"We'll have a good time, Mom.''

"I know we will, Princess. You can show me your apartment, and we'll sit and drink hot chocolate just the way we used to. We'll have all kinds of fun.''

"That sounds wonderful, Mom,'' Hilary said, closing her eyes and pressing her forehead against the wall. They ended the conversation a few minutes later.

The silence behind Hilary told her Sean had managed to clear his buddies out of the apartment.

"You were a little hard on her, weren't you?'' Sean said when he saw that Hilary had finished.

"What do you mean?''

"You didn't need to be so defensive with her.''

"I wasn't defensive,'' she snapped, unwilling to admit she probably had been. "You don't understand,'' she added, pleading with him. "My mother wants to dictate my life.''

Sean continued to clear off the kitchen table, stacking the chips in a round container. "I guess you're right. My own mother died when I was small— I barely remember her.''

"Did your father remarry?''

Sean nodded. "I never got along much with my stepmother.''

"She smothers me with her love.''

Sean's lips thinned slightly and he nodded, but Hilary could sense his censure. He didn't understand.

He couldn't. He didn't have a clue as to how oppressed she'd felt the last couple of years.

He slipped the deck of cards into the slot in the chip holder. "About the poker game—"

"Yes," she broke in, hands on her hips. "Let's talk about you bringing complete strangers into my home."

His jaw muscles tightened. "Are you looking for an argument, Hilary? Because I'll be happy to give you one."

She deflated her chest and slowly shook her head. They had made the first steps toward friendship, and she didn't want to crush that.

Sean sighed and shook his head. "You're right. I probably shouldn't have invited my buddies over, but I didn't figure it was any big deal."

"It wasn't," she admitted slowly.

He cocked his head slightly to one angle as if he wasn't sure he'd heard her correctly. "I should have cleared it with you first."

"I shouldn't have made such a fuss," she whispered, her voice wobbling. Exhausted to the core, Hilary walked over to a wall calendar and flipped to the following month.

"Hil, what's wrong?" How gentle he sounded, how concerned.

She turned away from the kitchen wall and gestured weakly with her hands. "We're in deep yogurt, Sean. My mother's decided to come visit."

Sean's brow condensed into thick lines. "When?"

"Mother's Day."

"No sweat," he said with what sounded like supreme confidence. He marched past her and examined the calendar, counting out the weeks until the holiday. His index finger stopped dead on the second Sunday in May.

"The Greers won't be back until the following week,' he murmured thoughtfully.

"I know."

"It's no big thing. I'll pack up my things and get a hotel room for the weekend. I might even be able to stay with Craig for a couple of days. He's another friend of mine. The guy wearing the baseball cap."

Hilary remembered Sean's friend as the one who whistled using two fingers when Sean announced she was his roommate. "You'd be willing to do that?" His offer surprised her even more than the efficient way in which he'd ushered his friends out of the apartment.

"Of course."

"I . . . I don't know what to say." It wasn't so much that he'd be willing to find somewhere else to stay for the weekend, but that he'd take the time and effort to remove every bit of evidence of his presence in the apartment. It was one thing to stay away a few nights and another to literally move out.

"She won't know I was ever here," Sean promised.

Hilary was overcome with gratitude. She mumbled her appreciation and then wandered aimlessly to her room. After she'd showered and changed clothes, she returned to the kitchen to find Sean straightening up the kitchen. Most of the food had been put away, and he'd swept the floor.

"I...I hope I didn't embarrass you in front of your friends," she said, feeling guilty about the way she'd stormed at him.

Sean shrugged. "Don't worry about it."

"I'm tired and out of sorts," she admitted. With him and with her mother, too. "I shouldn't have said the things I did."

Sean turned around, holding two empty beer bottles in his hands. "Did I just hear you right? Did you actually admit you might have been wrong?" A smile quivering at the edges of his mouth gave him away. Once more, Hilary felt herself responding to his grin.

"How about a cup of coffee before you go to bed?" Sean asked.

"Make that a cup of chocolate with miniature marshmallows and you've got yourself a deal."

"Hot chocolate?"

"I was teasing," she said, feeling lighter than she had since arriving home. "Actually, a cup of tea sounds perfect." She brewed a pot and carried it into the living room. They sat across from one another, awkward with the situation. Neither seemed inclined to speak.

Sean was sprawled across the sofa, his arms stretched out, a beer bottle dangling from his right hand. He balanced his ankle on his knee.

Hilary sat in the overstuffed chair, her back straight, knees together, holding the cup and saucer in both hands. The teapot and cozy rested on the coffee table between them.

He grinned and looked away.

"Is something wrong?" Hilary wanted to know. She certainly hadn't done or said anything amusing.

"No, it's just that...hell, you've got pretty legs, why don't you cross them?"

Hilary could feel the heat permeating her cheeks. She shifted positions and tucked her feet beneath her.

"That's better," he said, then smiled and took a swig of beer. When he'd finished, he leaned forward and set the bottle next to the ceramic teapot. "I got the job."

"Oh, Sean, congratulations." Hilary was genuinely pleased for him. His get-together with his buddies had probably been a celebration of sorts.

"Your friends seem ... nice," Hilary said as means of starting a conversation.

Sean nodded. "I met Joe, Craig and Dave in Saudi. They're good men."

"You were involved in the Gulf War?"

A sigh expanded his chest. "You could say that."

"Do you mind talking about it? Both Mom and I were intrigued with reports of the war. We sat by the television all hours of the day and night."

For the next hour Sean fascinated her with stories of his role in Saudi Arabia, of harrowing escapes, of his other adventures in the military. Hilary asked him several questions, enthralled by the life he'd led. He didn't mention much about his childhood, just enough for her to surmise it hadn't been all that happy. He talked briefly about his mother and her absence in his life. Hilary told him about losing her father and how it had drastically changed her and her mother's lives. Usually she found it difficult to carry on a lengthy conversation with a man, but that wasn't the case with Sean. He was easy to talk to, interesting and fun. She didn't know why she hadn't realized it earlier.

Sean intrigued her. She wouldn't have called him handsome, not even rugged looking. But there was something strongly appealing about him. His integrity, his decency, his willingness to make the best of an uncomfortable situation. Perhaps this wasn't going to be such an intolerable situation after all.

Hilary slept until late the following morning, not stirring until a quarter after ten. Since she didn't start work until early afternoon on Wednesdays, she wasn't in any rush to get out of bed. She didn't hear Sean and assumed that he'd left the apartment.

She paused outside the bathroom door. Curious, she wandered in and turned on the radio. To her surprise the soft, melodic strains of Rossini's overture from *La Gazza Ladra* was playing. Pleasantly surprised, Hilary smiled to herself. Sean had changed back the station, just the way he'd said he would.

She wandered into the kitchen and reached for the phone, dialing her mother's number. She owed her an apology. After the call, she felt vastly improved, and returned to the bathroom, intending to brush her teeth.

"Oh, sorry." Sean's voice came from behind her when she'd finished. "I didn't know you were in here."

"'Morning," she said, smiling up at him. Apparently he'd been working on his car, because his hands were covered with grease.

"Don't give me that disgusted look," he chastised with a knowing grin. "I'll clean the sink when I'm finished," he added, scooting past her. The opening between the sink and the door was narrow, and as they edged past one another, her breasts met the solid muscles of his torso. They both hesitated, and Hilary's startled gaze slowly rose to Sean's. He seemed to be holding his breath.

"That was nice what you did," he said, his voice barely above a whisper.

"What?"

"Apologize to your mother."

Hilary lowered her eyes.

"I didn't mean to listen in, but the kitchen window was open. I bet it meant a lot to her to have you call."

Hilary shrugged.

By tacit agreement they moved away from each other. "I...I have to get ready for work." Her voice was shaky as she slid past him.

Hours later, standing in the music store, the scene from the morning with Sean drifted into Hilary's mind. They had stood there in the bathroom, their upper bodies pressed against each other, and conversed as if unaware of what was happening. Her breasts had more than brushed his torso. They'd hardened to a painful tightness and he'd seen that. He couldn't have avoided noticing.

Hilary didn't know what Sean would think. Perhaps he was accustomed to living with women. He'd probably had several lovers over the years. The thought tightened the muscles of her abdomen.

A second wave of confusion washed over her, this one more forceful than the first. They were both trying so hard to make their arrangement work, to find ways to be cordial to one another instead of creating conflict. Only now, another conflict was developing. A sensual one.

Although they'd never discussed it, never set the ground rules for anything physical between them, it was understood nothing could or would happen. They'd crossed the line that morning.

They'd touched each other. Her breasts had met his chest, his thigh had brushed hers, and the heat of that light contact burned her skin still. Even now she could feel it, as clearly as if it were happening all over again.

Hilary dragged in a deep breath and prayed Mr. Murphy wasn't paying any attention to her.

Something else was happening to her, something just as puzzling and unexplainable. Hilary felt inexplicably possessive of Sean. It made no sense—for all she knew he could be dating ten other women. She had no right to feel these things toward him. None. Not only was it illogical, it could lead to all sorts of problems later.

She guessed they'd bonded, in a manner of speaking. People couldn't live together and not have it affect them one way or another. This was something neither of them had even thought to consider.

Sean was at the apartment when she arrived home. An instant rush of pleasure was marred by the memory of their last encounter.

"Hi," she greeted him carefully as she came in the door, almost afraid.

Her roommate was standing in front of the stove, a dish towel tucked into the waistband of his pants. He was holding a wooden spoon to his mouth, sampling his efforts. When he saw her, he smiled and kissed his fingertips in an expression of culinary excellence.

"I hope you're hungry," he said.

"Why?" Thus far they'd each cooked their own meals.

"Because I cooked up a batch of the world-famous Cochran spaghetti sauce, not to be confused with the actor who bottles his own. It just so happens we share the same recipe."

"Does this mean you intend to feed me?"

"What I intend, my dear, is to fatten you up. A woman who calls three measly shrimp her dinner is a woman who hasn't tasted my spaghetti sauce."

Hilary laughed softly. "I've never turned down a free dinner in my life."

"Who says this is free?" Sean asked, wiggling his eyebrows suggestively. "I cook, you wash the dishes."

"You've got yourself a deal."

Sean's world-famous spaghetti sauce was as good as he claimed. Hilary couldn't remember when she'd enjoyed a meal more. They talked and laughed and joked until Hilary was shocked to realize she was an hour into her practice time.

"Thank you," she said, pressing her hands against her stomach. "The meal was heavenly."

"I owed you a dinner, remember?"

"In which case you're welcome to eat my shrimp salad anytime you want." She stood to stack the dishes in the dishwasher when she remembered. "I...I picked you up something while I was at work today. Something small." She felt silly now, wishing she hadn't done it.

"A gift?"

"Sort of. A thank-you for your willingness to move out so everything will go smoothly when my mother visits."

"That wasn't necessary, Hilary."

"I realize that. It's just a small way of thanking you." She fished through her purse until she found the small white envelope.

"What is it?" Sean asked.

"A ticket to the symphony's Mother's Day performance."

A silence followed. "Me? At the symphony?" Then Sean burst out laughing. "Forget that, sweetheart."

Chapter Five

Sean realized almost immediately that he'd hurt Hilary's feelings. He hadn't meant to be insensitive, nor had he intended to threaten the fragile thread of their friendship.

"I didn't mean to laugh." Even as he spoke, Sean knew it was too late. The damage had already been done. "It's just that I've never paid to attend anything where I couldn't buy popcorn or beer."

"I...understand," she murmured, her eyes refusing to meet his. "If you'll excuse me, I need to practice. I'll close the door so you won't be troubled."

"Dammit, Hilary, I didn't mean to offend you."

"I'm sure you didn't," she returned with a quiet dignity.

Sean waited until she was completely out of the kitchen before he threw the dishrag down on the floor, thoroughly disgusted with himself. He'd made a mess of the whole thing, even the apology.

It had come as something of a surprise to discover he enjoyed Hilary's company. He'd never known a debutante before. His family hadn't exactly brushed shoulders with the upper crust. Although Hilary hadn't mentioned that her family had money, it was obvious. She reeked of culture—her manners were impeccable and her vocabulary had come straight out of an expensive private school.

Her persnickety ways had driven him to distraction their first week together. Sean was willing to admit their problems were mostly his doing. He'd gone out of his way to irritate her, wanting to know how far he could push her before she broke. He'd been looking for some way of breaking through her stiff politeness and uncommonly good grace. No matter how much he'd goaded her, she hadn't raised her voice, hadn't revealed a hint of anger.

She'd upheld her image of refined elegance. It was only when she'd lost her cool that Sean discovered how much he enjoyed her company. It was then that she'd become human to him. There was a problem, though; she had a thing about her mother. A mere mention of the woman and Hilary became as prickly as an Arizona cactus.

This wasn't the way he had intended their evening to end. The incident in the bathroom earlier had stayed on his mind all day. Their brief sensual encounter had baffled him, and he was sure it had confused her, as well.

Not that he intended to do anything about it. His roommate was strictly off-limits. Sean wasn't a fool. He knew trouble when he saw it, and Hilary Wadsworth spelled torment with a capital *T*.

He walked into the living room, plopped himself down on the sofa and reached for the television controller as the first strains of her flute drifted toward him. His finger froze on the controller button. Her music was hauntingly beautiful, delicate the same way she was.

His mind wandered back to the meal they'd shared. He liked the way she had of neatly smoothing out her napkin in her lap and the way she lifted her fork to her mouth as if it were as exquisite as the food she was eating. In cooking their dinner, he'd purposely chosen spaghetti just to see how she'd manage the long noodles with a knife and fork. And she'd done it, without a hitch. The dexterity with which she'd manipulated her fork and spoon had amazed him.

Then he'd done something stupid. He'd laughed at her.

Sean rubbed a hand down his face. Hell, he was acting like he was in love with her or something. Now, that would be a disaster. Their situation was rife with problems, and Sean could see he was going to have to be the responsible one. Hilary was just naive enough to fill her head with thoughts of love and apple blossoms. When she did find that special man, it would be someone a damn sight more cultured than he was. A man who appreciated attending a symphony. Someone who knew polo was more than a shirt style.

With that thought in mind, Sean flipped the buttons until he found a program that suited his mood—wrestling. He stared at that for several moments, then turned off the television.

He was on his feet before he realized what he was doing. He walked down the hallway to Hilary's bedroom. Her door was closed, and the sweet melody of some ditty was as soft as a caress. His fist was clenched, prepared to knock against the door, when he hesitated.

"Oh, what the hell," he muttered under his breath, and walked away. Making an effort to get along with Hilary had its downside. There hadn't been nearly as many problems when they were snapping and fighting with each other. He'd actually enjoyed an exchange of wits. As far as he could see, being friends wasn't ever going to work.

Hell, he mused darkly, that was the crux of the problem—friendship was working all too well. He needed to keep his own head on straight, too, now more than ever.

Hilary hurried into the apartment, carting two heavy sacks of groceries. She barely made it to the kitchen table before the bags spilled out of her arms.

With a growing sense of enthusiasm, she stepped back and sighed. Tonight would be a celebration. This was Sean's first day as an employee of Halfax. He was a helicopter pilot, flying geologists and other scientists into Mount Saint Helens to continue their study after the devastating 1980 volcanic eruption. But it was more than the job that had prompted this dinner.

The atmosphere between them had been strained ever since she'd given him the ticket to the symphony. This morning he'd been nervous about starting the job. Hilary wanted to do something to put their relationship back on an even keel once again.

She regretted this whole thing with the symphony, and she knew Sean did, too. He wasn't the type of man who would enjoy a symphony, and she should have recognized that earlier. He felt bad about laughing, and she was upset for having put him in such an awkward position. It was time to smooth the waters.

Although Sean had tried to disguise that he was nervous over starting his new job, Hilary knew he was. The position was perfect for him, with just enough adventure to keep him from growing bored.

She might have been concerned about the danger of such flights if she didn't have complete confidence in Sean's abilities. He'd flown in a war zone and survived several harrowing missions. A little thing like a mountain didn't even faze him.

Hilary had spent the better part of the afternoon, between customers, coming up with the menu. She'd had to drive halfway across Portland to assemble everything she needed. Their dinner would start off with an asparagus roll with ham, followed by an entrée of baked fresh halibut with champagne sauce. For dessert she'd found a quaint bakery and purchased a Neapolitan torte.

By six-thirty, her masterpiece was ready and waiting. Hilary set the table with care, using three ultrathin candles in a bed of pink carnations as a centerpiece. A streamer spelling out CONGRATU-

LATIONS in bold metallic colors was strung across the archway leading into the kitchen.

At the sound of Sean's car door closing, Hilary placed a party hat on her head. When he opened the front door, she blew a paper whistle and yelled out, "Surprise!"

Sean froze, looking as if he'd just stepped on a land mine.

"Congratulations," Hilary said, stepping forward and wrapping her arm around his. "I hope you're ready for one of the most delectable meals of your life."

Still Sean didn't move. "Hil, you shouldn't have...."

"Are you surprised?"

He nodded slowly, regretfully. He didn't reveal any of the excitement she expected. If anything, he appeared painfully embarrassed. Not knowing what to make of his mood, she moved to the table and detailed their menu.

"There's a problem," Sean said with the same hesitation she'd detected earlier.

"Oh?" She turned back to face him.

"Some of my friends already made plans, and..."

In a heartbeat Hilary understood her folly. She should never have arranged this without checking with Sean first. She forced herself to smile. "Then go with them."

"But—"

"Don't worry about it, Sean." She did her best to smile reassuringly. Yes, she was disappointed, but it was her own fault.

"I'd cancel, but a couple of the guys are waiting in the car for me now and . . . well . . ."

"Nonsense," she said, meaning it. Gripping her hands together, standing beside the enormous Neapolitan torte, Hilary couldn't remember feeling more foolish. "You go with your friends, and we'll have our dinner some other night."

"It'll keep?"

"Of course," she lied.

"Everything looks wonderful," he said, surveying the table.

"It wasn't the least bit of trouble," she continued, adding one more white lie to the list. Hilary swallowed hard and prayed she could keep her smile from cracking.

"This was really sweet of you, Hil," Sean muttered.

Sweet. He talked to her as if she were a sixteen-year-old with a crush on him. Sweet, indeed! She might have said something, but before she had the chance, the door opened and Sean's friend, the one with the piercing whistle, stuck his head inside.

"What's the holdup? You don't want to keep Carla waiting, do you?"

Carla, Hilary's mind repeated. There was a limit to how much her ego could take, and it had just about reached the breaking point.

Sean looked at her, his eyes pleading for understanding.

"Go on, I insist," she said, exhausting her energy to sound as cheerful as possible. "Don't keep your friends waiting."

"You're my friend, too."

His words went a long way toward soothing her disappointment. "I know, and you're special to me, but I made a mistake. We'll celebrate another night. Okay?"

Sean's nod revealed his reluctance.

"Have a good time, and we'll talk later."

His friend peeked around the door a second time. "Are you coming or not?"

"I'm coming," Sean assured him. He walked across the room, gently took Hilary by the shoulders and kissed her cheek. "Thank you."

"Don't worry about it." She waited until he was gone before she sank into the kitchen chair. Her knees were shaking, and she wasn't sure if it was because of the emotional energy required to disguise her disappointment or if it was the result of Sean's brief kiss.

By the very nature of their circumstances, their relationship had to remain strictly platonic. Hilary had accepted that from the first. Sean did, too, although they'd never discussed it. She couldn't risk involving her heart. But more than her heart had gotten involved. He'd bruised her ego. He called her "sweet" and went off to spend the evening with a woman named Carla.

It shouldn't bother her so much. But it did.

The evening dragged for Hilary. She ate what she could of the dinner, which was delicious, but she found her appetite was practically nil.

After cleaning the kitchen, she practiced her flute for two hours, soaked in a hot tub, filed her nails, then went to bed. Lying in the dark, her eyes focused on the ceiling, Hilary wondered if Sean would even bother to come back to the apartment or if he'd spend the night with his lady friend. The thought felt like a heavy concrete block pressing against her chest. Breathing became painful, and she forced the image from her mind because it was too painful to dwell on.

Sean had rarely spent a more miserable evening. Every time he looked at the blond beauty on his arm, he saw Hilary instead, smiling like he'd never seen her smile, throwing open her arms and shouting *Surprise!*

He'd gone with Craig and Dave because they were waiting in the truck for him, but he realized his mistake almost immediately. He didn't want to spend the evening with his friends; he would much rather have been with Hilary.

She'd been so disappointed and struggled so hard to hide it from him. It hadn't occurred to him that she'd do anything like this. After the fiasco over the symphony tickets, he'd walked on eggshells in an effort to make things right between them, but it hadn't worked. No matter what he did or said, the atmosphere remained strained and tense. They were both trying too hard, he guessed. And now this.

To his credit, Sean lasted until midnight, then made his excuses. His friends, especially Craig, seemed surprised that he copped out so early.

Sean made record time getting back to the apartment, hoping Hilary would still be up. He needed to talk to her, explain, do what he could to make matters right. But the only light shining was the one on the porch.

He let himself into the silent house, and paused. The living room was dark and still. He splayed his fingers through his hair and experienced a fresh wave of disappointment. It was important for them both right now to talk. Not because he felt guilty—he had nothing to feel guilty about—but he wanted to reassure Hilary, thank her for her thoughtfulness, tell her how much he appreciated the effort she'd made.

Wandering down the darkened hallway, he noticed that her bedroom door was half-open. He stood there for a moment, allowing his eyes to adjust to the dark. She was sleeping soundly.

The world stood still. Sean's heart felt heavy in his chest, and before he realized his intent, he wandered into Hilary's bedroom and sat on the edge of her mattress.

Immediately he knew she was awake. Their eyes met in the dark.

"I shouldn't be here," he whispered, his voice tinged with anger. He had no business being with her like this.

"I should have checked with you before I planned the dinner." Her voice was as fragile as a hummingbird's wings.

His gaze lowered to her mouth, her sweet, soft mouth, and he knew once more that he wasn't going to be able to stop himself. Sean moaned, fighting her with every ounce of will he possessed, but before he could pull away, Hilary lifted her arms, tucked them around his neck and drew his mouth down to hers.

Chapter Six

Hilary felt Sean stiffen, felt him resist her, but she didn't know who he was fighting—her or himself. She levered herself up until they were only separated by inches, their gazes holding one another's. His eyes were filled with doubt, with regret and something else she couldn't read. Fear? This man, who'd faced death many times over, who'd laughed when she'd trembled as he told her of his exploits in the Persian Gulf, was afraid? It didn't make sense.

Now it was Sean who was trembling, like a man fighting himself much too hard.

"Kiss me," she whispered, shocked that she would be so bold.

"You don't know what you're asking," he said, dismissing her.

"Yes, I do."

"Oh, Hil, damn it all, this shouldn't be happening." He groaned and caught hold of her. Hilary's heart stopped and then lurched as his warm mouth covered hers. His hand moved slowly downward from her hair to the small of her back, urging her forward to receive his kiss.

He raised his head, his breath quick and warm against her upturned face. "Why does it have to be you?"

Hilary's eyes fluttered open. "Instead of Carla?" she whispered.

"No," he rasped. "No," he said again, his tone husky with need. His hands cupped her face, and he kissed her with a fierce hunger that matched her own. She didn't understand him, didn't understand his question, but none of that mattered as long as she was in his arms, as long as he continued to hold her.

He kissed her as she'd never been kissed before, sweeping her mouth with his tongue, forcing a response from her. He drew her closer until their upper bodies were flush against one another. His chest moved against hers, and the summits of her breasts ached with need. He moved his restless hands up and down her back as if he couldn't believe he was touching her, as if he feared she would vanish.

"I knew you'd taste like this," he said, dragging his mouth from hers. "Like the sweetest angel in God's own heaven." She felt the tremor in him and he cupped her head and lightly rubbed his callused thumb over her moist lips.

"No more," he said.

"Sean..."

But he was gone before she could stop him. Hilary sat alone in the silence, willing him back. Her heart roared in her ears as she raised her fingers to her lips to investigate for herself what had happened.

They were softly swollen—otherwise she might have believed his kisses had been nothing more than a wildly romantic dream.

The following morning Sean was still furious, but he didn't know who he was upset with more—Hilary or himself. He should be dragged before a firing squad for the stunt he'd pulled. Walking into Hilary's bedroom was like pulling the pin on a hand grenade. Yet, knowing that hadn't been enough to keep him away. The situation between them was explosive and growing more so each passing minute.

Kissing Hilary had to rank as the most foolish thing he'd done in the last fifteen years. He was a man who'd cut his teeth on discipline, he was intimate with self-denial. The army had trained him well. For ten years he'd been part of the armed forces' most elite corps; he'd proudly worn the hat of the Green Berets. It had taken less than a month and one sweet virgin to crumble his defenses. The weakness he felt for Hilary made him downright furious.

He wasn't alone in this. She hadn't done anything to help matters. She'd practically begged him to kiss her. His roommate knew next to nothing about the intimacy shared between a man and a woman. She assumed it was all perfume and romance, while he knew the truth. Making love was hot and physically demanding, a grinding of lips, a meshing of bodies. She didn't know what she was asking for, and heaven help him, he wasn't going to be the one to initiate her into the rites of love. He'd save that for the husband her mother would handpick for her someday.

He was packing his lunch when Hilary wandered into the kitchen, all pink and soft in her robe. He ignored her as best he could as he assembled a sandwich, but he felt her presence as profoundly as he'd sensed danger during war. In many ways, Hilary was dangerous to him.

"Good morning," she greeted softly.

He made a gruff, nonsensical reply.

"I was hoping we'd have a chance to talk."

By the sound of her voice, she was only a few feet away. Too close for comfort.

"I've got to be out of here in five minutes." He refused to turn around and look at her, knowing whatever resolve he'd managed to collect would be threatened by the mere sight of her.

"It's about last night," she said in that delicate way of hers, making the words sound like lace.

Sean slammed the pieces of bread together with such force that the imprint of his hand was left on the sandwich.

"I won't pretend it didn't happen," she added.

"Forget it, then, because it won't be repeated." He stuffed the mistreated sandwich into a plastic bag and tossed it into the small brown sack open on top of the counter.

"How can you be so sure of that?"

"Because I won't let it happen." He made sure his voice was filled with a determination steel wouldn't dent.

"Sean?"

"What happened to all the oranges?" he asked, standing in front of the open refrigerator. "I could have sworn there were some—"

"Sean?"

"—left. They were in here the other day."

She walked up behind him and slipped her arms around his waist. "Will you kindly listen to me?"

His heart went wild when she touched him, her hands gliding across the hard muscles of his stomach. It would have been a simple matter to break free of her hold, but he found he couldn't do it, and hated himself for the weakness.

"Hilary, stop," he said in his sternest voice, the same one he'd used to lead men. Others would have followed him into hell without question, but this sweet debutante refused to listen. He felt her sigh against him and press her cheek to his back.

"All right," he said, breaking her hold on him. He whirled around to face her. "You want to talk about last night, then fine, I'll talk and you'll listen. Understand?"

She nodded and smiled up at him. "No one's ever kissed me the way you did."

"Listen, Hil, if you're looking for a little experience, find it with someone else. Initiating virgins lost its appeal years ago. You're sweet and innocent, but frankly, you don't tempt me. I like my women with a little more seasoning."

The color left her face as she stepped away from him. Her head jerked with every word he spoke, as if he were physically slapping her. She was blinking furiously in an effort to keep the tears at bay. Sean hated himself for being so cruel, but it was the only way he knew to put an end to this madness.

Someone had to bring Hilary back to earth, otherwise she'd walk around all day with her head in the clouds. One of them had to be responsible before living together became hell for them both.

"The . . . oranges are in the bottom bin of the refrigerator," she said, her gaze avoiding his. "I put your food in the lower bin . . . mine's in the upper."

Sean felt a muscle jerk in his jaw as he grabbed his lunch and headed out the door.

What was so painful, Hilary realized, as she readied for work, was that Sean was right. Not only had she made a fool of herself over him twice, but he'd pointed out one all-important fact: He didn't want her.

It mortified her every time she thought of the way she'd thrown herself at him, how she'd wrapped her arms around his neck and kissed him. Never in all her life had she been so bold with a man. No wonder Sean thought she was out to gain a little experience. She'd led him to believe she was using him.

He was older, wiser, more knowledgeable than she was. This was her first time away from home. It made perfect sense that she would spread her wings. If anything, she should be grateful he was gentleman enough not to take advantage of her.

They'd been together nearly three weeks now. How quickly that time had passed. Soon he'd be on his own, and it was highly unlikely their worlds would cross again.

It surprised her how much she yearned to talk to her mother. It would have been a simple matter to reach for the phone and spill out her tale of woe, but Hilary resisted the temptation. She'd made an issue of standing on her own two feet. She'd even gone so far as to ask her mother to stop mothering her. Contacting her now, at the first sign of trouble, was a sign of pure weakness. Hilary eyed the wall phone longingly as she walked out of the kitchen.

Sean had one big advantage, she mused as she dressed. He had several friends in Portland. Because she was shy, Hilary had trouble getting to know others. She promised herself she'd make more of an effort.

Her chance came sooner than she expected. Arnold Wilson, who played bass violin, asked her out for coffee following rehearsal that same evening. He was tall and thin with a long, domineering nose. His smile was warm. He was a gentle man, and Hilary thought highly of him, although they'd only spoken briefly.

"Coffee . . . sure," Hilary answered, pleased at the invitation.

"After practice, a number of us stop in at Lenny's, the coffee shop on the corner. I was hoping you'd come."

"I'll be happy to." There were several in the symphony who were close in age to Hilary. Rita, who played fourth-chair clarinet, had asked her to join them once before, but Hilary had been exhausted and declined. Now, however, she was more accustomed to the grueling schedule of working days and then attending lengthy practice sessions.

That evening, when they'd finished at the music hall, Hilary, Arnold, Rita and Bill gathered around the table at the all-night diner. Hilary's new friends shared an easy camaraderie and soon they were all chattering at once, being careful to include her in the conversation. It felt wonderful to feel part of the group.

Hilary was surprised to learn that Rita, a housewife and the mother of a five-year-old, was only three years older than she was. Hilary couldn't imagine herself as a mother. As Rita talked, relating a recent anecdote about her daughter, Hilary's thoughts wandered back to the need she'd experienced that morning to talk to her own mother. She'd been hurt and had instinctively reached out for the one person in all the world who would comfort her.

Sean was right—her relationship with her mother was far more complex than she realized. Never in a million years would she have thought she'd miss her so much.

Her mother was the only person who occupied her thoughts. Sean was there as well, bold as could be, gruff and impatient, barely looking her way. He was letting her know beyond a shadow of a doubt that he regretted kissing her. The problem was, Hilary couldn't dredge up any genuine remorse. She'd been thinking about it for days, wondering what it would be like if he touched her. The incident in the bathroom hadn't helped matters any.

Arnold said something and the others laughed. Hilary's gaze drifted to him. He was warm and witty and fun. He made her laugh and helped her to forget the hurt she'd carried with her most of the day, but she wasn't attracted to him. Her blood didn't grow hot when she looked at the violin player. How she wished it did. How she wished she could stop thinking about Sean. He didn't want her, he'd said so himself. He was a man who didn't mince words. What he said he meant. She was a complication he chose to avoid.

When he moved away, even if she never saw him again, she'd always be grateful. He'd taught her about herself, awakened for her an area that had lain dormant far too long—her own femininity.

For the first time in her life, she was more than Louise Wadsworth's daughter. More than a talented musician. She was a woman, one with a heart ripe for love. Sean had gently proven there was nothing wrong with her; he'd shown her how wonderful the physical aspect of loving between a man and a woman could be. How could she be anything but grateful?

By the time Hilary arrived back at the apartment, it was nearly one. The porch light was shining, illuminating the empty parking space in front of the duplex.

Sean was gone.

Hilary's heart constricted with uneasiness. She feared he'd been so disgusted with her that he'd decided to move out, to leave her. Biting into her bottom lip, she unlocked the front door and let herself inside the apartment. Several lights were on. The kitchen. The hallway. Sean's bedroom.

"Sean?" she called out hesitantly. He might have loaned out his car. She walked down the hallway and noticed his bedroom door was wide open. His bed was untouched.

She had just returned to the living room when the front door opened. Sean roared into the center of the living room like a fire fighter at a three-alarm blaze. His eyes narrowed when he saw her.

"Sean?"

His features didn't soften. "Just where the hell have you been?"

Chapter Seven

"Where have I been?" Hilary repeated, shocked that he didn't know. "I was at rehearsal, the same way I am every Thursday night."

"Until one o'clock in the morning?" The question was shouted with enough force to rattle the windows.

She motioned with her hands, not understanding his anger. "I went out for coffee with some friends afterward."

"For three hours?"

"Yes." Still she was at a loss to fathom his strange mood.

"Did it ever occur to you that I might have been worried? You could have been in a car accident or been mugged. For all I knew you might have been kidnapped."

"Oh, come on, Sean," she said, making light of his concern. "I'm a big girl, I carry Mace. You don't need to worry about me."

Sean rammed both hands through his hair as though he wished it were her neck he was throttling. He closed his eyes in a blatant effort to compose himself.

"I hate to say this, but you're beginning to sound like my mother," she told him.

"Maybe that's because your mother cares about you. Did that ever cross your mind?" he demanded.

"Can you imagine what I was thinking while I drove the streets looking for you? Have you any clue of what I was feeling?"

Chagrined, Hilary shook her head. Although he was practically shouting at her, his anger tangible, she couldn't help being warmed by his words. "Does this mean you care, too?" she asked in a soft, low voice, almost afraid of his answer.

"Yes, dammit, I care," he admitted with a heavy sigh. "Just don't ever pull a stunt like this again. You want to go out with your friends after the symphony rehearses, then fine, but have the common decency to call first and let me know."

"All right," she agreed, then headed for her room. She hesitated just before she rounded the corner leading to the hallway. "Sean?"

"Yes?" he barked.

"I'm sorry."

His lips tightened, but he said nothing more.

By the time Hilary was up and around the next morning, Sean had already left for work. She didn't know how much sleep he'd managed to catch, and felt guilty about that, although she never suspected he'd be so worried about her. It never occurred to her to let him know, although in hindsight she probably should have.

When she arrived home from the music store early that evening, Sean was sitting in the living room reading the newspaper. His hair was wet as though he was fresh from the shower. He didn't acknowledge her when she came in the door, but she was certain he was aware of her standing there.

"Hello," she said tentatively, keeping her voice light and breezy. "How was your day?"

"Good." He didn't lower the newspaper, nor did he seem to be in the mood for conversation. Hilary could appreciate that—she'd had one of those days herself. At least, that was what she told herself. After she'd changed clothes, she moved into the kitchen, taking a cold bottle of spring water from the refrigerator shelf.

When he heard her, Sean set aside the paper and came into the kitchen. He glared at her before speaking. "The time's come for us to clear the air here once and for all."

"All right," she agreed calmly, although her heart was racing.

"I don't want you to misinterpret what happened."

"When you kissed me?" Her eyes didn't leave his while she sipped the cool, refreshing water.

"No," he said, and smiled fiercely. "I'm talking about last night."

"Ah . . . and how would I misinterpret that?" She wasn't being facetious, only curious. "You were upset. Understandably so . . . and I really should have let you know I was going to be late."

"I realize you don't owe me any explanations," he said. The intense quality hadn't left his eyes.

"I know, but if *you* were planning to be out until all hours of the morning, I'd want you to tell me out of common courtesy." She took another sip of her bottled water, savoring the coolness in her throat.

Sean was frowning again as if he was surprised by her response. It was almost as if he thought she intended to argue with him.

"I'm playing poker with the guys tonight."

"Here?" She remembered what a disaster the last time had been.

"No, we're headed for Dave's. His father-in-law'll be playing with us." Sean stuffed his hands into his pockets and eyed Hilary. Something about his abruptness gave her the impression he needed to do something with his hands in order to avoid reaching for her. It was a heady thought, and one she dared not cultivate. Then, too, it might have been wishful thinking, because she so desperately wanted him to hold her.

"Enjoy yourself," she said, meaning it.

"I'm sure I will."

He left a few moments later, and it seemed all her joy went with him. She understood Sean's hesitation when it came to the physical aspect of their relationship. She felt it herself. It was dangerous living together the way they did, sharing the small intimacies of life. They'd only been together a short while, but already Hilary couldn't imagine what it would be like without Sean. She'd better get used to it, though, she told herself. When the Greers returned in another three weeks, he'd be gone and she'd be alone.

Sean wasn't sleeping well. For three nights in a row he'd tossed and turned, until the bedding was in terrible disarray. This problem was a new one and was due to civilian life, he suspected; and immediately he knew he was kidding himself. If he had a problem sleeping, there was a very good reason. Hilary Wadsworth. If he had assumed time would ease the tension between himself and Hilary, then he'd miscalculated. His roommate had a way of reaching him that left him feeling vulnerable and, worse, defenseless. Even ten long years of disciplined army life didn't make a difference in turning his thoughts away from her. Hilary hounded him, and what bothered him the most was that she hadn't a clue as to what she was doing to him. Leave it to him to lose his heart to a pampered debutante who was determined to prove something to herself, the world and her mother.

Living with Hilary, being this close to her, day in and day out, had redefined the word "torture." She was delicate and soft, and he couldn't be near her and not want to touch her. That one slip, those few chaste kisses, had opened a Pandora's box of need. Now it was there in the open, taunting him each minute they were together.

His life, by necessity and choice, had been hard. Being this close to someone so gentle, so fragile, had opened a floodgate within him. He'd lived so long without anything soft, until this petite beauty had bulldozed her way into his heart.

He didn't like it. He fought her every way he knew how and paid the price. What irritated him most was how badly he was losing. Sean wasn't a good loser. He didn't take defeat well because he wasn't accustomed to dealing with it often. He certainly never expected a woman to have this much control over him and, if the truth be known, that bothered him more than anything else.

Rolling onto his side, he glared at the illuminated dial of his clock and clenched his teeth when he noted the time.

He wasn't going to sleep. Every time he closed his eyes, Hilary filled his mind with all the things that could never be. Of making love to her, of holding her afterward and planning the future. Forcefully he pushed the image from his mind, determined to close his eyes and sleep.

Instead he thought of Hilary at his side through the years, of her marrying him, bearing his children. These weren't matters of life a man entertained lightly. He assumed he would marry someday, but he'd never met a woman who tempted him along those lines—until Hilary.

He supposed this all had something to do with their being together day and night for weeks on end. It had filled his mind with romantic fantasies, when he'd always believed he was immune to such foolishness.

Unfortunately he wasn't the right type for a debutante. Hilary should marry a bank president, or someone as sensitive and cultured as she was, perhaps another musician. Not a helicopter pilot with a family whose income barely qualified them as middle-class. Nor was her mother likely to accept him; and there was already enough dissension between Hilary and her mother. He didn't relish the idea of being another source of conflict.

Dawn stroked a brush of pink across the horizon when Sean rolled out of bed. He'd heard Hilary stir a few moments earlier and knew she was probably in the kitchen brewing her morning cup of *latte*. He would have preferred to avoid her as much as he could, but he needed to pack his lunch.

She was dressed in her robe, leaning against the counter, her head braced against the cupboard. Her eyes were closed, and she looked as though she'd gotten even less sleep than he had.

"Hil?"

"'Morning," she murmured dreamily. "Why are Mondays always so difficult?

"I wouldn't know," he muttered, wondering the same thing himself.

My word, she was beautiful with her dark hair softly mussed about her shoulders. Looking at her took his breath away, and try as he might, he couldn't keep from staring at her. She looked so damn kissable. It was more than he could resist.

It'd been nearly a week since Sean had touched her, and he yearned for the feel of her in his arms again.

His kiss came as a surprise to her, but it was even more of one to him. One minute he was thinking he'd better make his lunch and escape and the next she was in his arms, his mouth pressed urgently over hers. He didn't remember it being this good the first time. Wonder mingled with need, both sensations swamping his senses.

Hilary moaned softly and opened to him as naturally as if they were longtime lovers. Her arms automatically went around his neck and she nestled in his embrace, so trusting and confident that this was where she belonged. She was completely at home. Completely at ease.

His hand tunneled under the thickness of her hair to cradle the back of her head. Their kiss grew deep and long. Either he stopped now or he'd have her stripped and in his bed before he could stop himself.

He broke away abruptly. "Now," he said, breathing heavily, "it's a good morning."

With that, he walked out of the kitchen.

Chapter Eight

The kiss Hilary exchanged with Sean that morning filled her with a wild sense of hope. For nearly a week Sean had been doing everything within his power to avoid her. Yet she caught him watching her at odd moments, and she saw in him a look of longing that gave her no room for doubt. He wanted her, possibly he loved her; but the emotion frightened him. He was a man who'd lived without love in his life. The army had met his every need. It had been his ego, his pride. As a member of the Special Forces, he didn't have room for anything or anyone else in his life. Like her, he was on his own for the first time. They were two lost souls making their way in the world. Both were vulnerable. Both were unsure of what the future held.

Of one thing Hilary was confident: Sean was too much of a gentleman to take advantage of her. The barrier of his resolve had been breached that morning. It was exactly what Hilary had been waiting for, exactly what she'd hoped would happen.

The next move was hers, and she was ready. More than ready.

That same afternoon, when she arrived home from the music store, she discovered Sean sprawled across the sofa, napping. He didn't hear her come in, which was all the better.

She watched him doze for several moments, drinking in the sight of him so relaxed and comfortable. For long moments, she did nothing but stand there; her heart was so in tune with his that she was convinced they beat in unison. She'd seen him like this often, and each time was like a treasure. He wouldn't appreciate it if he knew how much she enjoyed studying him. She had to be quiet; he was an amazingly light sleeper— from years of training, she guessed. Often she suspected he was awake but feigned sleep in an effort to avoid her.

Well, she was finished with those games. Holding her hair away from her face, she bent over Sean and lightly settled her mouth over his.

When the warm possession of her lips met his, he reached up, enfolding her, and brought her down so that she was stretched out atop his hard length.

Hilary released a small cry of surprise and noted Sean was wearing a sly smile. "You were awake the whole time," she muttered.

"Not exactly, but I'm awake now. Wide-awake." His eyes delved into hers. "For the love of heaven, Hilary, what are we doing?"

"I...don't know anymore," she whispered, and kissed him again. Only this time it was more than a mere brushing of their lips; it was a full-blown kiss. His tongue parted her lips and she responded eagerly. Although the full length of her body was pressed against his, she wanted even closer contact. Her hips made small undulating movements against him.

"Hil...we've got to stop." His hands moved from her back to her buttocks in a futile effort to still her actions. "You don't know what you're asking."

"I do know," she whispered, kissing him again, deeper than before, ending only when they were both panting and breathless with need.

He made a low, rough sound in his throat and reached for the zipper at the back of her dress. Hilary thought she would die if he didn't hurry. Even as he was working the fabric from her shoulders, she was spreading a series of frantic kisses over his face, encouraging him.

She felt his hands fumble behind her and deftly unsnap her bra. He gently peeled it away from her shoulders and rolled sideways, taking her with him so they were both on the sofa, side by side, facing each other.

His eyes held hers, but whatever answers he sought he must have found, because his hands cupped her bare breasts and he sighed when they peaked under his attention.

Hilary made a soft, moaning sound that seemed to encourage him even more. His mouth, warm and wet, slid over her breast to take in the tightly puckered nipple. No man had ever touched her so intimately, and when his mouth sucked firmly, her entire body experienced the rush of wild sensation. She jerked slightly, closed her eyes and relished that she could give him something in return for all that he'd given her.

It was so good, so wonderfully different than anything she'd ever experienced. She moaned again as pulses of pleasure pounded through her.

"Sean...oh, Sean, no one ever told me it would be this good." Her hands were in his hair, and she was frantically moving against him. He caused an ache, a wonderful, pulsing ache to build within her, to mature to a crescendo until she was desperate to find its conclusion.

At first Hilary couldn't identify the sound, a pounding, beating rhythm that she found irritating. Sean moaned and stilled.

"No," she pleaded, not wanting him to stop. Not yet, not so soon. She didn't know what the noise was, but surely it would stop, surely it would go away.

"Hilary...dear God." Sean expelled his breath forcefully. "It's the phone."

"Let it ring."

"No, answer it," he said with a small groan.

The sound pierced the quiet. "Whoever it is will call back," she whispered.

"Perhaps, but something tells me it's your mother."

"My mother," she repeated slowly. The thought propelled her into action, and she scrambled off the sofa so quickly she nearly fell like a deadweight onto the floor. She would have if Sean hadn't held on to her.

The phone pealed again and she quickly righted herself, unable to understand her urgency. If it was her mother calling, Hilary wasn't in any mood to speak to her.

"Hello," she answered, sounding both breathless and guilty.

"Sean, please."

She held out the receiver to him. "The phone's for you," she said. His gaze narrowed as though he disbelieved her.

While he was dealing with the call, Hilary readjusted her clothing, confident her cheeks were a bright, fire-engine red. She was so preoccupied, she didn't hear anything of what Sean was saying.

It took her a moment to realize that although he'd hung up the phone, he continued facing the wall.

"Sean?" she asked when he didn't immediately turn to face her.

"That shouldn't have happened," he said gruffly. "None of it. We're playing with fire—and one of us has got to keep our heads clear."

"But...why?" Hilary wanted to know. It was hard not to slip her arms around him and bury herself in his warmth. It felt cold and lonely outside of his arms. When Sean held her, all her doubts disappeared, all her concerns vanished. Yes, there were differences between them. Major differences, but none so great that they couldn't be resolved, if they were both willing to work at it.

"I'm...in love with you, Sean," she said quietly from behind him.

He made a low, disbelieving sound as he turned to face her. His eyes were gentle, but one look told her he'd closed himself to her. Nothing she said now would make any difference.

"Have you ever been in love before, Hil?"

"Yes. Once, in my freshman year. I'm not completely inexperienced, if that's troubling you."

He gave a short, humorless laugh. "You're very sweet and much too honest to lie effectively. If we hadn't been interrupted just now, do you have any idea what would have happened?"

"Of course I do," she answered indignantly. "We would have made love, which is exactly what I hoped would happen."

His eyes grew dark and intense, as though the thought troubled him. "It would have been a mistake."

"I refuse to believe that. Loving you isn't a mistake...you'll never convince me of that. I know you're this macho guy, and it's probably much harder for you to admit your feelings for me, but—"

"Hil, listen," he said, breaking into her tirade. His voice was calm and reasonable and left little room for argument. "Do you have any idea what would have happened afterward? We'd go on making love, entwining our lives more and more."

"Is that so wrong?"

"Yes, for you it is, and for me, too."

"But why?" She was becoming agitated now and more desperate.

"You're on your own for the first time. We wouldn't be able to go back. It's inevitable that we'd become more and more involved. Before we could prevent it, neither one of us would have a life of our own."

Hilary didn't know what to say.

"I've spent the last ten years of my life in the army," Sean continued, "and I'm not looking to make another commitment. That's not what you want, either. If we share anything, Hil, it's that we're both completely on our own for the first time in our lives. We can't trust what we're feeling. It's much too soon to know if it's real."

Part of what he said made sense. This was her first time away from her mother, the first time she was completely self-sufficient, the first time she'd held a real job. She'd set out to prove something to herself and, more important, to her mother. She'd done that. Or, at least, she wanted to believe she had.

As for what he said about her not being able to trust her love for him, she did so implicitly. Perhaps she was more naive than she realized, because she did love Sean, without question, without a single second thought. It was true she hadn't planned on falling in love so soon, but it had happened, and she was thrilled even if he wasn't.

If Sean wanted to debate with her, then she had a long list of arguments why their being together was right. But she couldn't speak for Sean. If he loved her, the way she believed, then he'd discover that on his own. If he wanted her in his life, then he'd ask. She'd done everything she knew how to do. She wouldn't make the mistake of pressuring him, or manipulating him the way her mother had tried with her. She'd been on the receiving end of such treatment and had rebelled. If she was going to win Sean's love, then there was little she could say or do until he was ready.

"All right," she said, slowly, thoughtfully, fighting back her doubts. For the first time she could appreciate how difficult it had been for her mother to let her go, to release her.

"Where do you suggest we go from here?" she asked when she could.

"Nowhere," he said flatly.

His words took her by surprise. They made no sense, and she wasn't sure his suggestion was emotionally healthy, either. "In other words, you're suggesting we forget what's between us."

"Forget it?" he repeated with an abrupt laugh. "I wish I could. No, I say we ignore it, we pretend it doesn't exist and go about our lives as best we can until the situation resolves itself." He stalked away from her and down the hallway and into his bedroom. Hilary followed and stood in the doorway as he opened his closet and peeled off his shirt. He was going out. "In two weeks I'll be out of here," he announced flatly.

"Then what?" How hard it was to disguise her dismay.

"Then we can both go back to living our lives."

"I see," Hilary said softly.

In two weeks' time Sean would be gone. Out of the apartment and, from the sounds of it, out of her life, as well.

Hilary sat in the darkened living room watching the hands on the wall clock slowly circle the dial. Sean had been furious with her for staying out late, for worrying him, but he felt no such concern himself. He'd left without a word and been gone for nearly eight hours.

Hilary had phoned her mother earlier in the evening and they'd shared an enjoyable conversation. It was the first time she could remember talking to her mother without finding something to be upset about. Louise had always seemed so confident she knew what was best for Hilary. Now it was Hilary who felt equally certain she knew what was right for her and Sean and their relationship.

Louise had known there was something wrong almost immediately, but to Hilary's surprise she hadn't pressured her. Hilary was grateful, and when the conversation ended, she felt rejuvenated and pleased she'd called.

Sitting alone in the dark now, hours later, gave Hilary plenty of time to sort through her thoughts. It took her several hours, but she'd realized that what was concerning Sean most had been left unsaid between them: her name and her money.

Hilary was aware of it, because she'd faced it before. At age eighteen, with William Donahue. Sean had asked her if she'd ever been in love before, but he hadn't wanted to know any of the details. Hilary wished now that she'd told him.

She'd been eighteen and fallen head over heels for a young man in her English literature class. She'd spent long hours with William discussing the rich layers of meaning in classic literature. William had been Hilary's first love, and she had given him her heart. It wasn't until later, when he started asking for small loans, that she realized he wasn't attracted to her, but to the large trust account that would someday be hers. What had been so difficult was that her mother had never liked William and had done her best to end the relationship. Hilary had stood up to her and argued that William wasn't any of the things Louise had claimed, even when it was obvious her mother was right. In the end, she'd been forced to admit her folly.

It had been a painful and bitter lesson for Hilary, and she'd avoided men and relationships ever since. Money and position had stood between her and the man she loved before. This wasn't a new experience.

William had wanted her for what she could do for him, for her wealth and her name.

Sean *didn't* want her, for the identical reasons.

A flash of light signaled that Sean was home. His headlights were extinguished, and a few moments later the front door opened. He didn't bother to turn on the living room lights, but walked through the darkened room.

He paused at the hallway before he slowly turned around. "Hil? What are you doing up?"

"Thinking," she whispered.

"It's nearly two in the morning."

"I know."

He came to her then and knelt down in front of her. The scent of roses and sweet perfume hit her like an openhanded slap across the face. Hilary closed her eyes to the sudden sharp pain and waited for the hurting to subside.

"How's Carla?" she asked evenly, refusing to allow any of her pain to bleed into her voice.

"How'd you know I was with her?"

"I can smell her perfume."

Sean frowned and gently cupped her face between his hands. "I didn't touch her, Hilary. I swear to you I didn't go from your arms to hers."

"You don't have to tell me that. I already know."

Deep, disbelieving grooves bracketed his mouth. "How?"

"Because," she said softly, confidently, "you couldn't. You wanted to, though, didn't you? You wanted to prove something to yourself and failed." She waited for him to confirm or deny her words, but he did neither.

"You shouldn't have waited up," he said, easing away from her, his voice stiffening. "You've got a long day ahead of you."

"Please," she said softly, "answer me."

He didn't. Instead he turned and walked away from her, just as he intended to do the minute the Greers returned.

Chapter Nine

"You're sure you'll be able to pull this off?" Sean felt obliged to ask Hilary the following Friday afternoon. Her mother was scheduled to land early Saturday morning. He'd packed up his belongings and made the necessary arrangements to vacate the apartment for the weekend.

"Of course I'm sure," Hilary said with a warm smile. He dragged his gaze away, amazed at how easily she could sucker him in with a mere smile.

"I have the sinking suspicion that you're going to tell her about me, and that would be foolish in the extreme." He knew he was frowning as he spoke, but he couldn't help himself. He seemed to be doing a lot of that lately. He loved Hilary so damn much it frightened him, and therein was the problem. If she were a passing amusement, he would have had her in his bed the first week. Make that the second week. Those first seven days he'd been more inclined to strangle her scrawny neck. But once they were past that initial hurdle, he'd found himself fighting an upstream battle. Because he loved her, he refused to rush her into anything that had the potential of hurting Hilary.

For that matter, Sean wasn't convinced he could trust her feelings for him. Hilary was too inexperienced to recognize love. He didn't doubt she was fascinated with him; they were as different as any two people could be. He feared that her interest in him would fade once he was out of her life. Then, and only then, would she adequately be able to judge her feelings.

Hilary had nearly made it impossible for him not to touch her. She was never blatant about what she wanted, never overt, but she didn't have to be in order for him to read her mind.

She wanted him. What made it so damn difficult was that he loved and wanted her, too. He would have given in to what they both desired if he didn't believe her feelings would ultimately change. Within a few weeks she'd completely forget about him.

"Mom'll never guess you're living here."

Sean studied her once more. "You aren't going to say anything?"

"No."

He eyed her carefully. "Give me your word, Hilary."

She laughed softly. "I hereby solemnly vow I won't tell my mother the two of us are living together."

Still Sean hesitated. Hilary and her mother were an unknown element. There was friction and there was a deep abiding love, too.

"Don't look so worried," she chided gently. "I can't say anything to Mom. It'll prove everything she's been afraid would happen the moment I moved away from home. In her eyes, the world is unsafe for her precious daughter."

"She's right," Sean flared.

"Oh, Sean, not you, too." Hilary released a deep sigh. "If anything, I've been safer because you've been here with me. Now stop worrying. Mom and I are going to have a wonderful weekend together." Her eyes took on an intense look. "We're going to clear the air.... I doubt we'll have enough time to delve into my relationship with you."

Sean couldn't keep from scowling. He'd been through each room of the apartment at least three times, removing every shred of evidence of his presence in the apartment. But he couldn't help thinking he'd forgotten something.

"Are you going to miss me?" Hilary asked softly, her wide eyes staring up at him.

Sean didn't answer, because it was all too obvious he would. The Greers would be back in one more week, and not a moment too soon. He'd intended to search for an apartment that weekend. He had only one criterion. For his own peace of mind, he needed to be within ten minutes' driving distance from Hilary. The closer the better. Damn, but he'd grown accustomed to having her in his life. To finding her in his kitchen every morning and spending the evenings in her company. It was the kind of life he'd always imagined for himself . . . someday.

"I'm going to miss you something dreadful," she responded when he didn't.

Although she prompted, he didn't answer.

She followed him out to his car, her movements sluggish and reluctant. "Would it be too much to ask you to kiss me for luck?"

He'd almost forgotten her first performance with the symphony would be on Mother's Day. It was the reason for Louise Wadsworth's visit.

Heaven help him, he couldn't resist her. Drawing her into his arms, his heart raced at the eager way she nestled in his embrace, turning her face to his. He felt a groan working its way forward from the back of his throat even before their lips met. Her own soft cry of pleasure mingled with his. If the kiss they shared was for luck, one of them was sure to win the lottery.

They broke apart, eyes closed, chests heaving, shaking with reaction.

It demanded every ounce of strength Sean possessed to ease her from his arms. "I'll be back Sunday night," he said, weakening.

She nodded, her eyes round and sad.

Hell if he knew if he could wait that long to hold her again.

Hilary held a small bouquet of pink rosebuds and waited at the end of the jetway for her mother to walk off the plane.

She'd held true to her word about keeping her living arrangement with Sean a secret, but for none of the reasons he'd asked.

"Mom." Her eyes lit up as Louise stepped off the plane.

"Hilary, darling."

Before another moment passed, mother and daughter were hugging each other tightly. It felt good, better than she had thought it would.

It didn't take long for them to collect Louise's suitcase. They chatted about nonsensical things like the weather and old friends as Hilary drove to the apartment. Her mother frowned as they approached her neighborhood, but Hilary was prepared for an argument if her mother offered one. This was her home, her life, and she wouldn't idly sit by and have her mother attack it.

"This is my apartment," Hilary said, once they were in her living room. She held on to her mother's suitcase with both hands. "But it's my home and I love it," she added a bit defensively.

Her mother smiled softly and glanced around. "It's very nice."

"I'm happy, Mom, and isn't that what really matters? I know this apartment is smaller than some of your closets, but it's mine."

Louise Wadsworth nodded. "I know. Your voice tells me how very well you've adjusted away from me."

"Isn't that the point, Mom?" Hilary hadn't intended they have their discussion quite so soon, but it seemed to be for the best. "A child, any child, must eventually make a life of their own away from their family."

Her mother's lips thinned as she turned and walked into the kitchen. "You didn't have to move to Portland," she said, turning to face Hilary once more, rubbing her palms together.

"But I did," Hilary protested. "For a number of very good reasons. First off, this was where I found employment. Second, it was away from you."

"Hilary!"

"I'm not saying this to be cruel. I never appreciated you, Mom. My attitude, I'm ashamed to tell you, was so critical of you. I was convinced if I stayed in San Francisco another minute you were going to suffocate me with your love. I had to get away and I'm glad I did. You should be glad, too."

Hilary noted her mother's hands were trembling.

"In the last few weeks, I've discovered so many things about myself that I never would have if I'd been living in the Bay Area."

"I've discovered a few matters myself," Louise whispered, holding her hand out to Hilary. "Mostly I've discovered how very proud I am of you for having the courage to stand up to me. I don't always know what's right . . . I just think I do."

Tears glittered in their eyes as they laughed and hugged again, this time with a much deeper appreciation of one another.

When they'd composed themselves, Hilary led her mother to Sean's bedroom. "You'll be sleeping in here."

Her mother looked around the cheery room and frowned. Then she started sniffing, her nose making small telltale movements.

"Is something wrong?" Hilary asked.

"No...it's just that I thought I detected a whiff of spicy after-shave in here."

"The former tenant was a man." It was on the tip of her tongue to mention Sean, but it was too soon to shock her mother with the news she was in love.

Louise nodded, seeming to accept her explanation.

"Would you like a cup of *latte?*" Hilary asked.

"That sounds delightful," her mother answered; and followed her into the compact kitchen. While Hilary brewed the *latte,* her mother opened the refrigerator and removed a carton of milk. She set it on the counter and hesitated.

"Did you know you had a six-pack of beer in here?"

"Beer?" Hilary repeated, clenching her teeth. It'd been there for weeks, a leftover from Sean's poker party. She'd forgotten about it, and apparently so had he. "Ah...yes, I remember now. I bought it for a friend and forgot all about it."

"A friend," her mother repeated slowly. "Someone from the symphony?"

"No." She kept her back to her mother and squeezed her eyes closed, seeking wisdom. Louise had only been in the house fifteen minutes. It would have been so easy to casually mention Sean. If their living arrangement were different she'd do so immediately.

"Which friend is this, dear?"

Hilary wasn't any good at lying, and the only way out was the truth.

"It belongs to Sean."

"Ah, yes," her mother said, "your neighbor. You mentioned him once before. I'm hoping I'll get a chance to meet this young man who keeps beer in my daughter's refrigerator."

"He's away for the weekend," Hilary said quickly, and immediately regretted it.

"Visiting his own mother?"

"No," Hilary said, carrying the two tall mugs of *latte* to the table where her mother was seated. "She died when he was young. He barely remembers her."

"You know quite a bit about this young man, don't you?"

Hilary sat across from her mother, her hands cupping the thick ceramic mug. "Yes . . . we've gotten close. It's Sean who's helped me better understand my relationship with you."

"Oh?"

She looked away and smiled softly. "He told me what a neat-freak I was, and it made me realize how much you and I are alike. I have this precise way of folding the bathroom towels that drives him crazy and I realized it was the same way you do."

Her mother was silent for a moment. "This . . . neighbor uses your towels?"

A moment of panic erupted inside Hilary as her eyes flew to her mother. She wasn't sure what to say or do.

She might be able to lie her way out of this, but she'd rather not. Blurting everything out seemed the most logical choice, and she might have if her mother hadn't spoken first.

"Now tell me about your job and the symphony and the new friends you've made."

Hilary did as her mother asked, but soon discovered she was talking more about Sean than anyone. "He's really been wonderful to me."

"You say he's recently been discharged from the army?"

Hilary nodded. "He was a warrant officer with Special Forces. We both moved into the area at the same time and...we've become good friends."

Her mother didn't comment. "Now tell me if you've met any young men from the symphony."

Hilary bristled. "You've never even met Sean and already you're dismissing him."

Her mother looked surprised by the emotion with which Hilary spoke. Hilary was somewhat surprised herself.

"He's a former soldier, Hilary. Trained to kill and..."

"I've never felt safer with anyone in my life. He's big and tough and gruff around the edges, but I've never known a gentler man."

Her mother said nothing for a long moment, and then, "I see."

"I did go out with one...a fellow from the symphony," she added. "His name is Arnold. You'll have a chance to meet him yourself tomorrow afternoon at the performance.''

"This is going to be the best Mother's Day gift you could have given me, Hilary.''

"What is, Mother?''

"Being able to sit in the audience and watch you perform. Your father would have been so proud.''

Hilary nodded, her heart heavy because she knew, deep down, her mother had categorically dismissed Sean without ever having met him.

That afternoon they went shopping, but Hilary's heart wasn't in it. She made the motions and allowed her mother to buy her a new outfit. She was almost grateful when it was time to leave her mother for the last rehearsal before the Sunday performance.

Sean couldn't remember the last time he'd put on a suit and tie. The only reason he did so now was because he figured it would be expected of him. The symphony was for the upper crust and certainly nothing that would have interested him if it hadn't been for Hilary.

She'd given him the ticket weeks earlier. He hadn't intended to use it, and wouldn't now if he weren't so damn curious. His desire to see Hilary give her first performance with the symphony was his initial reason for his being there. It also gave him the chance to get a good look at Hilary's mother. Once he did, he just might be able to judge how receptive she'd be to her daughter falling in love with a nobody like him.

The usher escorted him to his assigned seat, and Sean was grateful it was at the end of the row. He hated the cramped feeling.

He began reading over his program and was completely lost. Sean liked to think of himself as an intelligent man, but there were letters and numbers listed with each composer, and he couldn't make heads nor tails out of the thing. This wasn't going to be the least bit of help.

"Excuse me," he said to the attractive woman seated beside him. "Would you help decipher this for me?"

"I'd be happy to," she said warmly.

Sean thanked her with a smile when she'd finished the explanation, and eased his finger along the inside of his collar. The damn thing was slowly asphyxiating him. He noticed the woman was watching him. "In case you hadn't guessed, this is my first time at a symphony. I feel as out of place here as a chicken in a nest of eagles."

She laughed softly. It wasn't until she turned to him that Sean realized she wasn't nearly as young as he first thought. He'd assumed she was in her late twenties, but upon closer examination he realized she was closer to forty.

"I have a friend playing with the symphony," Sean explained, proud of Hilary's talent. He didn't normally speak to strangers, but he felt a bit awkward and strangely talkative. "She's the third-chair flutist."

"Ah," the woman said softly. "Is she a good friend?"

"Very good." Sean relaxed and crossed his long legs as his gaze scanned the audience. "Her mother's here someplace."

"Are you hoping to meet her?"

"Not exactly," Sean said, resisting the urge to laugh. "She'd take one look at me, and it would be the end of my relationship with Hil."

"What makes you say that?"

"Hilary's family has got money, lots of money."

"And that troubles you?"

"Not exactly, but I don't think her mother would approve of someone like me. Not that I blame her—if Hilary were my daughter I'd want the very best for her, too."

"And you're not?"

This conversation was beginning to get a little more personal than he'd intended. "Yes, in some ways I am. But I doubt that her family would see it like that."

"Then you love her, and would whether she had money or not?"

Sean looked away, surprised he would openly admit his feelings to a stranger and not Hilary. "I love her."

"I see. I take it you intend to marry her?"

He thought for a good long while before answering. "No, I probably won't. She should marry someone in her own league. Take, for example, the fellow playing violin. His name is Arnold something-or-other. He's a nice guy from everything Hilary's said about him. He's asked her out a couple of times, but she always makes an excuse. I think once I move out, Hilary will agree to date him. I've got a wait-and-see attitude when it comes to Hilary and me. I want to give her the time and space to know her own mind before I broach the subject of marriage.''

"Once you move out?'' she repeated. "Are the two of you living together?''

"In a nontraditional way,'' he explained quickly, hoping to sound casual. "There was a mix-up and we both rented the same apartment. The couple who manage the place are out of town for several weeks. We didn't have any choice but to share the place until the owner returned with the deposit and first month's rent.'' He could feel the tension ease from the woman. "Can you imagine what her mother would think if she found out about that?''

"I can very well imagine, since I have a daughter of my own. She's in her twenties.''

Sean had trouble believing the woman was old enough to have a child that old and said so.

"Thank you for the compliment, but it's true. I know exactly how this . . . other mother would feel.''

"Then you understand why it's better for everyone concerned that Hilary's mother never finds out about me.''

The woman frowned. "I can't say I agree with that. If this young woman—what did you say her name was again?''

"Hilary."

"Right. If Hilary's mother were to learn about the two of you, what do you think would happen?"

"For one thing, she'd be furious with Hilary, and their relationship is already a little rocky. Hilary's had this chip on her shoulder about proving herself to her mother. See, Hilary is headstrong and opinionated. She claims she inherited both traits from her mother."

"I see," the woman returned, laughing softly. "You know, this mothering business isn't as easy as it looks."

"I'm sure you're right. I don't remember my own mother, so I feel at a loss when it comes to advising Hilary about hers."

His companion relaxed. "Being a mother means far more than changing a few diapers and showing up for parent-teacher conferences. In fact, it's downright tricky business. We love them, guide them, give them our hearts and then are supposed to set them free."

"I never thought of it in those terms," Sean said.

The woman smiled softly and sighed.

He didn't entirely understand why he was talking so freely with this stranger, possibly because this issue was weighing so heavily on his own shoulders.

"There's a rhythm to being a mother.... I know that sounds odd, but it's true," she continued, sounding faintly emotional. "It's the part of parenting I've found the most trying. It fills me with self-doubts and worries, which I know are mostly unfounded, it's just that I can't keep from fretting about her. I know she hates that and I can't say that I blame her." Just the way the woman exhaled told Sean she felt as uncomfortable sharing with him as he had with her.

"A rhythm?" Sean repeated.

"Yes... I hope you don't mind my talking so freely."

"I confided in you, too," Sean admitted, wondering at this bond he'd formed with a virtual stranger.

"I appreciate that because it's helped me define my feelings. Strange how you can meet someone you've never known before and learn so much about yourself."

Sean nodded, experiencing the same feeling himself.

"It doesn't help matters that she's an only child. I fear I, too, hold on to her tighter than most mothers, because she's all I have. It was hard for me when she first learned to ride a bicycle. I was afraid she was going to fall and hurt herself, but that was only the beginning.

"Then she went off to college, and I was dreadfully lonely without her. Her freshman year she fell in love and was so badly hurt that she wanted to drop out of school. I wouldn't allow that, although I badly wanted to be there to protect her."

"You did the right thing."

She smiled softly. "It wasn't easy, any more than it was just recently."

"Recently?"

"Yes, she's fallen in love for a second time. I believe she intends to marry this young man. I'm not certain he realizes it yet, but then, he doesn't know how stubborn my daughter can be."

"You don't approve of him?"

"She's young, but then, I'd been married a year at the same age and was pregnant with her. I . . . don't really know this man she's chosen. We've only just met, but from what I've seen, I think he'll make her a good husband. But you realize what that means, don't you? It means I'll have to let go of her all over again."

"She'll always be your daughter."

"Yes, I realize that. It's just another step in this process, this ebb and flow of life. The holding on, the letting go. You know, the holding-on portion is the easy part, it's the letting go that's so damned difficult."

Just then the thick curtain parted, and the audience applauded. Sean glanced over the program, the very program that had initiated this intense conversation with a stranger. They had each shared a deep part of themselves.

"Thank you," Sean said, holding the other woman's eyes.

"No," she said, her dark eyes intense. "Thank *you*."

The music started after the round of applause. Sean assumed he'd be bored stiff. He'd never attended anything like a symphony performance and he wouldn't be here now if it weren't for Hilary.

He had to admit halfway through the schedule that it was enjoyable. Nothing he'd bring his friends to, exactly. The experience was... He searched for the right word. Pleasurably different, he decided.

During the second half of the performance, Sean found himself relaxing, blocking out the world and savoring the music. With his eyes shut, the immediacy of the music took him by surprise. It was as if he were in a small raft heaved about a storm-tossed sea. He gripped the edges of his seat, amazed at the amount of emotion he felt in the music. It swelled and surged like nothing he'd ever known.

When the orchestra finished, he rushed to his feet and applauded with all his might. Soon others were standing, too, including the woman next to him. She, too, had apparently found the same richness as he, because she was dabbing her eyes with a lace-edged hankie.

"It was wonderful, wasn't it?" she asked above the din.

"Magnificent!"

"Then you should let your young lady know."

He hesitated.

"Go on, tell her," she urged. "She deserves to know how much you enjoyed her music."

Sean decided she was right. When the music hall started to empty, he headed for the stage. The older woman was directly behind him.

Hilary's gaze widened with delight when she saw him. "Sean," she said, easing her way between other symphony members to get to him. Her eyes sparkled with pleasure. "You came . . . you came."

"You were fabulous," he said, kissing her cheek. He longed to hold her against him and tell her everything he'd experienced through the music, but he wasn't sure he could put it into words.

"I'd like you to meet my mother," Hilary said, reaching for his hand, her fingers closing tightly over his.

He'd asked for this, coming onto the stage, but now was as good a time as any, Sean decided. The woman he'd talked to earlier had given him a good deal of insight into a mother's heart. For the first time since Hilary had mentioned her mother, he was looking forward to meeting her.

"Sean," Hilary said, slipping her arm around his waist, "this is my mother, Louise Wadsworth. Mom, this is Sean . . . the neighbor I was telling you about."

Sean felt as though someone had kicked him in the stomach. Louise Wadsworth was the woman who'd sat in the seat next to his own.

Chapter Ten

"We've already met," Sean replied stiffly. "Isn't that right, Mrs. Wadsworth?" He'd tensed at her side, and Hilary wasn't sure she understood why.

"Indeed we have," her mother continued, smiling softly at Hilary. "You've helped solve a complex puzzle for me, young man. I was beginning to have some serious questions about my daughter."

"About what, Mom?"

"The scent of a man's after-shave was my first clue something wasn't right at the apartment. Then I found the beer in the refrigerator."

"I left the beer," Sean muttered beneath his breath, and his tone told her he was furious with himself.

"But the real clincher was turning on the radio and finding some man singing in a pleasant twang about being a rodeo clown. I know my daughter, and her tastes in music don't extend to country and western."

Sean looked as if he were a mouse with his tail caught in a trap.

"I think it might be an excellent idea if we all adjourned to dinner. I've made reservations at the Ritz."

"I think you two should go on without me," Sean said, excusing himself.

"Nonsense," Louise countered. "I spilled my heart out to you, young man, so if you're feeling foolish, you shouldn't. Our conversation told me far more about you than ten arguments with Hilary."

"Conversation?" Hilary demanded. "What went on out there?"

"Tell me, sweetheart," her mother asked, grinning broadly, "did you purposely arrange for our seats to be next to each other?"

"Your seats... You mean...?" Her gaze went from her mother to Sean and then back again. "No...I had no idea.... I didn't even think Sean was coming.... I'd hoped, but I..." She let the rest fade.

"I was just wondering the same thing myself," Sean said to Louise. "It was the perfect setup."

"But I didn't... I suppose I should have, but the thought never crossed my mind."

"Don't worry, sweetheart, we believe you."

"You like him, don't you?" Hilary asked, slipping her arm into her mother's. Then she glanced up at Sean. "She's not nearly as intimidating as you thought, is she?" She wrapped her free arm around his.

Louise laughed softly. "I must say, Hilary, when you move out on your own, you certainly do it with a bang."

"Listen," Sean said. "This is Mother's Day. I'd be intruding."

"Nonsense."

"One thing you'll discover about my mother," Hilary said, smiling up at him. "She doesn't know how to take no for an answer. She's both stubborn and strong willed.''

"Nonsense. Hilary is the one who is stubborn and strong willed. And she picked up those traits from her father," Louise announced. "Heaven knows she didn't get them from me."

Sean wasn't sure what he was feeling as they dined in the most expensive restaurant in town. Surprise, certainly, but a certain amount of relief, too.

He'd have preferred that Hilary's mother hadn't learned they were living together quite so soon. He wondered if she believed the two of them were strictly roommates and not lovers. He didn't know that he would himself.

Louise Wadsworth amazed him. He wasn't sure what he'd pictured in his mind, but not the strikingly attractive woman he'd introduced himself to at the concert. In his mind, he saw her as much older, far more domineering. What he found was something else again. A woman struggling with her role as a mother, giving everything she had to be the best parent she knew how to be.

What amazed him even more was that he liked her. He genuinely liked her, which shouldn't be so amazing once he thought about it. He was crazy about Hilary, so it only made sense that he would feel kindly toward the woman who'd raised her. It surprised him that he hadn't realized that sooner.

The question was, where did they go from there? Hilary's mother made it plain that she was leaving the decisions in this relationship up to Hilary and to him. Although Sean appreciated what it cost her to say that, he had several concerns of his own.

Their dinner was enjoyable, but Sean couldn't help feeling ill at ease. He was intruding on a day reserved for mothers and their children. When he could, he made his excuses and left. He felt Hilary's eyes follow him as he walked out of the restaurant, but he had no reassurances to offer her. He loved her, but that and four bits would buy her a cup of coffee.

"Sean," Hilary cried, her eyes shining, when he came into the apartment early Monday morning. "Where have you been . . . ? I expected you back Sunday evening." There was no chastisement in her words, only relief and a good deal of delight. She threw her arms around his middle and squeezed tight.

He resisted the urge to hug her, realized it was a lost cause and wrapped his arms around her waist. Closing his eyes, he drank in the warm scent of her.

"Mom thinks you're wonderful. We talked and talked and talked. I don't know what you said, but whatever it was has changed everything."

Sean frowned. "I didn't say anything."

"Not according to Mom. She claims you helped her realize I was an adult now, capable of making my own decisions. It's time to let me soar on my own power."

"Your mother's a special woman, Hilary. So are you."

"We had a marvelous time. I can't remember ever feeling closer to her."

"I'm pleased to hear it." He knew his voice sounded stiff and unnatural.

Hilary eased back enough so she could look up at him. "Is something wrong?"

How beautiful she was. His fingers stroked her cheek before he steeled himself and said, "I found an apartment this weekend, Hil, and I've already moved in."

"But...what about the deposit and the first month's rent the Greers owe you?"

"I'll collect that later."

"But I thought you said you didn't have the extra cash. You told me you couldn't afford—"

"I couldn't. I got my first paycheck this Friday."

The sunshine seemed to drain from her eyes. "In other words, you're outta here." She broke completely away from him and laced her fingers together so tightly they went white.

"I want to give us time, Hil, away from each other, so we'll know if what we have is real."

"Of course it is. How can you doubt it? It doesn't get any more real than this."

"What we feel might well be the result of our living together. Any two people in such close proximity—"

"You don't honestly believe that, do you?"

Sean sighed. He'd known this was going to be hard, he just hadn't known how hard. "Yes, Hil, that's what I believe."

"But that's—"

"I want you to promise me that you'll start dating other men."

For a long moment, she didn't say anything. He could almost see her erecting a shield against him so he wouldn't see her distress. "Is that what you want?" she asked, her voice a monotone of pain.

It wasn't, but it was the best way he knew to figure everything out. "Yes."

"What about you...will you be dating other women?"

"Yes."

Her eyes filled with tears. "I see." She did her best to put on a cheerful facade. "All right, you're on. We'll give it a few days—a week at the most—then we'll—"

"It's going to have to be longer than a week, Hil."

"Two weeks?"

"More like two months. We'll meet at the Ritz for dinner." He walked over to the calendar, flipped the pages and checked the date. "At seven," he said.

"Two months... You're sure you want to wait that long?" she moaned.

He nodded, thinking sixty days was an absolute minimum. "I don't want there to be any room for doubts when the time comes. Agreed?"

An eternity passed before she reluctantly nodded.

* * *

Hilary had never known time could pass so quickly. It helped that she was extraordinarily busy. She'd taken Sean at his word and dated several times. First she'd gone out with Arnold, and then someone else she'd met through Mr. Murphy at the music store. Both were very nice young men, but she'd experienced none of the spark, none of the excitement she'd had with Sean.

She'd missed him dreadfully, and wondered about him each and every day.

"There's an old saying," her mother had repeatedly told her in their weekly telephone conversations, "about setting someone free, and if he returns, it's meant to be."

"There's also an old saying about hunting him down and making his life miserable if he doesn't," Hilary reminded her.

Louise laughed. "You do love him, don't you, sweetheart?"

"Very much."

"Have you decided what you're going to do if he finds someone else he loves more?"

Hilary bit into her lower lip, refusing to entertain the notion. "It won't happen."

"I'd hate to see you hurt."

"I'm not exactly looking forward to that, either, you know." Hilary felt closer to her mother in the last two months than ever before. She had Sean to thank for that, and she would thank him when she saw him again.

"Whatever happens, you know I'll always be here for you."

"Yes, Mom, I know. We're here for each other."

The evening she was scheduled to meet Sean arrived bright and clear. He was waiting outside the restaurant for her, pacing the sidewalk, looking a thousand times more handsome than she remembered. Her heart was in her throat as she approached him. She clenched her hands into fists at her sides for fear she'd reach out and touch him, and she dared not.

"I'm not really hungry," she said, glancing toward the restaurant door. "How about if we go for a walk instead?"

"All right."

"So," she said when they'd gone about half a block. "Did . . . you follow through with your word and date other people?"

He nodded. "Dozens. What about you?"

She nodded. "Two."

"Arnold and who else?" he asked brusquely, then apologized.

"Carla and who else?" she answered.

He laughed and stuffed his hands into his pockets.

"Well," she said, when she couldn't stand it any longer, "what do you think?"

"That I could get accustomed to listening to symphony music."

"What about becoming accustomed to the third-chair flutist?" she asked softly.

"I don't know how it happened, Hilary, but you're in my blood. The hell if I know what I'm going to do about it."

It was just what Hilary had been waiting for. Before another moment could pass, she launched herself into Sean's arms. "You idiot, there's only one thing to do about it. Marry me."

His thick arms circled her waist and lifted her from the sidewalk. "I guess there's no help for it. I'm crazy about you, Hil."

At once laughing and fighting back tears, she spread eager kisses down his face. "Can we call my mother? She's sitting by the phone, waiting."

"She is?"

"Of course she is. I know my mother."

Hilary and Sean were married five months later in December. The church was decorated in a profusion of red and white poinsettias. When it came time to give the bride away, Louise Wadsworth stood, and with happy tears in her eyes, whispered, "I give my daughter."

It was just another small step like all the others she'd taken over the years in learning to let go.

*　*　*　*　*

Debbie Macomber

Yesterday I spent the day at my son, Dale's, high school. I was being interviewed by the history class. They wanted to talk to someone who was alive when President Kennedy was assassinated, hear my views about the Vietnam War and Watergate. These teenagers were aghast when I mentioned party-line telephones and life before television. These kids have grown up with VCRs, microwaves and cellular phones.

I feel we both came away with a renewed appreciation of the richness of our lives. It just seems to get better and better. My editor phoned and asked me to write up a short biography, so with my experience at the high school in mind, I'll tell you: I was born the year of the Berlin airlift. I was five when our family bought our first television and in junior high when the transistor radio became popular. John Kennedy died when I was a high school sophomore, and by the time Nixon was facing Watergate, I was a young wife with three small children and another on the way, and my life was consumed with being a mother.

Jody, Jenny, Ted and Dale are young adults now. It's hard to imagine where the time went. It seems only a year or so ago that I was changing diapers and involved in car pools. Just a short while ago my life revolved around soccer meets, Boy Scouts, clarinet lessons and *Sesame Street*. The world has changed and so have I. But one thing remains constant. I'm a mother. Through determination, talent and to some degree luck, I've accomplished several goals in my life that make me proud. But none so great as having raised my children to be productive, emotionally healthy adults.

A Special Request

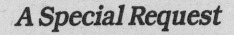

JUDITH DUNCAN

A Note from Judith Duncan

The interesting thing about motherhood is that you have to go through childhood to get there. I can't say that my own childhood prepared me that well for motherhood; nothing on earth can prepare you for toilet training, an epidemic of chicken pox or the absolute terror of turning your sixteen-year-old loose with the family car for the first time. It's enough to give you hives.

On the other hand, my childhood was exemplary. Not that I was an exemplary child. Far from it. I was a brat. Actually, I was a spoiled brat. I was the kind of kid who, at the age of five, would sit on the woodpile and watch until I saw my oldest brother (who was seventeen) leave the barn; then I'd turn on the most pathetic, heart-wrenching, woebegone tears, sobbing that I was so small, and the wood was *so* heavy, and that there were big spiders in the woodpile—or maybe even mice—and that I got slivers in my teeny-weeny arms from all that heavy, heavy wood. The ploy worked at least twice. Then my father bought me a big red wagon.

My other brother, who was ten years older than I, was just as malleable. I remember the time that he let me use my mother's best chenille bedspread as a queen's robe, which I fastened with her prized cameo brooch. My queenly attire was accessorized by Mom's best button-pearl earrings, lipstick and a splash of hand lotion, and he played a nice somber, regal march on the piano as I swept into the living room. It was wonderful. And the bedspread was back on the bed by the time she returned home.

My sister had to endure much on my behalf. I'm sure there were times she would have liked to stuff me down a hole, but she still let me have the lunch box with the red thermos in it, and I knew she would have fought like Attila the Hun if anyone had ever laid a hand on me. She also taught me to ride her bike.

It was a great childhood. Frankly, I don't know how they all put up with me, especially my mother. I had these wonderful, Scarlett O'Hara fantasies about houses with grand, sweeping staircases. The only stairs in our house were the dark, dreary ones leading up to the attic, which didn't quite cut it as far as I was concerned. So I'd gather together a hodgepodge of chairs, piano benches and mandarin orange boxes and build my own staircase in the living room, with the second floor being the top of the piano. Mother never said a word. She allowed me my fantasy world where I could see fairies in the frost on the windowpane, shapes in the clouds, and pixie faces in the white wood violets. She sewed me doll clothes that were the envy of every kid in the district, made homemade ice cream that tasted like sin and fixed me a playhouse in the trees where I made dandelion-decorated mud pies for my imaginary friends. She gave me home perms (which I hated) and French braids (which I loved) and sewed every stitch that went on my back. She made angel costumes for our one-room-school Christmas concerts, knitted me gloves with every finger a different color and made chocolate birthday cakes with treasures in them. She rubbed my back when I had bad dreams, and she taught me the words to "Twenty Froggies" one rainy Sunday afternoon. She never told me I couldn't do something because I might get hurt, and only looked slightly exasperated when I got my rubber boots full every spring when I'd go wading for tadpoles. She gave me the space to pretend, to make believe, to explore the world around me; she also taught me to read when I was five years old.

So for all those very wonderful and very special memories, I thank you, Mom. It was the very best of times.

Judith Duncan

Chapter One

Dear Grandpa,

I guess you know I just had my birthday, Grandpa. Mom put those candles on my cake—you know, the ones that start up again when you think they're out. I just about blew my brains out, trying to get all nine of them to stay out. Mom sure laughed—you know, when she laughs so hard she gets tears in her eyes.

I didn't get what I really wanted for my birthday. You know, those three things I told you about. I asked for a dog again, but she said no and really meant it. I haven't told her (now that you aren't here, Grandpa) I really want a dad. She'll freak out for sure. And I don't know if I'll ever get Wayne Gretzky's autograph. I'd do almost anything for one. Scot Lauder says he thinks that's stupid, but he's just jealous because everybody thinks Wayne Gretzky is the best hockey player ever. Scot can be such a dweeb sometimes.

I got into trouble at school on Tuesday. We were supposed to be learning the stupid times tables, and Mrs. Martin caught me looking at Jason Smith's mashed up Wayne Gretzky hockey cards. If they're mashed up, they're no good to trade, Grandpa. Anyhow she phoned Mom and told her I was wool-gathering again. What does wool-gathering mean,

Grandpa? I was going to ask Mom, but she was all upset because I wasn't paying attention again. I think Mrs. Martin must have been teaching for a hundred years. Jimmy Manson says she looks like a prune. You know, like all wrinkled. I felt bad after I laughed. Mrs. Martin was really nice to me after you went away. It was like she knew I was feeling bad inside, and she'd give me jobs, like clean the black board brushes, so I wouldn't have to go outside at recess.

Mom doesn't know I write to you, Grandpa. I didn't tell her, because I think it would make her feel bad. I think she still misses you. That's why we need a dad. Not just for me but for Mom, too. If I can get a dad, a dog and Wayne Gretzky's autograph, boy, would I be happy. I'd like a Nintendo Game Boy, too, but I'm saving up my own money for that. But I might need some help with the other stuff, Grandpa. You know, like when you showed me how to whistle through my teeth. Because I'm not real good at doing things on my own yet. Well, I guess I'd better go. Mom says we have to go to Millard to get groceries. Yuk. I'll write you real soon, okay?

Your grandson, Davy

Friday, May 5

Davy Jefferies trudged up the back alley, the canvas bag that held the spare newspapers bumping against his leg. Boy, what a crummy day. Old Mrs. Prowski had given him heck because he'd tracked mud up her sidewalk when he delivered her newspaper, and then

Mr. Olsen was mad because he had walked on his grass. He was going to be glad when he was big enough to get a real job, so people wouldn't treat him like a kid. And then there was Mrs. Martin.

Davy sighed and hitched the strap higher on his shoulder. He shouldn't have taken the mice to school. And he sure shouldn't have turned them loose in the girls' bathroom, but Jimmy Manson had dared him to. A grin worked its way free. It had sure been funny when Marcy Brown went screaming down the hallway, waving her hands in the air like some dweeb. Served her right for telling on him. He should have put a mouse in her jacket pocket and really fixed her.

He moved to the other side of the alley so he could wade through the big puddle behind the Mansons' garage, wishing Mr. Manson hadn't filled in the pothole. It used to be fun, wading through that puddle, wondering where the hole was.

Once clear of the puddle, Davy started carving a network of channels in the remnants of ice with the heel of his boot, allowing one puddle to drain into the next. When he grew up he was going to be an engineer and build dams and canals and stuff. Spotting a piece of copper pipe lying in the dead grass, he picked it up and squinted through it, pretending to blast alien spaceships from the sky. Captain Kirk and the Starship Enterprise. Maybe he would be an astronaut instead.

Sarah Jefferies rested her forearms on the rail of the back porch, savoring the smell of spring, the wind cutting through her heavy sweater and whipping tendrils of hair across her face. She turned into the wind, allowing the brisk breeze to blow back the annoying strands, drinking in the sensation. Lord, but she loved spring. She loved the smell of damp earth and melting snow, loved the sound of water dripping off the eaves. Spring made winter worth living.

Smiling to herself, she rested her weight against the railing and gazed at the overcast sky that was heavy with moisture. She always loved that first spring rain, the one that washed away the last grimy vestiges of winter. And she was especially going to love it this year. She was sick and tired of watching massive snowdrifts shrink into gritty patches of ice, only to be replaced by another heavy snowfall, the fresh drifts deeper and wider than the ones before.

But now spring was truly in the air, and when she closed her eyes and took a deep breath, she could smell its arrival—the smell of green grass, of budding leaves, of—

Of burning pizza.

The pizza! She'd forgotten the pizza! Swearing under her breath, she slammed into the house, the screen door clipping her heel, the acrid smell of burnt cheese wafting out to meet her. She snatched up the pot holders lying on the counter and yanked open the oven door, releasing a cloud of blue smoke that billowed up to the ceiling and set off the smoke detector. Waving her hand to clear a path in front of her, she opened the window by the table and sent the smoldering pizza sailing out into the yard, then dropped the pan in the sink. Her eyes smarting, she waved a tea towel under the alarm, trying to get it to shut off before the whole neighborhood heard it. Damn it, this was the second meal this week she'd ruined because she hadn't been paying attention. She was as bad as Davy.

The alarm finally stopped its earsplitting scream, and she exhaled heavily. Her house was probably the only one in the whole damned world that regularly suffered smoke damage from scorched meals. Heaving another disgusted sigh, she tossed the towel on the counter and opened the cupboard door under the sink. She located a can of furniture polish and sprayed it around the room, knowing from experience that it was the only thing that would effectively cloak the smell. Her mother would be so proud—she'd finally found a use for it.

The smoke had settled and she was in the process of preparing another meal when the back door slammed and Davy came in. He kicked off his rubber boots in the back hall, then entered the kitchen and dumped his newspaper sack on the table. Wiping his nose on his sleeve, he snitched a cookie out of the cookie jar.

Sarah gave him a stern look. "Put that cookie back and get a Kleenex, David. You don't eat cookies five minutes before supper, and you don't wipe your nose on your sleeve."

He rolled his eyes and heaved a sigh of resignation. But he put the cookie back and got a tissue out of the box by the telephone. Giving his nose a token swipe, he leaned against the counter, his expression alive with excitement. "Guess what, Mom! I saw Mr. McGregor's dog come running out of our yard with a pizza in his mouth. It was a big one, too—like one of those humongous ones you buy."

She pretended innocence. "Really?"

Caught up in the adventure, he dragged his sleeve across his nose, enthusiasm bubbling out of him. "Yep. It looked like one of those double cheese, pepperoni and mushroom ones."

Sarah felt like banging her head against the wall. Why couldn't she get away with anything?

She had no choice but to try and bluff it out. "So," she said, her tone bland. "You could see all that from the alley, could you?"

He considered the cookie jar with unfettered longing, then looked back up at his mother. "Yep. And it looked burnt on the bottom."

"No kidding."

He started to answer, then narrowed his eyes and glanced around the kitchen. "You've been spraying furniture polish again," he said, his tone accusing.

Sarah turned her back and began stirring the creamed corn, humor rising up in her. If he found out about the pizza, he would never, ever let her live it down. Not in a million years.

When he spoke again, his tone was shrewd. "You were spraying furniture polish, weren't you?"

"Hmm."

Davy knew all about the furniture polish trick, and he made a beeline for the garbage can under the sink, his voice shrill with glee. "Your face is all red, Mom! I know! I'll betcha there's an empty pizza box in here."

Cursing her red face and desperate to protect her already-dubious reputation, Sarah blocked his move, her voice breaking when she tried to wrestle him away from the cupboard. "No! Darn it, Davy. Let go!"

Davy hung on to the sink, delighted that he'd found her out. As he struggled to maintain his hold, he discovered the final damning piece of evidence. "There's a pizza pan in the sink, Mom!" he announced, maintaining a death grip on the counter. "And it's all burnt on the bottom!"

Victorious, he squirmed away, pleased as punch that he'd put it all together. "Boy, are you going to catch it. Mr. McGregor doesn't like anyone feeding his dog, Mom."

Laughing and out of breath, Sarah leaned against the sink, feeling as though she'd just been mauled. She gasped out her response. "Thank you, Sherlock."

Knowing how her son relished spilling the beans on her, she considered her options, realizing it would be all over town by Sunday morning if she didn't negotiate with this little Benedict Arnold. That was one of the disadvantages of living in a small town like Alton, everybody knew everybody—and everybody's business.

Resting her hand on her hip, she fixed her gaze on her son, trying to shame him. "You know what a traitor is, don't you?"

Grinning broadly, he rested his elbow on the counter, then propped his chin on his hand and nodded.

She tried pleading. "You wouldn't do that to me, would you?"

The sparkle in his eyes didn't give her much hope. He nodded again.

Narrowing her eyes at him, Sarah tried to brazen it out. "If you say one word, so help me, Davy, I'll ground you for a week."

Enjoying himself immensely, he shook his head. "No you won't. You say you will, but you won't. The only time you ground me is if I've done something *really* bad. It wouldn't be fair, and you always say people have to be fair."

He had her there. This kid was getting too darned good at this. Giving him a narrow look, she made her next move, which she liked to think of as negotiation. What it was was bribery, plain and simple. She sighed in capitulation. "Okay, what do I have to do to keep this quiet? Make popcorn? Let you stay up late? Help you deliver papers? What?"

He gazed at her, his expression perfectly deadpan. "Well, I've been thinking. It's a toss-up between a dog and a dad."

He'd caught her broadside with that one, and Sarah nearly choked. Knowing she didn't dare give an inch, she responded, her tone dry, "Nice try, Mr. Jefferies."

He grinned again, flashing a set of dimples that already had little girls acting silly. "Yeah. I thought so."

Sarah gazed at him, her chest suddenly tight. God, but she loved him. She loved his determination, his sense of fun, his enthusiasm for living, his need to *experience* life. Which reminded her of the mouse episode at school. Trying to ease the tightness in her chest, she reached out and ruffled his hair. "You'd better go wash up for supper, kiddo. It's just about ready. And comb your hair."

Davy rolled his eyes and heaved a put-upon sigh, grudgingly dragging his arm off the counter. Sarah watched him, knowing how he hated being mothered. Davy figured that sort of stuff was for sissies and dweebs.

She gazed at him a moment, then turned back to the stove and stirred the corn again. Her tone was mild when she said, "By the way, how was school today?"

There was a brief hesitation, then Davy answered, a thread of caution in his tone. "It was okay." Then he sighed and flopped his hands down by his sides, knowing what was coming. "Mrs. Martin phoned, didn't she?"

"No. Why?" Which was true. Mrs. Martin hadn't phoned. Sarah had heard about the mouse episode at work, when one of the school janitors had come into the bank to deposit his check. Old Joe had thought it was hilarious. Sarah had been thankful for small mercies. The last time, it had been a jar full of wasps that Davy had caught for a science lab and one of the kids had dropped in the library; the time before that it had been three garter snakes because they were studying reptiles; and the time before that it had been a can full of earthworms, which he dumped in Mrs. Martin's terrarium, because "worms were good for the soil." She had tried, with weary patience, to explain that not everyone was turned on by wasps and snakes and earthworms. But that was something Davy could not fathom. Why would anyone be scared of worms? Worms were no big deal. In comparison to eight kids getting stung during the wasp episode, she figured two mice were no big deal either.

Davy heaved another heavy sigh. "I took two mice to school today, for Mr. Matheson's science class, but I let them go in the girls' washroom." He sighed again, dispirited by the confession. "I knew Marcy Brown was in there, and she's so mean to everyone."

Biting the inside of her lip to keep from laughing, Sarah glanced at him, wishing she could just let it go. Marcy Brown was a rotten, spoiled kid who was not only mean and nasty, but also loved to lord it over everyone. Sarah suspected that was one reason Mrs. Martin hadn't phoned—because she figured Marcy had it coming. Clearing her throat, she scrambled to find a lesson in all this. "You shouldn't have gone into the girls' washroom, David. You could have really embarrassed someone."

He looked down at his feet. "Yeah, I know."

Sarah gazed at him, pride rising in her. His grandfather had taught him that, to own up to his mistakes and accept the consequences. She turned back to the stove, her voice uneven when she said, "Go wash up, okay? Supper's almost ready."

Saturday, May 6

Davy sat at the breakfast table, his head on his hand, watching his mother cut up a grapefruit. He hated grapefruit. Well, he didn't *hate* it. Not if it were one of those really pink ones and she put lots of brown sugar on it. But sometimes she forgot to get brown sugar, and then he *really* hated it. It made his teeth feel all fuzzy and dry. He wished he could just have a bowl of cereal and a banana like he did on school days, but she always wanted to have a "real" breakfast on the weekends, whatever that meant. She was also making French toast. He hoped she didn't burn it. If she didn't burn it, Mom made the best French toast. He grinned, thinking about Mr. McGregor's big black Lab running off with the pizza in his mouth. That old pizza had stuck out from Triffle's mouth just like a board.

Shifting, Davy watched the sunlight make patterns on the wall by his mother's head. Jimmy said that his mother was a carrottop, but that wasn't true. Her hair wasn't the color of carrots. It was exactly the color of a penny, and it was frizzy all over. Jimmy's big sister, Alicia, said his mom had "big hair" in that dopey tone, as though big hair were something real. Which was dumb. How could someone have "big hair"? It wasn't like having big feet or a big nose, was it?

His mom brought the grapefruit to the table, the light dusting of freckles on her face and arms making her look almost tanned. Davy kinda' liked his mom's freckles. They made her seem nice, somehow. Sorta like cinnamon toast.

She passed him his dish, then sat down and opened the *National Geographic* she'd brought with her, laying the magazine by her plate. Davy knew if he wanted to sneak something past his mother, the best time to do it was when she was reading *National Geographic*. Feeling as if he were cheating, he looked down and started digging the fruit wedges out of the rind. "I was going to go for a bike ride after breakfast, then maybe play some road hockey with the guys, okay?"

His mother never even lifted her head. "All right. But you have to clean up your room sometime today."

It wasn't that he *couldn't* tell her where he was going. He just knew it would make her feel real bad if he did. He nodded, his throat kind of achy and tight. He didn't like being sneaky—not with his mom.

The road out to the west railway crossing skirted a small slough that was encircled by dried-up bulrushes and red willows. Davy got off his bike and waded through the bulrushes in the ditch, looking for frogs' eggs. Last year Jimmy Manson had tried to smoke one of the brown things on the end of the bulrushes, the thing that looked like a brown velvet wiener, and he'd burnt all his eyelashes off. Davy had thought it was the funniest thing he'd ever seen when Jimmy stuck that thing in his mouth like a cigar. Mrs. Manson never could figure out why Jimmy's jacket had smelled all smoky. Boy, they'd laughed over that.

There were no frogs' eggs, but there were pussy willows. Davy decided he would pick a big bunch for his mom on the way home; she really liked pussy willows, and he knew she'd put them in that big Chinese vase that used to be Grandma's. Whistling through his teeth, Davy checked the inside pocket of his jacket for the letter, then got back on his bike and headed off toward the west crossing.

The road ended in a T intersection. North was the way to Billy Martin's farm. South and over the railway crossing was the main highway. Straight ahead was the cemetery. Davy pushed his bike onto the grassy approach in front of the big double wrought-iron gates, then leaned it against one of the stone pillars. Taking off his baseball cap, he squeezed through the gate and walked down the track until he came to two gray granite headstones inside a retaining wall.

Fishing the envelope out of his pocket, he sat down on the cement retaining wall. Swallowing hard against the funny lump in his throat, he rubbed his hand against the smooth stone. "Hi, Grandpa," he whispered softly. "It's me, Davy. I brought you another letter."

Davy hadn't known he could miss anyone the way he missed his Grandpa when he died. He couldn't remember his grandmother, but his grandfather had been his best friend, next to Jimmy. Grandpa never got upset if he forgot to brush his teeth or ate with his elbow on the table, or even if he came into the house with frogs in his pocket. Grandpa went to ball games and hockey practice with him. And he had always, *always,* laughed at Davy's jokes; sometimes he even laughed over things that Davy didn't think were funny at all. But it had been awful after, when Davy would wake up at night with a big hollow hurt in his stomach. He hadn't wanted to cry, because his mom was already feeling bad, but then one night, when he'd wanted to talk to his Grandpa, when he just couldn't *not* cry, his mom had come into his room. She'd held him real tight and told him that Grandpa was probably in heaven fishing, and that Grandpa would always be there for him, because he was alive in Davy's heart. She also said that she was sure Grandpa would be able to hear him if Davy ever really needed to talk to him. All Davy had to do was believe that Grandpa could.

Davy wasn't so sure about this hearing thing, but it made him feel better, thinking about Grandpa sitting in heaven fishing. And it took the ache away, thinking that maybe, just maybe, Grandpa *could* hear him. And that was when he started writing him letters—he'd been writing for almost a whole year now.

Leaning against the headstone, Davy gazed off across the field on the other side of the road. If he squinted real hard, he could see the very tip of the spire on top of the church. Someday he'd like to climb to the very top of that spire.

Hooking his ball cap on his knee, he patted the stone. "So how are you doing, Grandpa? We're doing fine. Mom got a raise at work, and I'm doing okay at school." He sighed and scratched his cheek. "But I got a problem, Grandpa. I think Mom is really feeling all by herself since you went away—like I told you in the letter—and I've been thinking that maybe we need a dad. But Mom just gives me that funny look of hers if I say anything. Then the other day she said she guessed she could ask Old Boogie Cruthers. Old Boogie must be a hundred years old, Grandpa. She won't get serious." Davy sighed again, this time a little heavier. "And I really want a dog, Grandpa. But Mom keeps saying no, that we don't have a place to keep one.'' He stared off into space, pondering his problem. It was too bad Grandpa couldn't just send him a sign.

A whistle sounded, and Davy turned to watch the freight train rumble around the curve, the big diesel straining against the slight grade. Davy counted the cars, the sun warming the granite stone at his back. As he watched the freight cars flash by, the heat from the sun and the rhythm of the train made him feel all warm and fuzzy.

His eyes were getting heavy when the caboose finally flashed by, and suddenly he got the funniest feeling in his stomach. He couldn't believe it. Sitting on the other side of the crossing, right in the middle of the road, was the most beautiful dog Davy had ever seen. It was a big black-and-white husky, and when the dog stood up, his tail curled over his back. The animal lifted his head and looked at Davy, then he turned and started down the railway track toward town. Davy sat stone-still, the strange feeling getting stronger. Alton was a tiny town, and he knew every dog in it. And there wasn't one husky in the bunch. And besides, the only things on the other side of the track were an old road and the highway. And there was nothing between the old road and the highway except a bunch of yellow-and-white trailers that had been hauled in for the road construction.

And Davy knew. He just knew. The dog jogging

into town was just like Lassie. It was a sign. For sure, it was a sign.

Davy's voice was hushed with awe. "Wow. Thanks, Grandpa."

Chapter Two

Nathan Cassidy cautiously climbed out of his truck, wincing as he jarred his ribs, trying to will away the spots that kept dancing in front of his eyes. He was beginning to wish he'd never laid eyes on this damned town. In fact, he was beginning to wish he'd told Kenner Benson to stuff it when he first suggested that Nat come to Alberta for a couple of months.

At the time, Nat had figured it was an okay idea. The hydro-electric project he'd been working on for the past three years in Northern Quebec was completed, and he didn't have to leave for the big dam project in South America until the end of June. He'd had time to kill, and Kenner had been in a bind. He'd landed the contract for fifty miles of new four-lane highway just west of the Saskatchewan border. Then, two days after Kenner had moved his equipment in, his foreman had broken a leg. Kenner needed someone to replace him temporarily, someone who had the necessary experience. And Nat certainly had that. He'd been operating heavy equipment since he was seventeen. In fact, he'd put himself through university working heavy equipment during the summers. Yeah, he was a hotshot, all right. That was why he was walking around with a damned concussion and two cracked ribs.

Totally ticked off, Nat collected the cellular phone from the dash and slammed the truck door, disgust boiling through him. Served him right for trying to fix the hydraulics on the D9 by himself. Served him bloody-well right. The damned wrench must have weighed five pounds, and he had a gash on the back of his head to prove it.

His boots caking with mud, he headed toward the foreman's trailer, the pounding in his skull intensifying. If he hadn't needed stitches, he wouldn't have bothered going to the hospital in Millard. He'd been here three lousy days, and the way things were going, he doubted if he'd survive those two lousy months. If the trip across Canada had been any kind of an indication, he should have known he was heading into disaster. It had had all the makings of somebody's nightmare. He'd taken the transmission out of his truck in Northern Ontario, been nailed with two speeding tickets in Manitoba, then hit a hailstorm in Saskatchewan that had left dents the size of dimes in the body work. Then, *then,* he had hit Alberta at twilight, and he'd had to take to the ditch to avoid a deer on the highway. Now he was sporting one hell of a headache, cracked ribs and an ugly mood.

Swearing under his breath, he skirted Kenner's truck, his boots collecting more mud with every step. The camp was nothing but a big mud hole. The location was convenient—just on the outskirts of Alton—but to his way of thinking, that was all it had going for it. Mud, mud and more damned mud.

Stopping by the trailer, Nat tipped his head back and exhaled heavily, trying to get a grip. Okay. So things hadn't gone all that well. Tomorrow was a new day. Tomorrow would be better.

Exhaling again, he straightened, a sharp jab making him wince. Damn his ribs, anyway. Taking a measured breath, he reached for the door. Suddenly it dawned on him that Scout wasn't around. He grinned ruefully. The dog had a brain; he'd probably moved to higher ground. One thing about Scout; he was a sticker. Nat had rescued him from an ugly situation three years before. He'd been just a pup, one of a string of sled dogs that Nat had seen chained outside a shanty in Fort Churchill. Vicious, snarling and wild, the dogs were on the verge of starvation. But there had been something about Scout that got to him, and it infuriated him to think anyone could abuse animals that way, especially a puppy. He'd paid the trapper one hundred dollars, bundled Scout up in his parka and taken him back to camp. Since then, the dog had barely left his side. And the only reason he'd left Scout behind today was because he hadn't known how long it would take him in the emergency room, and he didn't like leaving the dog locked up in the truck for very long.

Nat whistled, waiting for Scout to come bounding around one of the trailers. Nothing. Not even a yap. Nat yanked open the trailer door. If something happened to that dog, he really would throttle somebody.

Kicking off clumps of mud on the metal step, Nat entered the trailer. Kenner was hunched over a battered metal desk, an untidy clutter of papers spread out before him. George, his heavy-duty mechanic, was seated across from him, puffing on a cigar, his feet propped on the desk. Leaning back in his chair, Kenner folded his arms across his chest and grinned. "Damned decent of you to show up, Cassidy. Even if it is five hours late."

Nat gave him a murderous look. He wasn't about to explain to Kenner where he'd spent the afternoon. The last thing he needed right now was a hard time. "Where's Scout?"

George dropped his feet and leaned forward, scraping the ash from his cigar into an old sardine can. "Can't say for certain. Saw him up at the crossing with a kid. Saw that new man, Vic Whatshisname—Manson—stop and talk to 'em."

Nat jammed his hands on his hips and stared at the ceiling, thinking thoughts that could get him arrested. What he needed was eighteen aspirins and bed; what he got was more aggravation. Now he was going to have to go looking for his dog. Couldn't anything go right for three hours at a stretch?

After spending an hour driving around town looking for Scout—especially when there wasn't much of a town to drive around—Nat was not a happy man. Alton was, at best, eight blocks by eight blocks, with a scattering of new houses on the south side of the railway tracks. Not a booming metropolis by any stretch of the imagination. Not much of anything, in anyone's imagination. But in spite of its size, he couldn't find hide nor hair of his dog. If anything had happened to Scout, he would definitely throttle somebody.

It was getting dark when he came across a group of boys playing road hockey. Nat could tell, the moment he asked about Scout, that they knew exactly what dog he was talking about. By then he felt as if he were going blind from the headache, and his ribs were screaming for a horizontal position. He was in no mood to play games. As much as he wanted to shake the information out of them, he offered a ten-dollar reward instead. He figured he would take it out of the kid's hide who'd stolen his dog.

It was dusk when Sarah picked her way through the puddles in the alley, her mother's intuition on red alert. She'd spent the afternoon at the senior citizens' drop-in center helping with the spring tea. Joyce Manson, Jimmy's mother, who sat Davy after school, had phoned just as they were finishing breakfast, wondering if Davy wanted to spend the afternoon there. The Mansons lived across the alley, and when Sarah had stopped by on her way home from the center Joyce had said Davy had gotten bored watching TV and had gone home to rake the backyard. Since Davy's TV time was carefully monitored, and knowing that her son would watch TV until his eyes rotted, Sarah was instantly suspicious. Davy would rather walk across broken glass than rake the yard. When she stopped to think about it, Davy had been acting strange when he'd come back from his bike ride, but she'd been in such a rush to get out of the house on time, it hadn't registered then. But it registered now.

Her son was up to something. No doubt about it. She just hoped the broken-glass association wasn't Freudian. The last time her son had voluntarily done anything in the yard was when he'd put a baseball through Mr. McGregor's garage window.

The light from the kitchen cast a faint rectangle of light into the early evening gloom, and Sarah frowned. Davy wasn't supposed to go into the house when Joyce was sitting him—not unless he had Joyce's permission.

She rounded the lilac bush by the corner of the garage, nearly tripping over the rake. Through the gloom, she saw a big pile of dried grass in the middle of the yard. Not a good sign.

"Hi, Mom."

Sarah looked up. Davy was sitting on the back step, his arms wrapped around his knees.

Pausing at the bottom of the stairs, she stared up at him, but before she had a chance to say anything, he spoke, his tone quavery as he quickly assured her he hadn't broken the rule. "I only went inside to put something in my room, Mom. I didn't stay in or anything."

A heavy sensation unfolded in Sarah's middle, a feeling that was closely related to guilt. She hated having to scold him. In spite of all his escapades, he was a good kid. Swallowing against the sudden tightness in her chest, she climbed the steps, the tightness compounding when she saw the anxious expression on his face. She crouched down in front of him and brushed back his hair, her voice husky and soft when she said, "What's up, Skeeter?"

He gazed up at her, then got up and anxiously wiped his hands on his jeans, his eyes wide with nervous anticipation. "I got something to show you, Mom."

Attuned to the anxiety, to the hope that flared in his eyes, Sarah brushed a smudge of dirt off his cheek, then motioned him into the house. They had shed their coats and were heading down the hallway to his bedroom before Davy screwed up his courage. "I found him, Mom. I couldn't leave him without anywhere to go. So I brought him home. I just had to bring him home."

Knowing what was coming, Sarah closed her eyes and braced herself. The last time he'd "just had to" bring something home was last spring. That time, it was seven frogs he'd corralled in an old aquarium under his bed. She took some solace in the fact that it was too early in the year for frogs.

No, it was definitely not frogs. It was a dog. A big dog, who was stretched out on Davy's bed, his head on his paws, looking as though he had just discovered doggy heaven. When Davy entered the room, the dog perked up his ears and lifted his head, his tail thumping against the bed. Davy knelt beside him, burying his face in the husky's ruff. The dog nuzzled his nose against Davy's chest, and Sarah rolled her eyes heavenward. A dog. How on earth was she going to get out of this one?

Davy smoothed down the fur on the dog's head. "This is my mom, Buddy," he said, his tone significant, as though Sarah had been the topic of a previous conversation. With the polish of a politician, Buddy lifted his head, looked straight at Sarah and gave her the most fraudulent, ingratiating grin she had ever seen. She nearly laughed. Just what she needed, another con artist.

Shaking her head in wry amusement, she leaned against the door frame. "Don't overdo it, dog. And you," she said, leveling a warning finger at her son, "had better have a good explanation."

Sensing he had a foothold, Davy couldn't make his explanation fast enough. He told her about finding the dog, how he had trotted off down the railway track, how Davy was sure he was a stray. "I bet whoever owned him didn't want him anymore, and they were driving down the highway and saw the town." Getting all caught up in his theory, Davy expounded, enthusiasm bubbling out of him. "He's a stray, Mom. And he was hungry and thirsty, and he was so glad when I brought him inside. I bet he's been lost for a long time, and he doesn't have a collar or anything." Knowing exactly what buttons to push, he moved in for the kill. "And he doesn't have anyone to look after him but us. And we just can't leave him outside."

Folding her arms in front of her, Sarah studied her son, knowing full well that he was working her. She glanced back at the dog, who had his head up, his ears alert, as if poised for her response. Sarah repressed a smile. Lord, he was as bad as Davy. She fixed her attention back on her son, considering the situation. Finally she spoke. "Okay, kiddo. This is the deal. He can stay here tonight and tomorrow. But Monday morning, I'm going to check around and see if anyone knows who he belongs to. If I can't find out anything, I'm going to run an ad in the *Millard Times*." Seeing the sudden sagging of her son's shoulders, she explained softly. "There's a chance that he was stolen from his owner, Davy. And maybe there's another little boy out there looking for him."

Bending his head, Davy silently fiddled with a hole in his T-shirt. There was a long silence, then he rubbed his hand through the dog's fur. Raising his head, he looked at his mother, his expression a mixture of hope and disappointment. "If nobody comes for him," he said softly, "can we keep him?"

Sarah gazed down at him, knowing she could not dash his hopes. "If no one claims him, we'll think about it." By the look on her son's face, Sarah knew he thought he had her backed into a corner. And she had the uncomfortable feeling that was exactly where she was.

And Master David James worked it for all he was worth. After supper, he and Dog stretched out on the living room floor to watch TV, the two of them presenting a picture that, as far as Sarah was concerned, was a deliberate bit of manipulation. Davy lay with his head propped on the dog's ribs, absently scratching the animal's ears, offering comments to the dog that were clearly meant for his mother's ears. And the dog was no dummy, either. Every time Sarah walked into the room, he raised his head, wagged his tail and gave her that wheedling grin, doing his doggy best to worm his way into her good graces. She sighed, wondering how much it would cost to fence the backyard.

Setting the bowl of popcorn down on the floor by her son, she spoke, her tone dry. "I suppose he'll want his own bowl."

Not taking his eyes off the TV, Davy grinned. "Naw. He can eat out of mine."

Sarah cocked one eyebrow, wanting to smile and knowing she didn't dare. David James was feeling pretty cocky. "Just so you know—if he gets sick all over the floor, I'm going to wipe it up with your favorite hockey jersey."

Davy swiveled his head and shot her a scandalized look. "You'd use my Wayne Gretzky hockey jersey to wipe up *dog* barf?"

"If he gets sick on the carpet I will."

Davy was about to answer when the dog's head came up, his ears cocked; then he scrambled to his feet just as a loud knock sounded on the front door. The dog let out a woof, and Sarah experienced a flicker of alarm. This was small-town Alberta. *Nobody* used their front door.

Nat stood on the darkened front step, ready to hammer the damned door into kindling. He was in no mood for this crap. His head felt as if it were going to explode, his ribs were killing him, and he was fed up to the teeth with all the bloody inconveniences he'd had to put up with today. And when he got his hands on the damned kid, so help—

The light above the door flashed on, and Nat jammed his hand on his hip, ready to do battle. There had better not be a hair out of place on that dog.

The door opened and Nat was ready to let whoever it was have it, but nothing, not one single sound, came out. Nat felt as if his equilibrium had just been knocked off its axis.

A strong wind could have blown her away. Slight to the point of thinness, she stood poised in the pool of light, her eyes wide, her copper-colored hair a wild tumble around her solemn, waif-like face. It was the way she stood with her hand on the door, the way her deep green oversized sweater hung from her slender frame, that kicked off images in his mind, and all Nat could think of was Joan of Arc. There was a hint of the warrior in her, the steadiness in her solemn gray eyes making him feel oddly insignificant. Nat did not like feeling insignificant.

There was a coolness in her tone that irritated him. And he was already damned well irritated. Shaking off the sensation that he'd just been poleaxed, he went to take a deep breath, but his ribs had other ideas. That irritated him even more. "Is this the Jefferies residence?"

Her chin came up a notch, and she stared right back at him. "Yes, it is."

"Do you have a son named Davy?"

The eyes narrowed ever so slightly, a defensive glint appearing. "Yes."

Not liking the way she pointed her chin at him, Nat shifted his weight onto one hip and glared back at her. "Lady, your son stole my dog, and I want—"

Her eyes narrowing even more, she put her hand on her hip and interjected. "He did not *steal* your dog. He—"

A loud barking drowned her out, and Scout bounded around her, pushing through the narrow space between the wall and her legs, nearly upending her. With eighty pounds of momentum, Scout jumped up to welcome Nat, catching him squarely in the chest. Stifling a groan, Nat closed his eyes and swore, feeling as though the damned dog had just caved in what was left of his ribs. Clenching his teeth against the pain, Nat pinched the bridge of his nose, wondering what in hell he'd done to deserve this. All because he'd wanted to help out a buddy.

"Is something wrong?"

Annoyed by the whole lousy scene, annoyed by his initial response to her, annoyed by his annoyance, but especially annoyed by that snooty tone in her voice, he eased in a careful breath, then raised his head and stared at her, the muscle in his jaw taut. "I just want my dog," he said through gritted teeth. "Then I want to get in my truck, go back to the camp and inhale a whole bottle of codeine." He snapped his fingers and motioned for Scout to heel, then gave her one final warning. "And you'd better tell that kid of yours to stay away from my dog."

A small, tearful, uneven voice spoke up, remorse in every syllable. "I'm sorry about your dog, mister. I didn't know."

Suddenly feeling like a first-class jerk, Nat turned, meeting the gaze of a small boy. A small, miserable, ashen-faced little boy. *Way to go, Cassidy,* he thought disgustedly. *Now you're taking your ugly mood out on little kids.*

Before he had a chance to respond, to try to make amends, the woman drew the boy against her in a protective, consoling gesture. She gave Nat one final glare, then moved back and shut the door. The outside light went out, and Nat looked up at the sky and swore. Damn it, it was just a kid, not some bloody criminal. Exhaling a heavy sigh, he lowered his head and rubbed his eyes, acknowledging the fact that he'd acted like an absolute fool. Upsetting the kid was bad enough, but upsetting her was even worse. And he had upset her. He had caught the expression on her face just before she'd shut the door. Great. Now he was running around intimidating women and children.

Heaving another heavy sigh, he motioned to the dog, his voice laced with disgust when he muttered, "Let's get out of here, boy. Next thing you know, I'll be running over little old ladies."

Sarah stood at the living room window, her arms tightly folded, watching the streetlight flicker through the naked branches of the tree in the front yard. It was eleven o'clock, and she should be in bed, but she knew she wouldn't be able to sleep.

It wasn't often that the past came back to haunt her. But for some reason the dark, angry stranger at her door had fired up old emotions, memories of how devastated and alone she had felt when Davy's father, who'd been little more than a boy himself, had walked out, leaving her with no money and a two-year-old. She had just turned twenty-one, and she had been so scared, so emotionally bruised, so ashamed, that she couldn't look anyone in the eye when she moved back to Alton. She had believed that Jeff's walking out was all her fault, and she was sure the good people of Alton saw it the same way. They didn't, of course, but she was so humiliated by what she saw as her own personal failure that she had practically gone to ground. It had taken her years to shore up her self-esteem, to see the whole mess for what it really was, to realize that Jeff had hit the road because he was immature and couldn't handle responsibility. But every once in a while, when something happened that made her feel inadequate or foolish, she suffered an unsettling flashback. Suddenly she would be twenty-one years old again, feeling alone and inadequate and stupid. And for some reason, the angry man who had turned up on her doorstep had kicked off those feelings all over again.

Shifting her gaze, she picked a piece of lint off the sleeve of her housecoat and rolled it between her fingers, her expression solemn. A perfect stranger shouldn't be able to make her feel that way. *Nothing* should be able to make her feel that way. She managed a wry half smile; he hadn't been, in the strictest sense of the word, perfect, either. Granted, he had a face with billboard appeal—dark, rugged, with an unshaven, gunslinger look. But perfect? He'd been too much of a jerk to be perfect. Her eyes narrowed. A jerk who had accused her son of stealing his dog.

"Mom?"

She turned, a surge of empathy lodging square in her chest when she saw Davy framed in the archway. Her tone was soft when she answered. "You're supposed to be in bed, Davy."

"I know. But I'm real sorry about the dog," he said, his voice catching. "I thought he was a stray, Mom. I wouldn't take someone's dog."

"I know that," she said quietly.

Davy rubbed his eyes with the cuff of his pajamas, then spoke, his voice thick with misery. "He said 'camp.' Do you suppose it's the construction camp for the new highway?"

"I expect." Feeling so badly for him, she went over to him and crouched down, gently smoothing back his hair. "You were just trying to do what was right, Davy," she said softly. "You thought the dog needed someone to take care of him, so you brought him home. You don't have to feel badly about that."

His face awash with unhappiness, he swallowed hard. "I don't like having someone mad at me."

She stroked the side of his neck with her thumb and gave him a wry smile. "Neither do I."

In an un-Davy-like gesture, the boy put his arms around his mother's neck, and Sarah closed her eyes and hugged him hard. Sometimes Davy's conscience was just too big for such a little boy. Swallowing against the awful thickness in her throat, she cradled her son's head against her neck.

Anger flickered through her. So Mr. Billboard lived at the camp, did he? Well, when he came into the bank to deposit his paycheck, she hope it bounced.

Chapter Three

Sunday morning was the pits. It was cold and overcast, with a persistent spring drizzle fogging the windows, and to make matters worse, the propane tank in Kenner's fifth-wheel trailer was empty. Tossing the coffee grounds back into the can, Nat slammed the pot down on the front burner and reached for his jacket. He could hear Kenner snoring in the bedroom at the back of the trailer, and that did nothing to lighten Nat's mood. Especially when he'd gotten maybe two hours' sleep the night before.

Scout was lying under the table in the nook, and Nat patted his thigh, signaling the dog to come. "Come on, boy. He can fill his owned damned propane tank. We're going to town for a cup of coffee."

By the time the heater in the truck was blowing warm air, Nat was shivering, and he shrugged deeper into his leather jacket. The physical aftereffects of a lousy day. The back end of the truck fishtailed slightly as he pulled onto the blacktop, and Scout perked up his ears. Nat reached out and ruffled the dog's fur.

They bounced across the railway crossing and were about to take the narrow Y to the road to town when a movement at the gate of the cemetery caught Nat's attention. He braked, his expression altering when he recognized the kid squeezing through the gate. A disquieting sensation settled in his gut as he watched the boy approach a grave with something that looked like a piece of paper in his hand. Feeling like a heel all over again, Nat continued to watch, wondering what brought a small boy out to a cemetery so early in the morning, especially in the chilling rain. The boy stood by the headstone for a moment; then he crouched down out of the line of sight. When he stood back up, the piece of white was gone.

Letting the truck roll ahead slightly so it was behind a clump of willows, Nat switched off the ignition, the feeling of disquiet intensifying as he watched Davy squeeze back out the gate and pick up his bike. It was at that moment that Scout, who had been lying on the seat, scrambled up, his ears perked, his tail wagging. Nat knew by the intentness in Scout's pose that a bark wasn't far behind, and he reached out and clamped his hand around the dog's muzzle. "Easy, boy. I don't think that would be a good idea."

His expression becoming reflective, Nat watched the boy get on his bike, then head back to town. Nat didn't move for a moment, then he reached for the door handle. "Stay, Scout. I'll be right back."

The trail of small footprints through the wet, brown grass led Nat to a family plot surrounded by a low retaining wall. One grave was relatively new, an observation confirmed by the marker. *Matthew James "Scotty" Beaumont, beloved husband, father and grandfather.*

Stuffing his hands in his jacket pockets, Nat somberly studied the dates. Scotty Beaumont had died in

June of the previous year and had been sixty-three years old. Glancing down, Nat looked for the paper the boy had had in his hand.

He would never have seen it if he hadn't been looking for it. But a thin edge, just a sliver of white, showed in the crack between the headstone and the retaining wall. Driven by something he couldn't identify, Nat dug his Swiss army knife out of his jeans, then crouched down, carefully extracting the piece of paper, a hollow sensation forming in his chest when he realized it was an envelope. His expression turning somber, he turned it over. It was addressed to "Grandpa."

Grandpa. Nat looked away, a sudden twist of comprehension cutting through him. The kid had ridden out here in the rain because he needed to bring a letter to his grandfather. Bracing his elbow on his thigh, Nat rubbed his eyes, trying to ease the cramp in his throat. He couldn't have been a bigger SOB if he'd worked at it.

Nat's morning was all downhill from then on. The coffee was weak, the eggs were runny, and the toast was cold, but he figured he deserved a lousy breakfast. He would have given anything to know what Davy Jefferies had put in that letter to his grandfather, but he'd returned it unopened. He owed the kid that much, at least.

Kenner had set up a meeting with the project engineer for later that morning at the camp office, and Nat found himself only half listening as they discussed a difficult piece of roadbed. His leg cocked across his knee, he rocked back in his chair and folded his arms across his chest, his expression preoccupied. He kept thinking about the kid. Nat flicked a piece of mud off his jeans. He wasn't normally a hothead. If he hadn't been feeling so beat-up and ticked off the day before, he wouldn't have lost his cool the way he had.

"It would be real nice if you'd check in here, Cassidy," Kenner said, his tone a lazy drawl. "These three culverts are going to take some doing, and any suggestions from the engineering expert *would* be appreciated."

Nat raised his head and looked at his friend, giving him an insolent grin. "I suggest you stick all three of them up your—"

"Hey, Nathan!" George stuck his head through the trailer door, a cigar clamped in his mouth. "Someone's here to see you." He plucked the cigar out of his mouth and motioned with his hand. "Said he wanted to talk to the man with the dog. Unless he's referring to my ex-wife, I figured you're it."

Kenner thought the ex-wife crack was pretty funny, and he let out a loud guffaw just as the front two legs of Nat's chair hit the floor.

Davy was standing outside the camp trailer, nervously fidgeting with Scout's ruff, the freckles across his nose standing out like beacons against his ashen face. He looked scared to death. Right beside him, crowded right against his leg, was Scout, who was clearly anxious about how Nat was going to handle this visit from his small friend.

A touch of amusement glinted in Nat's eyes. Obviously he had overrated the dog's sense of loyalty. Sticking his hands in the pockets of his jacket, he fixed his attention on the boy. "You wanted to see me?"

Davy swallowed, then spoke, his voice quavery with fear. "I came to tell you I was sorry about the dog, mister." He swallowed again, his voice shrinking with remorse. "I took him home because I thought he was lost. I didn't mean to steal him."

Remembering the letter he'd found earlier that morning, Nat solemnly watched the boy, knowing the kind of courage it had taken for the kid to come here and face him. He wondered if Davy's parents knew about this little trip. Fingering the loose change in his pocket, he spoke, his voice quiet. "Did you tell your dad you were coming here?"

Looking down at the dog, Davy stroked Scout's ear. "I don't have a dad." He hesitated; then he looked up and met Nat's gaze, his voice wobbling even more when he continued. "There's just Mom and me—and I didn't tell her. She wouldn't have let me come."

Nat's head suddenly stopped hurting. So it was just the kid and his mom. Interesting. Flicking away an old toothpick he'd found in his pocket, he stepped off the planking and crouched down, his hand inches from the boy's as he scratched Scout's neck. He considered everything that had happened, then he looked at Davy, his expression solemn. "I think I owe *you* an apology, Davy. I kinda' went off half-cocked last night, and I shouldn't have lost my temper the way I did." He paused, his expression thoughtful as he rubbed dirt off

Scout's nose. Finally he looked up, hoping like hell that he could find the right words to erase the abject misery in the kid's eyes. He didn't say anything for a moment, then said, "You don't have to apologize for what you did yesterday, Davy. Taking care of Scout the way you did." Startled, Davy met his gaze, his eyes wide with uncertainty. Nat gave him a wry half smile, then explained. "Most people wouldn't have bothered with a stray dog, let alone have taken him home and looked after him." He looked down and began stroking the dog's head, not liking how his voice had suddenly thickened. "I was just afraid something had happened to him."

Davy's response was instantaneous. All it took was Nat's admitting that he'd been worried about the dog and Davy's misery evaporated. His face suddenly animated, he dropped to his knees, his arm around Scout's neck. "He's such a neat dog," he said, his voice rushed with enthusiasm. "He wouldn't get on my bed until I told him it was all right, and he went and sat by the sink when he wanted a drink. I didn't figure that out, but my mom did." Davy chuckled and scrubbed the dog's jaw. "And every time he saw Mom looking at him, he'd give her that silly grin—you know, when he rolls his lips back over his teeth. She said he knew which side was up and that he was too smart for his own good."

Nat watched the boy, amusement glinting in his eyes. So Scout had Mom's number, did he? Mom, with the enigmatic gray eyes, the hint of defiance and the wild red hair that made her look like a Celtic warrior. Even more interesting.

"What did your mom say when you brought him home?"

Davy heaved a resigned sigh. "She said he probably belonged to somebody."

"Were you going to keep him if no one claimed him?"

Davy gave a dejected shrug, his expression losing its animation. "She said she'd think about it." He let go another heavy sigh, then met Nat's gaze. "I've been bugging her for a dog for a long time, but she says we don't have anywhere to keep one because our yard's not fenced." He gave Nat a resigned look.

Nat got the message. He studied Davy, his eyes narrowing in speculation, amusement tugging at his mouth. This kid was truly a piece of work. Knowing he was probably going to end up in Mom's black books, but recognizing the boy-dog thing between the two, he made a decision. "How would you like a job dog-sitting?"

Davy's head shot up, his expression transfixed by surprise. "Pardon?"

Nat grinned. "Dog-sitting. I've got a bunch of running around to do, and I don't like to leave Scout locked up in the truck for too long. And since he wandered off yesterday, I can't leave him here." He paused, watching the kid, seeing enthusiasm blossom in him.

"You mean it?"

The laugh lines around Nat's eyes deepened. "You bet."

Davy scrambled to his feet, excitement bursting from him like the Fourth of July. "All *right!*"

Nat stood and did up the bottom snap on his jacket. "But before we work out a deal, I think we'd better run this idea past your mom, sport."

Davy's expression suddenly changed, an odd, calculating look narrowing his eyes. "You mean you're coming home to meet my mom?"

Nat wondered about the kid's change of mood. "I think that would be a good idea, don't you?"

Suddenly Davy grinned, a bright gleam appearing in his eyes. "I think that's a *real* good idea."

Nat watched Davy, not quite sure how to handle the trip back to town. "Can I give you a lift home?"

Davy shook his head. "Naw. Mom would have a fit. I got my bike, and I know a shortcut. I'll just meet you in the back alley behind my house."

Smiling slightly, Nat nodded. Davy rubbed his hand against his thigh, looking a little sheepish. "Maybe I should know your name, mister. You know—for Mom."

Nat grinned and stuck out his hand. "Nathan—Nat—Cassidy."

Davy shook hands, then gave Nat a sly grin. "My Mom's name is Sarah. My Grandpa used to call her Sarah Anne."

Sarah Anne hardly ever swore. But she swore when she knocked the plant she'd just finished repotting off the end of the table. Realizing the plant next to it was tottering, as well, she made a lunge for it, knowing full well that if it went, so would the bag of potting soil and the pail of gravel she used to line the bottoms of the pots. She managed to grab the pot, but in the process spilled the drain tray of muddy water down the front of her clothes. For an instant she thought she had averted disaster, but then the gravel pail toppled over the side, allowing the bag of potting soil to sag, spilling rich black dirt on the floor. Totally disgusted, she was all set to smash the plant she was holding on top of the whole rotten mess, but just as she was about to let it fly, she remembered it was her favorite pink azalea.

Swearing again, she slammed it down on the table, sending another geyser of muddy water all over herself. Gritting her teeth, she closed her eyes, forcing herself to remain calm. What was it with her, anyway? How could she manage to turn the simplest task into a disaster?

Letting the air out of her lungs with an exasperated rush, she stepped over the broken shards of pottery and went to the sink, trying to find something to wipe the speckles of mud off her face. Just as she turned on the tap, she looked up, and her heart went dead-still. A big black Bronco with tinted windows and glinting chrome, the sides heavily splattered with mud, was just pulling to a stop behind the house. She suddenly had an awful gut feeling, and she knew something rotten was about to happen. When she recognized the man who got out of the driver's side, she closed her eyes and covered her face with her hand, wondering what she had done to deserve this. He'd gotten his damned dog back, hadn't he? What was he back here for, a pound of flesh?

Heaving a big tired sigh, she rubbed the bridge of her nose then dropped her hand, wishing heartily that she could be someplace else. She glanced out the window again, confirming his destination, but this time her heart went into full cardiac arrest. Her son, her one and only son, came around the corner of the garage, pushing his bike, chatting away as if this man were a long-lost buddy, the dog romping around in front of him. She barely noticed the dog; it was the sly grin on her son's face that filled her with foreboding. And what in the name of heaven was he *doing* talking to this person?

"Oh, God," she breathed, realization settling in. The dog. Davy had been hanging around the dog. After Mr. High-and-Mighty had given her explicit orders about keeping Davy away.

Skidding on the gravel-covered floor, she headed toward the back door, prepared to defend her son to the death. As she turned into the small back hall, another thought occurred. Just *why* was David James smiling like that? Like the cat who ate the canary?

Caught in a panic, Sarah frantically looked left and right, trying to come up with an escape plan. But she was too late. The door swung open and she was face-to-face with her small son. But it wasn't her small son who made her lungs seize up and heart lurch and stammer; it was the tall dark stranger filling up her doorway. Lord, he was big. And gorgeous.

Embarrassed by that unexpected thought, Sarah tucked her hands behind her back, determined to brazen it out.

Nat had to work hard to hold back a smile. She was something, all right. And that pointy little chin of hers was too adorable for words. He wanted to find out why she had globs of mud speckled all over her face, and why she looked like she'd been dragged through a buffalo wallow. But in a situation like this, discretion was the better part of valor.

Davy kicked off his boots, exuberance bubbling from him. "Guess what, Mom? I went to the road camp to apologize for taking Scout, and guess what? Mr. Cassidy asked me if I'd like to dog-sit Scout once in a while." He paused in the midst of stripping off his jacket, an undercurrent of anxiousness creeping into his expression. "But he said we'd better talk it over with you first. You'll let me, won't you? That'll be okay, won't it? Just once in a while?"

Hooking his thumbs in the pockets of his jeans, Nat watched confusion blossom on Sarah Jefferies' face. And he watched the beginnings of a deep blush creep up her neck. Experiencing a sudden urge to hug her so she would have some place to hide her face, he met her gaze, his mouth quirking into a wry half smile. "If this is a bad time, maybe I could give you a call later." He held her gaze, his expression sobering. "But before I go, I want to apologize for last night. I kinda' jumped the gun, and I'm sorry about that."

"He was worried that something had happened to Scout—that's the dog's name, Mom. But it's okay now. We had a *long* talk about that."

It was pretty clear from Sarah Jefferies' confused expression that she didn't know what in hell was going on, and she looked from one to the other, her flustered state deepening. Nat smiled at her and spoke, his voice soft. "I just thought that since your son and my dog have this thing going, maybe we could work something out."

Davy broke in, his tone anxious and beseeching. "Please, Mom. Please. He won't be any trouble. I promise." As if realizing he'd messed up on his manners, he glanced up at Nat, then back at his mother. "You remember Mr. Cassidy—Nat Cassidy—don't you, Mom? Mr. Manson's going to be working with him." He looked up at Nat. "This is my mom, Sarah, Mr. Cassidy."

Her name suited her, Nat thought. He could tell by the way she was standing that Sarah Jefferies had her hands tightly clasped behind her back, as though she'd been caught in some mischief. She also looked as if she wanted to bolt. He looked right into her eyes, smiled and held out his hand. "Pleased to meet you, Sarah Jefferies," he said softly.

She hesitated, uncertainty flickering in her eyes; then she hesitantly took his offered hand. "I—" She took a deep breath, then tried to smile. "Hello."

Nat liked the feel of her small hand in his, he liked the warmth. But most of all he liked the way the pulse in her neck was beating in double time. He remembered the time he'd caught a swallow with a broken wing, and how he could feel the bird's frantic heartbeat against his palm. Sarah Jefferies' pulse was just as frantic.

She stared up at him, something more than just uncertainty darkening her eyes. After a long, still moment, she swallowed and lowered her gaze. Reluctant to sever the physical connection, Nat released her hand.

Sarah shot him a startled look, then stepped away, clasping her hands tightly together. Moistening her lips, she turned to her son, her voice tight. "You'd better put your boots on the mat, Davy. They're covered with mud."

Rolling his eyes in exasperation, Davy did as he was told, then straightened, wiping his hands on his jeans. "I can look after Scout once in a while for Mr. Cassidy, can't I, Mom?" He gave Nat an urgent look over his shoulder, clearly hoping to win a little support. Suppressing a smile, Nat placed his hand on the back of the boy's neck, giving his head a little shake. "I don't think now is a very good time for your mom, sport, so I'm going to check out. Maybe you can let me know what you decide later, okay?"

Sarah Jefferies' eyes widened, and Nat could have sworn he saw traces of guilt. "Oh, I—well—perhaps—" She closed her eyes, her expression revealing that she felt like an utter fool. Nat grinned, wanting to hug her again. Drawing a deep breath, she finally looked at him, her cheeks pink with embarrassment. "It's fine. Really. We can talk about it now."

A loud knock sounded, the door swung open, and Vic Manson stuck his head in. "Yo, Sarah. I'm here to pick up the deep fryer for Joyce." Spotting Nat, he stepped in, surprise registering in his expression just before he grinned. "Well, hell, Cassidy. What are you doing here? You lost or something?"

Sensing that something unexpected was about to unfold here, Nat stuck his hands in his pockets and grinned back. "I never get lost, Vic. Only misdirected."

Vic snorted, then gestured toward the kitchen. "Are you sticking around for coffee? I'll go get Joyce if you are."

Vic Manson didn't know it, but he had just put Sarah Jefferies on the spot. Nat could tell, though, and he didn't mind one bit. Now all he had to do was wait her out.

It was obvious she didn't know what to do, but after receiving a pleading look from her son, she relented. "I just made a fresh pot of coffee, if you'd like some."

Davy shot Nat a triumphant look. Vic motioned to the box sitting by the door. "Is this it?"

Her expression a little dazed, Sarah nodded. Vic hoisted the box and opened the door. "Joyce and I'll be back in a flash."

Davy flashed Nat another smug look as he hung his coat on a hook. Feeling a little smug himself, Nat shed his muddy joggers, then started to follow Sarah and Davy. But at the archway leading to the kitchen, Sarah Jefferies pulled up short, muttering something that sounded suspiciously like "Oh, hell." Davy plowed into his mother's back, and Nat saw her slap her hand over her face. Nat moved behind her, wondering about the fresh flood of color spreading up her neck.

He glanced into the kitchen and nearly laughed. The place was a disaster. He'd seen a few jungles in his time, but never in someone's kitchen. It looked as if someone had taken a greenhouse and upended the whole thing on her kitchen table and floor.

"Mom! Why have you got dirt and gravel all over the floor?"

"Maybe," Nat said, his tone laced with dry amusement, "she's building a road."

Her shoulders started to shake, and for a split second Nat thought she was crying, but then she made a choked sound, followed by a burst of the most unrestrained, infectious laughter he'd ever heard. Nat grinned, pleased with himself for making her laugh, but more pleased with her for seeing the humor.

Finally Sarah Jefferies let go a big sigh, wiped her eyes and looked at him, her expression alight with humor. "A road wasn't part of my original plan, but maybe it's not a bad idea."

Amused by her response and intrigued by the deep dimple in her left cheek, Nat gazed at her, liking what he saw. There was something about this lady that was definitely worth knowing.

Sarah held his gaze for a moment, then another fine blush crept up her cheeks, and she looked away, making a disconcerted little gesture toward the opposite arch. "Davy, why don't you take Mr. Cassidy into the living room, and I'll bring the coffee in there."

Nat watched her, cataloging her unease. Feeling unexpectedly protective, he spoke, his voice husky. "Could we can the Mr. Cassidy routine? It makes me feel like my father."

Sarah shot him a quick, startled look, a hint of amusement appearing. "Davy, would you take—Nat into the living room?"

Nat wanted to offer to help clean up the landslide in the kitchen and move the jungle of plants for her, but he sensed an undercurrent of wariness in her that kept him silent. The lady was skittish; that was obvious. And he sure as hell didn't want to rush his gates with this one. This one intrigued him.

If the kitchen had been a revelation, the large living room was doubly so. It was cluttered, it was jammed— it was fantastic. It was an old-fashioned room with dark woodwork, deep baseboards and delicate peach-and-beige wallpaper. There were several excellent prints on the wall—beautiful travel posters of Greece and Italy, a print of a Paris street scene by Renoir, a grouping of miniatures that included sketches of a Swiss village, shrimp boats off the Louisiana coast and the pyramids of Egypt. The bookshelves on either side of the fieldstone fireplace were stuffed with books, all of them well-used and worn, and there was a huge bouquet of pussy willows arranged in a Chinese vase.

Feeling as if he'd walked into someone's secret hideaway, Nat wandered around the room, absorbed by the countless knickknacks. Most of the furniture was old—an old walnut rolltop desk, a three-legged table, a cane-backed bentwood rocker, an oak sea chest that had to be a hundred years old. But jammed in amidst it all were a chrome-and-glass wall unit and a couple of end tables that came from one those trendy, inexpensive furniture stores. The sofa was a budget model in a deep brown corduroy, the love seat was a deep rust right out of the thirties, and the big, old leather easy chair was overstuffed and inviting.

The wall unit held a hodgepodge of things—an earthenware jug, an old copper teakettle, a grouping of pieces of carnival glass, a tin tea can that had to be fifty years old, a battered pewter jug full of peacock feathers mixed with some dried wheat.

The whole scheme should have been a disaster, but it wasn't. It was warm and inviting, and, for Nat, as fascinating as hell. He couldn't remember ever being in a room that he felt so totally at home in.

Davy moved a stack of books from one end of the sofa and set them on the coffee table, which looked like an old round harvest table that had had the pedestal shortened. There must have been fifteen candles grouped together on that table—fat ones, tall ones, thin ones, some long white elegant tapers—some stuck in bottles, some in candle holders, and a couple of large ones stuck in the lids of pickle jars. There was also an old-fashioned candy dish full of homemade fudge. Nat grinned. No wonder Scout wanted to come back.

Davy motioned to the sofa. "You can sit there. Then you'll have someplace to put your coffee." He popped a square of fudge in his mouth, then remembered his manners and offered the dish to Nat as Nat sat down. "Want some? Mom makes the best fudge."

Nat took a piece of fudge and settled into a comfortable slouch on the sofa, stretching his legs out in front of him. The fudge lived up to Davy's estimation. Davy helped himself to another piece and put the dish down, then sat cross-legged on the table. He took another bite, considered it, then looked at Nat. "At least, it's usually the best. Sometimes she forgets what she's doing and then it turns out pretty awful."

Nat studied the kid, amusement lurking around his mouth. "So how's her coffee?"

Davy shrugged and grimaced, his eyes full of mischief. "I don't know. But Mrs. Manson—that's my baby-sitter—says when Mom's hot, she's hot, but when she's not, a pig wouldn't eat her cooking."

Nat's amusement deepened. For some reason, that bit of information didn't surprise him. He took another piece of fudge when Davy offered it to him, savoring the thick, dark richness of the candy. "What grade are you in, Davy?"

Davy heaved a heavy sigh. "Four. I wish I was in Five."

Nat gazed at Davy, seeing traces of his mother in him. Traces he liked. "What's wrong with Grade Four?"

Davy gave another resigned sigh. "My teacher. She says I don't pay attention in class, but it's just that there's better things to think about, you know?"

Nat did indeed know. "Do you like sports?"

Davy's face lit up. "Oh, yeah. I like 'em all. Especially baseball and hockey. I play right wing in hockey and shortstop in baseball, and I've got a whole collection of hockey and baseball cards—you know, the ones you trade." He bounced to his feet, enthusiasm bright in his eyes. "Do you want to see 'em?"

"No, he does not want to see them," said Sarah as she entered the living room, carrying a tray.

"Aw, Mom—"

"No," interjected his mother, her tone indicating she didn't want an argument.

Davy rolled his eyes and let out a disgusted sigh, and Nat glanced up at Sarah and grinned. "Moms are such spoilsports."

She avoided meeting his gaze, but he caught the hint of a smile around her mouth. "Before you take sides here, maybe you should know that he has five hundred and forty-three cards. And a story to go with every single one of them."

Nat winced and raised his hands in surrender. "I get the picture." Sarah looked at him with a twinkle in her eyes, and in that instant of shared intimacy, Nat knew he was in big trouble. This lady was different from the others. This one was special. She was also a puzzle. One he wanted very much to figure out.

Chapter Four

Sarah stood behind the teller's wicket, wrapping rubber bands around bundles of one-dollar bills, feeling like an overextended rubber band herself. She was in such a muddle that she'd gotten up in the middle of the night and vacuumed the living room. If that wasn't bad enough, she'd made coffee that morning without putting any coffee in the basket, and she'd almost come to work with two different shoes on. She felt like Alice after she'd fallen down the rabbit hole.

She stopped and stared at the stack of bundles, realizing she hadn't recounted a single one of them. There could be forty bills in each of those bundles for all she knew. In fact, for all she knew, she could have been bundling grocery coupons. Drawing a deep, stabilizing breath, she closed her eyes in exasperation, totally disgusted with herself. She wished she could go home and start the morning all over again.

"Is something wrong, Sarah?"

Letting her breath go in an irritated rush, she turned and looked at Edith Graham, her long-time manager, dredging up a wry smile. "No. I just forgot my brain today, that's all."

Edith chuckled and picked up a sheaf of papers, giving Sarah an amused look. "Well, that's not as bad as forgetting your lunch."

Sarah watched the older woman leave the front area, experiencing a sudden urge to smash open every single roll of change in the cash drawer. Yes, there was something wrong. She'd lost her mind, that was what was wrong. She should have grounded Davy for a week for going over to the road camp on his own. She should have said no to the dog-sitting thing. But most of all, she should never have let Nathan Cassidy past the back door. Her self-disgust renewed, she sighed and rubbed her eyes, wishing she had one iota of sense. Why hadn't she grounded her son, why hadn't she said no to the dog-sitting, and why, *why,* had she invited a perfect stranger into her house?

Sarah dropped her hand and stared dismally across the bank. She *was* losing her mind. She'd trusted some man in her house because he'd been upset over his *dog?* What sort of recommendation was that? She rolled her eyes heavenward, shaking her head in disbelief. Lord, she shouldn't be allowed out of the house by herself.

She started unwrapping a bundle of bills. Well, she might have lost her mind, but at least her living room was thoroughly vacuumed, and Davy was thrilled about the dog. But Nat Cassidy? No way. That man was a load of dangerous goods if she'd ever seen one. Closing her eyes and taking a deep breath, she forced herself into a calm, rational state. Okay, now she was going to count money. That was all. She wasn't going to think about kids or dogs, and she was *not* going to think about Nat Cassidy, about how he had stayed exactly one hour, his very male body sprawled on her sofa, eating her fudge and drinking her coffee—and charming the bejeebers out of her son.

But her mind refused to turn off. Joyce Manson had got him talking about the things he'd done and the places he'd been. And Nathan Cassidy had been almost everywhere—on every continent, on every ocean, on nearly every major river system in the world—places she'd only read about, places she could only dream about. God, it had been wonderful, listening to him talk about the jungles of Peru, the steppes of Russia, the great vast pampas of Argentina. He had opened whole, new fascinating worlds to her, worlds of unfamiliar cultures and people and customs. She could have listened to him talk all night, his deep lazy drawl just as absorbing as his tales. But he had stayed only an hour, and never had sixty minutes gone by so fast. When he had stood up to leave, she had very nearly blurted out an invitation to supper. That out-of-the-blue reaction had caught her so by surprise that she'd gone speechless with mortification. People like Nathan Cassidy were way out of her league.

"Good morning."

Sarah jumped, scattering the bills she'd been holding, her heart lurching with startled alarm. Nearly toppling from her high stool, she closed her eyes and clutched her hand against her breast, certain her heart was going to leap right out of her chest. Inhaling deeply, she opened her eyes, her heart getting its second jolt for the day.

Nat Cassidy stood at her wicket, his arms folded on the high counter, his stance pulling his shirt tight across his broad shoulders. Feeling the rush of heat to her face, Sarah stared at him, part of her wanting to hide behind the counter, another part—that tiny, wayward part—mesmerized by the sparkle in his dark hazel eyes. Lord, with eyes like that, he could walk into any bedroom in town.

Scandalized by her own thoughts, Sarah blushed again, fervently wishing she had a bag to put over her head. She was twenty-nine years old, for heaven's sake; she wasn't some fourteen-year old with a massive crush. Feeling like an utter fool, she made herself meet his gaze. "Good morning, Mr. Cassidy."

Resting his weight again the counter, he continued to study her, the laugh lines around his eyes creasing just a little, the twinkle in his eyes warm and inviting. "I thought we decided to can that 'Mr. Cassidy' stuff last night."

She held his gaze for a second, then looked down, her confusion compounding as she began fussing with the loose bills. "Yes, well—" She took a deep breath and looked back at him, lifting her chin, determined to see this through if it killed her. "Is there something I can help you with?"

He didn't say anything for a moment but just continued to study her, the twinkle suddenly glinting with more than amusement. His gaze fixed on hers, he cocked one eyebrow and gave her a slow, sexy smile that sent Sarah's insides into a series of rolls and loops. And she knew darned well that whatever he was thinking had nothing to do with banking. Feeling as though her lungs were about to seize up, she took a steadying breath, hoping that her knees didn't cave in beneath her. Lord, she was going to faint if he didn't quit looking at her like that.

The twinkle in his eyes intensified, enfolding her in a crazy, effervescent sensation. It was as though they were old friends sharing some private joke, and Sarah found herself gazing back at him, a smile lurking around her mouth. She felt as if she were suddenly floating, her body lighter than air.

The sound of a file drawer slamming jarred her back to reality, and she inhaled deeply, trying to reconnect.

Nat released a small sigh and straightened, pulling a leather portfolio toward him. "Yeah, I need to get a couple of things straightened out." He drew out a sheaf of papers. "First of all, I need to open an account, and then I'd like some funds transferred from my branch in Edmonton. I also have some checks to deposit to the Benson Construction account and one to my own."

Avoiding his gaze, Sarah took the papers he handed her and began flipping through them. They could have been written in Greek for all she knew. Realizing that nothing was registering in her befuddled brain, she stopped, gritted her teeth in determination and started all over again. If she didn't get her damned head together, she was going to end up in a major wreck here. Finally something made sense. "You won't need to open another account. We can just manage the one in Edmonton from here if you like."

He gave her an easy shrug. "Sounds fine."

What sounded fine was his voice; what sounded fine was that rich mellow drawl. Disgusted with herself, she turned off the sound of her own internal voice. Somehow or another, she had to get through this transaction.

Somehow or another, she did. By the time she finished, there were two other customers in the bank, which helped. She experienced a funny, let-down feeling when Nat, his business concluded, gathered up the deposit slips, bank books and records and stuffed them into his portfolio, thanked her, then turned and left. Realizing what was happening, she silent berated herself. Good grief, she hadn't been this silly when she'd *been* fourteen.

Determined to ignore that let-down feeling, she waited on the other two customers, stamping the back of Mrs. Wong's utility bill "paid" with far more force than necessary. Mrs. Wong moved down the counter to put away her receipts, and Sarah stuck a plastic smile on her face, ready to serve the next person in line. The smile stuck like hardening cement and her stomach went into another series of rolls and loops. She was staring at Nat Cassidy again, fighting the urge to turn around and run.

Resting his arm on the counter, Nat propped his chin on his hand and stared at her, his mouth quirking in a maddening half-smile. Sarah considered quitting her job and leaving town. Still staring at her, he leaned a little closer and murmured, "We have a little problem, Ms. Jefferies."

Problem? Her whole morning had been one big problem. The silly fourteen-year-old ninny running around in her mind was a problem. His closeness was a problem. Sarah forced herself to speak, her voice coming out in a breathless squeak. "A problem?"

Still watching her with that same half-smile, he nodded.

Feeling about as stretched out as she could get, Sarah waited for him to explain. His gaze didn't alter, and his expression remained the same. Sarah had to clench her hands to keep from fidgeting under his unnerving scrutiny. Finally he spoke. "Tell you what. I'll make a deal with you. If you come for coffee with me, I won't tell your boss you screwed up two accounts."

Sarah stared at him, a flicker of irritation catching hold. She *never* screwed up accounts. Never. Determined to hang on to her annoyance, she ignored the little voice that reminded her that she had done nothing *but* screw up all morning.

As if sensing her intended rebuttal, he pushed two deposit slips toward her, giving her an ingenious smile. "You deposited my check to the Benson Construction account, and one Benson check to mine."

She stared at him, trying to assimilate what he'd told her, then she looked down at the two pieces of paper lying before her. As soon as she saw the figures, she knew that was exactly what she'd done. Staring at the two offending deposit slips, she muttered under her breath. She should have stayed at home with her vacuum. Feeling like a total fool, she drew the two pieces of paper toward her, keenly aware of the heat rushing into her face. All she'd done since she'd met this man was blush.

"Sarah," he said softly.

She looked up, mentally framing an apology. But he never gave her a chance. He smiled, the creases around his eyes crinkling, the warm assurance in his gaze making her heart pound. "It's not a big deal," he said in that same gentle tone. The twinkle in his eyes intensified, his gaze becoming warm and intimate. "In fact, I consider it some sort of omen."

Sarah stared at him, so befuddled she wasn't sure what was going on. "Pardon?" she whispered, not sure she'd heard him right.

The smile deepened. "I think it means you're supposed to come for coffee with me."

Feeling more like Alice by the minute, Sarah rubbed her hands against her thighs. "I can't."

"If you say no, I'm going to be forced to go see your boss."

Amusement flickered through her; he looked just like Davy when he was trying to get his own way. "No you won't."

"I will."

She was sure he was joking until he picked up the two deposit slips and turned toward the side counter where Edith was doing some paperwork. Tipping his head, he indicated Edith and raised his eyebrows in an expression that clearly asked, *Well, what's it going to be?* Sarah didn't know what to do. If she said no, the whole office was going to find out about her silly blunder, and they would never let her live it down. If she said yes—oh, God, if she said yes, she was setting herself up for an emotional upheaval. And an upheaval it would be, because Nathan Cassidy was someone who could definitely rock her nice quiet, staid, stable boat.

Sarah stared at him, wanting to go in the worst way, knowing she shouldn't. She was just too susceptible to his brand of masculine appeal, his aura of adventure, his dark, sexy, sparkling eyes. But oh, how she wanted to.

His voice was soft, gently querying. "Sarah?"

Sarah hadn't even been aware she'd made a decision until she heard herself answer, her voice shaky and a little breathless. "I can only take twenty minutes."

Late that night, Nat sat in the eating nook of the trailer, absently picking at the label on the bottle of beer he had cradled in his hands, the only light coming from the small fixture over the sink. He hadn't really wanted the beer. And he sure as hell didn't want to be prowling around at three o'clock in the morning, unable to sleep for the images that kept taking shape in his mind. He felt as if he'd been caught by a fast-moving train. There were a whole lot of things he wanted to do with Sarah Jefferies, and they didn't have one damned thing to do with his bank account.

Shaking his head in self-disgust, he took a swig from the bottle, then set it back down, twisting it around in the circle of moisture on the table. He couldn't shake this feeling that he had just been confronted with one of the most significant turning points in his entire life.

He exhaled heavily and took another long swallow, the wind making a mournful sound as it rattled the vents on the trailer. Somehow he had to sort out his thoughts or he would never get any sleep. But that was easier said than done. Sarah Jefferies wasn't just another woman he was mildly attracted to, not by a long shot. But in this case, even a heavy dose of attraction didn't cut it. He was here for two months; then he would be moving out, and he wouldn't be back in Canada, except for visits, for at least three years. And she wasn't the kind of woman he could simply have a good time with, then leave—at least, not with a clear conscience. She was too damned vulnerable, too damned sweet and unspoiled. He realized she wasn't some timid little mouse; he'd seen sparks of temper, and it was pretty clear she had a mind of her own. But that didn't mean she could walk out of a short-term relationship without being hurt. Besides, he suspected that she already carried some scars, and he sure as hell didn't want to inflict any more.

Nat picked away another corner of the label, a wry smile appearing. Maybe he was crossing bridges that weren't even there. After all, their coffee break hadn't exactly been a roaring success. They'd had maybe five minutes on their own, then some old geezer had come over—an old friend of Sarah's father's—and had made himself right at home in their booth, referring to Sarah as "our Sarah," making sure he knew what Nat was all about, then talked up a storm about the new highway. Nat had the uneasy feeling that there would be quite a few townsfolk checking him out if he started hanging around "their Sarah."

Nat polished off the last of the beer, then pushed the bottle aside and went to stand in front of the door. The lights of town twinkled through the naked branches of the trees, the huge grain elevators along the track faintly visible in the fading darkness. Bracing his hand on the wall, he stared out, his expression somber. If he had six months here, he wouldn't hesitate about pursuing an involvement with Sarah Jefferies. But he didn't; he had two months. That was it. He was committed to the job in Bolivia. And even after spending less that two hours with her, he knew she was far too special for some short, casual affair. Sarah Jefferies was the kind of woman who made him think about station wagons and white picket fences. And white picket fences just didn't fit into the jungles of Bolivia.

Wednesday, May 10

Sarah stood at the kitchen window, hugging her sweater around her, watching Davy romp with the dog. Maybe it was for the best. Maybe her guardian angel had managed some sort of divine intervention Monday morning, arranging for George Prowski to show up at the café when he did. A man like Nathan Cassidy would never become a permanent fixture in her life; she knew that. But, oh Lord, he made her feel young and alive. She gave a small smile. There was a flip side to that, of course; he also made her feel threatened, insecure and alone, and in record doses. But what was worst of all was that he made her feel small-town, drab and unsophisticated.

Sarah sighed, disgusted with herself. Who was she trying to kid? She *was* small-town, drab and unsophisticated. She'd lived in Alton most of her life and had traveled outside the province maybe—*maybe*—ten times. Hardly the making of a scintillating woman.

She sighed again, wishing that, just for once, things could be different. That just once she could experience something wild and exciting. That just once she could have something more than her humdrum existence. Just once.

Realizing she was dangerously close to feeling sorry for herself, Sarah straightened her shoulders and shifted her gaze. She just felt so damned alone, but maybe that was nothing more than a delayed reaction to losing her father. Or maybe she'd been reading too many romance novels. She experienced a small flicker of amusement. Maybe she was just losing her mind.

She caught a movement at the corner of the garage, and she turned, her pulse doing a wild skip and flutter when Nathan Cassidy came into view, her son dancing backward in front of him. She hadn't seen Nat since Monday, and that made her throat ache for some reason. She finally realized just how very much she'd hoped he would call.

Scout's owner looked up, his expression altering when he saw her standing in the window. He stood staring at her for a moment, his hands rammed deep in his pockets, the breeze cutting through his hair. He was solemn, dark and dangerous, his angular jaw shadowed with five-o'clock stubble, his stance containing a raw masculine grace that made her think of dark nights and predators. And Sarah knew with a shiver of awareness that this was the man who could shake up her existence, who could make her want things, feel things. Things she had no business wanting or feeling. Like excitement and expectation and adventure—and impossible dreams. Things she didn't even dare think about.

His expression narrowed, and he stared at her an instant longer; then he abruptly shifted and turned his attention back to her son. Hugging herself, Sarah closed her eyes, trying to will away the sensations pumping through her. She couldn't afford to let herself indulge in the kind of fantasies that were taking shape in her mind. Not the kind that made her pulse race and her whole body hum. Not the kind that made her want to break out of her everyday existence and soar. But God, just once she would like to soar, to experience life at its fullest. Just once.

Nat stood in the backyard, his hands buried deep in his pockets, only half listening to Davy tell him about how he'd spent his two hours with Scout. His thoughts were focused squarely on the kid's mother. Nat wondered if he was really losing it. Here he was, standing out in the yard, freezing his butt off, his ribs feeling as if they were separating from his spine, and all he could think about was touching Sarah Jefferies' hair. Maybe he was in deeper than he thought. When he'd seen her standing in the window, that riot of curls framing her face, something had kicked loose in his chest. Something he'd been trying to contain ever since Davy had told him there was no one but him and his mom. The corner of his mouth lifted in a wry expression. Hell, who was he trying to kid? He'd been thinking about her all day, and now he was out here, dead tired and cold to the bone, still thinking about things that he had no business considering.

He was only passing through, and he was going to have to do his damnedest to remember that.

Chapter Five

Friday, May 12

Dear Grandpa,
I'm supposed to be in bed—well, I am in bed, but I've got my flashlight under the covers. You know, the one you gave me the Christmas before you went away. I hope I don't sifixiate—Jimmy Manson says he heard about a kid that sifixiated from reading in bed. I don't think I spelled sifixiate right, Grandpa. We had a spelling bee at school today, and I won. Mrs. Martin says I'm the best speller she ever had. I guess it's because Mom makes me look up words in the dictionary.

Guess what? Billy Martin taught Jimmy and me how to belch. Marcy Brown heard us at recess, and she said we were disgusting. I told her the way she picks her nose when nobody is looking is more disgusting. Jimmy really thought that was a good one.

I kinda need to talk to you, Grandpa. Sunday is Mother's Day, and I feel bad because I can't do anything special for Mom—you know, like take her to dinner like we used to. I wish I could do something nice for her. You know, to let her know I'm glad she's my mom. I got her a card and some of that bath stuff with my own money, but I wish I could do something else.

I looked after Scout today. Remember, I told you about him. Mr. Cassidy is real nice. He drives a big black truck and he has a neat leather jacket—you know, one of those ones with all the pockets like a pilot's jacket. Maybe I'll be a pilot when I grow up. I think it would be really neat to fly jets.

I got to go, Grandpa. I hear Mom locking the front door, so I have to turn off the light. The last time she caught me reading in bed, she kept my flashlight for two weeks. I'll let you know about Mother's Day.

Your grandson, Davy

Saturday, May 13

Nat parked in the alley behind the Jefferies home, noticing the changes that had taken place over the past two days. The trees were beginning to show a tinge of green, and he'd come across a whole patch of crocuses when he'd been out with the surveyors this morning. He wondered if Sarah liked crocuses. Giving his head a wry shake, he started up the walk beside the garage. He needed to give his head more than a shake.

He stopped when he saw Davy sitting on the bottom step of the back porch, his chin propped in his hands, a dejected sag to his shoulders. The kid looked as if he'd lost his best friend. Scout was sitting beside him, looking just as sorrowful as his small friend. Nat repressed a grin. He didn't trust either one of them.

Sticking his hands in his pockets, he studied Davy. "Hi. How's it going?"

Davy heaved a big sigh and looked up, giving him a despondent shrug. "All right, I guess."

Restraining his amusement, Nat watched him. "It doesn't sound all right."

Davy sighed again. "Tomorrow's Mother's Day, and I really wanted to do something nice for my mom."

Nat didn't say anything for a moment, then he spoke, his voice quiet. "You mean like getting her something?"

Davy gave another despondent shrug. "I got her some of that smelly bath stuff she likes, and I got her a card." He bent his head, his voice uneven when he said, "But other moms get to go for dinner, or they get flowers and stuff. Grandpa—" He stopped, and Nat saw him swallow hard. His voice was even more unsteady when he finally continued. "Grandpa always took us to Millard for dinner, and he used to take me shopping for something really nice." Avoiding Nat's gaze, Davy began fiddling with Scout's new collar. "I just feel bad, that's all."

Nat looked away, a lump the size of a baseball taking shape in his throat. This kid had a big heart, that was for damned sure. Doing some heavy swallowing himself, Nat crouched down in front of Davy, his own voice gruff when he spoke. "Tell you what. How about if we work something out?"

Davy's head came up, hope kindling in his eyes. "You mean you and me?"

Nat gave him a lopsided grin. "Yeah. That's what I mean."

Davy stared at him a moment; then his whole face lit up. "You mean like dinner or something?" Then, as if realizing he'd put Nat on the spot, he quickly added, "Or pizza. If we could take her for pizza, then I could pay. I have money from my paper route and my allowance."

Nat had never wanted to hug a kid as much as he wanted to hug this one. He smiled at him instead. "Tell you what. I'll take care of dinner, and you take care of your mom."

The boy's eyes narrowed, and a sly smile appeared. "You mean like a surprise?"

The kid was no dummy. Nat had a suspicion that if Sarah Jefferies knew what they were cooking up on her back step, she would nix it pretty damned fast. And Nat also suspected that Davy knew that. Nat grinned at him. "Yeah. Something like that."

Davy gazed up at him, mischief glinting in his eyes. "I'm real good at secrets."

Nat laughed and ruffled his hair. "I figured you would be." He stood up, indicating Scout. "Can you watch him for a bit? I'll have to make a run to Millard."

Putting his arm around Scout, Davy grinned and nodded. "Don't phone or anything, okay? She might figure things out if you phone. You can just tell me what time and stuff when you come to get Scout."

Nat almost smiled. The kid had a few things figured out himself.

Sunday, May 14

Sarah sat at the kitchen table, intent on the dough figurines spread out before her, splashes of brightly colored paint smeared on the slab of cardboard she had used to protect the table. Davy's school was having a spring tea and bazaar the following week, and she had to get these damned things finished. They were plaques of plump little people, comic caricatures that she molded out of a special dough, baked, then painted. They had become a kind of collector's item in town. Mrs. Berkowitz, the town cleaning lady, liked to boast to anyone who cared to listen that she had nineteen hanging on her kitchen wall.

Sarah was heartily sick of the things, but the school library fund made a small fortune off them, so she was doomed, she was sure, to a lifetime of roly-poly butchers, bakers and candlestick makers.

"Mom?"

"Hmm?"

"Uh—are you going to be working on those all day?"

Wiping off her brush, Sarah looked up. Although she could have sworn she heard a trace of anxiety in Davy's voice, he was looking at her with wide, innocent eyes. But he was all fidgety and . . .

She narrowed her eyes, suspicion taking root. It looked as if he had just taken another shower. They had gone to church that morning, and he'd had a shower before they went. And now he was standing in front of her, freshly scrubbed, with his hair combed. And Davy *never* combed his hair unless she made him.

Sighing, knowing, just *knowing,* that Davy hadn't suddenly become fastidious without a reason, she set down her brush. Okay. It was Mother's Day. He had spent three months' allowance and all his weekly newspaper earnings on a bottle of her favorite bath oil and a beautiful card that had made her cry. No matter what, she was not going to give him a lecture.

There was, however, a hint of exasperation in her voice. "What have you done this time, Davy?"

He shot her a startled look, then fidgeted some more. "Uh—um, well, nothing. I just thought because it was Mother's Day, maybe you could get dressed up, and maybe we could do something. It's just about five o'clock, so I thought if you got changed now, maybe we could go to the café for supper or something."

Her throat suddenly so tight she could barely swallow, Sarah stared at him, her chest clogged with emotion. God bless him, he wanted to make it a special day in the only way he knew how, or was able. Alton boasted only one restaurant, which was little more than a coffee shop, and the menu did not exactly provide an epicurean night on the town. Still she wanted to hug him for being so sweet and thoughtful.

She inhaled carefully, not sure just how close the tears were. "That would be really nice, David," she said softly. "I'd really like that."

Davy shifted his weight from one foot to the other, glanced toward her bedroom, then gave her a hopeful smile. "Well, maybe you could start getting dressed now. You know."

She glanced at the dough bodies on the table, then back at him, her expression regretful. "Could I just finish this, Skeeter? All I need is another twenty minutes."

Davy shifted his weight from one foot to the other again, only this time he glanced toward the back door. "Well, um, do you think you could finish faster?" He shifted and looked out the kitchen window, his eyes widening. "Oh-oh."

There was a knock at the back door, and Davy responded instantly. "It's for me, Mom!"

Frowning slightly, Sarah watched him, wondering what was going on. One minute he was in a hurry to leave, and the next minute he had friends arriving. If whoever it was would just keep him busy for twenty minutes, everyone would be happy.

Sarah was aware of some whispering, an awed sound from Davy, then some rustling. A few moments later she heard Davy return. "Mom? Happy Mother's Day."

She looked up and went stock-still. She couldn't even see her son; he was completely obscured by a huge bouquet of flowers—a glorious arrangement of purple irises, yellow daisies and the most beautiful orange tiger lilies she'd ever seen. It was beautiful. And expensive.

Coming out of her shock of surprise, she started to speak, but Davy cut her off, his voice wobbling with anticipation. "It's part of a surprise, Mom." Carefully setting the arrangement down on the end of the table, he tipped his head so he could see her, his wide-eyed expression revealing anxiety. "There's more, Mom. We're taking you to Millard for dinner."

Nat figured this was his cue, and he moved so Sarah could see him, amusement overriding his doubts about this whole plan. The look on her face was certainly worth the price of admission. He realized she'd had no idea he was there. "Hello, Sarah."

She looked at him, a stunned look on her face, then blinked as reality set in. She made a helpless gesture with her hands, looking from him to her son in dazed confusion. Nat waited for the blush to come, and he tried not to smile when it did. She was so predictable. Sticking his hands in the pockets of his slacks, he spoke, his voice tinged with amusement. "Our reservation is for six o'clock."

She looked from him back to Davy, then back at him. Her voice came out in a confused squeak. "Reservation?"

Nat grinned, enjoying her reaction. "For dinner. It *is* Mother's Day, you know."

Raising her hands in a frantic gesture, she looked down at her paint-splattered smock. Then she closed her eyes and covered her face with her hand, her neck turning even pinker. "Oh, God."

"Come on, Mom," Davy urged. "We gotta hurry. It takes us half an hour to get there."

She didn't move; she just sat there, her hand plastered to her face. Nat's grin deepened. "I think it's going to take her a while to get it together, Davy. I think we surprised her pretty good.''

Davy grinned up at him, satisfaction and delight sparkling in his eyes. ''We did, didn't we?''

''I think so.''

Taking a deep breath, Sarah dropped her hand, avoiding Nat's gaze and looking at the flowers. ''They're just beautiful,'' she said, a funny catch in her voice. ''Thank you so much.''

Davy went over and gave her a quick hug, then made an embarrassed gesture. ''You're welcome. They're from me and Nat.''

Nat knew it took considerable effort for her to look at him, but she did, meeting his gaze with a directness that made his heart roll over. ''Thank you,'' she said softly.

He gazed at her, his chest tightening with some very potent feelings. His own voice was husky when he answered. ''My pleasure.'' She didn't shy away from his gaze; something sweet, special and oddly intimate was revealed in her eyes, and Nat knew that any ideas he'd had about staying away from her had just gone out the window. Right or wrong, he was going to make the most of what little time they had.

''Come *on*, Mom,'' Davy urged, tugging at her arm. ''We're going to be late if you don't hurry.''

She held Nat's gaze an instant longer, then made another flustered gesture, the familiar blush reappearing. ''Yes—I—yes, I guess I'd better.'' She looked at the mess before her, then down at her smock, before she stood up, nervously wiping her hands. "I—I won't be long."

Davy darted out of the room behind her, but it wasn't long before he was back, a twenty-dollar bill crumpled in his hand. He offered it to Nat. "This is for the flowers." He gave Nat an embarrassed shrug, fidgeting a little. "I know it's not enough, but I can give you some more when I collect from my paper route next week."

Nat wanted to tell him to forget it, but he sensed this was a big deal for the kid, that it was important for him to shoulder part of the responsibility. Reluctantly, he took the money. "Thanks. But you don't owe me anything else." He folded the bill and stuck it in his pants pocket, then lied. "That'll cover half of the flowers, and the deal was that dinner was on me."

Davy stared at him a moment, as if pondering the fairness of that arrangement. Finally he nodded. "Okay, but then you can't pay me for looking after Scout, okay?"

Experiencing an unexpected pride in the kid, Nat nodded. "Deal."

Davy nodded back, then grimaced. "I gotta go get changed, too. I had to wait until you came, or she'd have got suspicious for sure." He turned to go. "I think there's still coffee in the pot if you want some."

His hands still rammed in his pockets, Nat wandered around the spacious, plant-filled kitchen, studying the prints hanging on the walls; then he returned to the table and studied the shapes spread out on a sheet of cardboard. Dragging one hand from his pocket, he reached down and turned one plaque around, smiling when he recognized a plump farmer with a plump pig tucked under his arm. It was an exceptional piece of work—funny, appealing, with a strong streak of whimsy about it. He studied the rest of the figurines, amazed at their detail and craftsmanship. There was no question about it—the lady had talent.

He was at the kitchen window, watching a blue jay at the bird feeder, when Sarah came flying back into the kitchen. He turned, experiencing such a jolt that he couldn't move.

She was dressed in a soft yellow dress with long full sleeves, the swirl of the fabric accentuating her slenderness. Her hair was in its usual riot, but she had pulled it back from her face and fastened it with two big combs, the style revealing her delicate bone structure, her slender neck and heart-shaped face. She wasn't beautiful—not in the classical sense—but there was a wholesomeness, an air of whimsy, something that bordered on the unusual, that fascinated the hell out of him. And suddenly he wanted to touch her in the worst way.

She sounded totally distracted when she muttered, "Where are my darned shoes?"

Trying to ignore the stampeding sensations in his chest, Nat shifted. He spotted them on the chair closest to him, and he reached out and picked them up. "Are these the ones?"

She made a disgusted sound and reached for them. "Yes."

She took them from him and slipped them on, sunlight catching in her hair when she stood up. Nat only had so much willpower, and it was fading fast. But when she tossed her head to clear her hair from her face, he totally lost it. His palms itched, and he knew he had to bury his hands in that hair.

"Sarah."

She looked up at him, clearly caught off guard by how close he was. Her lips parted, and a startled look appeared in her eyes, but what did him in was the catch he heard in her breath. His gut clenching into a tight knot, he cupped her head in his hands, then tipped her face up, his own breath jamming in his chest when he brushed a light kiss against her parted lips. For just an instant she remained frozen beneath his touch, as if stunned by what was happening, then he felt her body sag and she exhaled with a low sound, her mouth going all soft and pliant beneath his. Her response was like a jolt in the chest, and Nat tightened his hold on her face, his lungs seizing up as his pulse rate took off. Lord, but he'd been thinking about this moment for so long that one small kiss was not enough. Not nearly enough.

Knowing that Davy could return at any moment, he eased away from her and looked down at her upturned face, feeling slightly intoxicated. She was standing perfectly still, her eyes closed, her lips parted, but what crippled his determination was the wild pulse in her neck and the rapid rise and fall of her chest.

Unable to stop himself, he shifted his hold, his fingers tangling in her hair as he kissed her again, moving his mouth against hers in a slow, languid way that made his heart pound. She was so damned sweet and so damned delicate, and the softness of her mouth sent his blood pressure skyrocketing. Fighting the urge to crush her against him, he deepened the contact, reveling in the taste of her and the tantalizing warmth of her body just inches from his. His heart laboring, he moistened her bottom lip, then took her mouth in a long, thorough kiss, his lungs malfunctioning as the frenzy in his chest expanded.

Realizing that he had to stop before things got out of hand, he reluctantly withdrew, tucking her face against his neck as he drew her into a full embrace. Swallowing hard, he smoothed his hand up her back, then pressed a gentling kiss against her temple, aware that her heart was hammering just as frantically as his. Releasing his breath, he dragged his hand through her wild tumble of hair and nestled her closer, a small smile appearing when he realized she was trembling.

He wanted to pick her up and carry her off, but instead he gave her another light kiss on the temple and massaged her shoulder, his voice soft and husky as he whispered, "I think I like this Mother's Day thing."

She gave an unsteady laugh and tried to ease away, but he knew she would go all shy again if he let her go. Shifting his hold, he put both arms around her, then kissed the curve of her neck.

"Nathan, I—"

The breathy way she said his name made his heart roll over again, and he closed his eyes and hugged her hard, feeling a grin coming on. God, she was too sweet for words.

Hearing the toilet flush, and knowing Davy was about to come tearing into the kitchen, he slid his hands down her arms, then eased away so he could see her face. She surprised him by meeting his gaze—a little hesitantly, but she didn't shy away. Realizing she didn't know what to say, he gave her an out. He dropped another light kiss on her nose, then smoothed back her hair. "Happy Mother's Day, Sarah," he murmured.

She gazed up at him, then gave him an unsteady smile. "Thank you, Nathan."

The way she looked up at him turned his insides to mush, and it was all he could do to keep from pulling her back into his arms. Instead, he touched her small pearl earring, then smoothed his hands back down her arms. "You're very welcome."

"Hey, Mom! Where did you put my jacket?"

Sarah gave Nat a look that was tinged with regret, then reluctantly eased away. And Nat reluctantly let her go.

He knew she was shaken by what had happened between them, and it took nearly the entire trip to Millard before she started to relax. It wasn't until Davy made the comment, his tone hushed with awe, that their waiter walked like he had bricks in his underwear that the last trace of hesitancy disappeared.

Doing her best to look stern, Sarah tried to scold her son, but Nat started laughing. Partly because she looked so damned adorable when she tried to be stern, and partly because the waiter *did* walk like he had a load of bricks in his shorts. By the time they finished dinner, she was scolding *him,* and she only blushed a little when he lifted a tendril of hair back off her face.

He had intended on taking them to a movie, but Davy had started fidgeting and looking uncomfortable. He whispered that it was okay, that there was a special on TV his mother wanted to watch. Nat had a hunch that Davy was feeling guilty. He had seen the kid sneak a peak at the bill, and he'd also seen the look that had flitted across Davy's face when he'd seen the total. But Nat never let on that he'd noticed. As soon as he got the chance, he was going to have to make it clear to the kid that he'd wanted to take his mom to dinner, anyway; Davy had just provided a good excuse.

There wasn't even a trace of strain on the trip back to Alton, and during the drive, Nat managed to find out quite a bit about Sarah. No mention was made of Davy's father, however, but Nat strongly suspected that he was the cause of her wariness. He decided the guy needed his head caved in.

Sarah's invitation to come in for coffee disrupted his dark thoughts about Davy's father, while Davy's burst of enthusiastic chatter made him grin. If nothing else, he had an ally in the kid.

At Davy's insistence, Nat went back to the trailer and got Scout. By the time he returned, Sarah had made coffee and popcorn and had changed into a fuzzy gray sweat suit exactly the same color as her eyes. Davy, sporting a Wayne Gretzky hockey jersey and a scruffy pair of sweatpants, welcomed the dog with an exuberant hug and an old tennis ball. Scout obviously knew what that was all about. He crouched down, poised for action, and Davy giggled and chucked the ball down the hallway. Sarah's only precaution was to shut the bathroom door so they didn't kill themselves.

But the evening really began for Nat when Sarah came into the living room carrying a second bowl of popcorn. He was sitting on the sofa, flipping through the TV listings when she entered. Tossing the paper aside, he took the bowl out of her hands, set it on the table, then caught her wrist and pulled her toward him. "Come here, Sarah Jefferies," he said, his tone soft.

She stared down at him, giving him the same look she used on Davy, a hint of humor in her eyes. "Are you going to behave?"

Lacing her fingers through his, he gave her a lazy grin. "Depends on how much butter there is on the popcorn."

"This popcorn doesn't have *any* butter, Nathan," she said in that same censuring voice.

Amused by her tone, he pulled her down beside him, then lifted her legs across his lap. "Hell," he said, running his hand up her calf. "But then," he said, looking her squarely in the eyes, "I didn't stay for the popcorn."

He saw her pulse falter, and he heard her breath catch. "Nat . . ."

Cupping his hand along her jaw, he pressed his thumb against her parted lips. "Shh." He leaned over and brushed her mouth with a feather-soft kiss, his own pulse faltering. Withdrawing before things got too heavy, he slowly raised his head and waited for her to open her eyes. Smiling at her, he stroked her bottom lip with his thumb. "We're going to sit here, eat dry popcorn and watch the special. Then I'm going to get up and go home, okay?"

She swallowed hard, her smile just a little wobbly. "Okay," she whispered.

Slipping his arm around her, he drew her closer and snuggled her head on his shoulder. Reaching for the remote control, he switched the channel, then propped his feet on the coffee table and nestled deeper into the sofa.

He half expected her to move when Davy and the dog came into the room, but she only asked her son to shut off the hall light. Davy gave them a wise look and a slightly discomfited grin. Nat grinned back; the kid was all right. He patted the space on the other side of him. "Come sit with us, sport."

"Naw," said Davy, pulling a throw off the love seat. "Me and Scout are going to lie on the floor."

"Scout and I," his mother corrected.

Davy rolled his eyes. "Scout and I." He looked at Nat. "Can he have popcorn?"

Nat lightly pinched Sarah's waist. "Seeing as there's no butter on it, I guess so."

"Mom says too much butter isn't good for you." He dragged his own bowl closer and gave Scout some popcorn. "Did you know popcorn is good for your teeth?" he said, exposing his teeth in a leer. Scout lifted his head and exposed all of his in an equally phony leer.

Sarah tipped her head back and laughed, and it was right then—at that precise moment—that Nat knew he was head over heels in love with her. A week—he had known her one lousy week—and she had him tied up in knots. It wasn't supposed to happen that fast—and it certainly wasn't supposed to happen now, when he would be heading out of the country for a three-year stint.

Blocking out that very sobering thought, he tightened his arm around her and rested his chin on top of her head. He wasn't going to think about leaving—not now, not with her all soft and warm in his arms.

Sarah shifted her head against his shoulder, then slid her hand down past his wrist, lacing her fingers through his. Swallowing hard, Nat shut his eyes and closed his hand around hers, his chest suddenly tight. Too little time. They had too little time. Pressing a kiss against her hair, he stroked her arm, shutting out all thoughts of what was ahead of them. One day at a time. He would take it one day at a time.

Chapter Six

Dear Grandpa,

I'm writing this under the covers again, so if it's kind of messy, you know why. I was going to do it after supper, but I had homework, so I couldn't.

I got lots to tell you, Grandpa. Remember how I was all worried about Mother's Day? Well, guess what? Nat—that's Mr. Cassidy, but he told me to call him Nat. Anyway, I told him I was feeling bad about not being able to do anything special with Mom—you know, like we used to do. So we made a deal. We bought her a big bouquet of flowers—it was really humongous, and really nice. Then he took us out for dinner. I wanted to pay for half of dinner but he said no, that dinner was his treat. Boy, was Mom surprised. Then he came to our house after to watch that special on the rain forest. I think he likes Mom, Grandpa, and I think maybe she likes him, too. They sat on the sofa together, and I saw him, you know—kinda kiss her when he didn't think I was looking. You'd like him, Grandpa. Mr. Manson works for him and he says that Nathan Cassidy is a real straight shooter, and a "hell of a good guy." It's okay to swear when I'm telling you what someone else said, isn't it? That's why I put it in quotation marks, just so you know. It made me feel really good inside when Mr. Manson said that—like it would if he was my dad.

Anyhow, Mom has asked him over for supper a few times, and he took us to the movies last night, and he's come to my ball practice twice. And if he doesn't come over, he phones every night, and he teases Mom. I bet you he was a real good ball player, Grandpa. He can throw the ball all the way from center field to home plate.

The track meet is this Friday and Saturday. Nat's not going to be able to come to anything because he has to work, but he's taking Mom and me to the dance Saturday night. Mom says I can go for a little while. Jimmy's going, too, then I'm going to sleep over at his house. His grandma is there, so she's going to look after us.

I'm getting kinda sleepy, Grandpa, so I'm going to put this away and turn off the flashlight. I'll write you again real soon. And I'll tell you how I do in the track stuff on Friday. Mr. Benson thinks our team should win our division. I hope so. I hate the team from Barryville—they're all a bunch of dweebs.

Your grandson, Davy

Saturday, May 27

Sarah stood in front of the mirror, muttering to herself, trying to wrestle her hair into some kind of order. But she wasn't having much luck. She'd spent the whole day at the tournament, and she looked like a wreck. It had rained in the morning, then gotten hot and windy in the afternoon, and her hair looked as though it had been dried in a wind tunnel. For the nine-hundredth time she was tempted to get it all hacked off. Heaving a disgusted sigh, she slammed down the brush. Some choice—if she got it cut off, she'd end up looking like Little Orphan Annie.

"Hey, Mom! Nat's here!"

Closing her eyes, Sarah drew a deep breath, trying to ignore the wild flutter in her chest. Lord, she was nervous. It would be the first time that she and Nat had gone anywhere together in Alton. Oh, he had taken her for coffee that one time, and he had taken them to the movies in Millard, but that wasn't the same. Tonight would be the first time everyone would find out that Sarah Anne Jefferies wasn't spending her evenings at home alone, making dough men in her spare time.

"Mom! Come *on.*"

Fortifying herself with another breath, Sarah opened her eyes and stared at herself in the mirror. Great. On top of everything else, a whole new crop of freckles had sprouted after a day in the sun.

There was a knock on the bedroom door, and Davy spoke. "What's taking you so long, Mom?"

Girding herself for her first confrontation, Sarah squared her shoulders and opened the door.

Davy looked at her, his eyes widening, his expression frozen in awe. "Wow," he whispered reverently. "Do you ever look nice, Mom."

Sarah gazed down at her small son, a smile working its way free. Too bad Davy wasn't her date. *A date.* In a matter of minutes, she and Nathan Cassidy would be walking into the school gymnasium together, and what had been private would suddenly become public. The butterflies in her stomach took flight again.

Nat flipped through a magazine that had been lying on the kitchen counter, enjoying the silence. After ten hours of listening to the rumble of heavy equipment, of dealing with a crew of men and the demands of the job, this was a real treat. Tossing the magazine on the counter, he straightened, slipping his hands into the pockets of his slacks as he stared out the window. In fact, every hour he spent in Sarah's house was a treat. It was beginning to feel a lot like home.

Hearing a sound at the archway, he turned, his expression altering when he saw Sarah. She took his breath away. If he had liked her in yellow, she was a vision in pink. Well, he supposed the color was more peach than pink, but the shade did something wonderful to her skin and added highlights to her hair. The dress itself was feminine, with a pleated skirt and a deep V neckline that was emphasized by a wide collar, the tiny white flowers adding to the impression of femininity. She looked as if she'd just stepped out of the sunset and got wrapped up in the color.

He wasn't sure he was going to be able to speak for the sensation in his chest. "You look lovely, Sarah," he said gruffly.

She looked down and fingered the pleats, then looked back up at him, giving him an uneven smile.

Nat gazed at her, amusement building in him. So she was going to go all sweet and shy, was she? Taking his hands out of his pockets, he walked across the room and took the ivory shawl she was holding out of her hand. Needing to touch her, he draped the shawl around her shoulders, then gently pulled her hair free from the loosely woven fabric. He wanted to kiss her, but Davy was watching them with that sly smile again. The kid was nobody's fool.

Tucking back a stray tendril of hair, he smiled down at her. "So, Cinderella, are you ready for the ball?"

A tiny sparkle appeared in her eyes. "This is Alton, Nathan. We don't go to balls."

His amusement deepening, he fingered her hair as he continued to gaze down at her. She was so damned adorable and so damned readable. He knew she was nervous about the dance tonight, and he even knew why. Sarah Jefferies was going public. His grin deepened. And he was going with her.

They ended up walking to the school, which was only a block away. By the time they got there, Sarah's nervousness had disappeared, but Nat kept a firm hold on her hand, half expecting her to bolt. The sounds of a country band with a rock-and-roll beat blared from the gym, and a few people were standing in groups in the wide corridor adjacent to the auditorium.

Nat was well aware of the looks and whispers when they entered the gym, and he was also well aware of the fine color creeping up her cheeks. He didn't know why that touch of bashfulness delighted him so much, but it did. As he gazed down at her, he saw her chin come up a notch, and he almost laughed. It was a damned appealing mix, her bashfulness and that touch of defiance. His Sarah might be shy, but she was no marshmallow.

He let go of her hand to pay the lady at the door, and something warm and wonderful happened to his heart when she didn't move away from him, but instead edged a little closer. Suddenly he had an overwhelming need to shield her.

Slipping his wallet in the back pocket of his slacks, he put his arm around her shoulders to ease her out of the stream of traffic. Davy caught his other arm, giving it an excited tug. "Come on. The Mansons are waving to us. See? Over at that table by the exit doors."

Nat looked in the direction Davy was pointing and caught a glimpse of Vic Manson past the people on the dance floor. Knowing a few more eyebrows were going to go sky-high, he rested his hand on the back of the boy's neck. "We'd better go around, sport. We'll never make it through the crowd on the dance floor."

Nat had grown up in a city, and he'd spent a good portion of his adult life in construction camps, so this was his first real experience with a small town, and he liked what he saw. Yeah, everyone might know everyone else's business, but there was a real sense of community, an air of hospitality, that kept him from feeling like a stranger in their midst.

And when people started stopping by the table, it was Vic Manson who quietly intervened, introducing Nat as his boss. Nat wondered how the good people of

Alton would respond if they knew how he had first met Sarah Anne Jefferies. He suspected they would run him out of town on a rail.

He was pleasant and sociable to every single, solitary soul who stopped by the table. But he didn't want to be pleasant and sociable. He wanted to dance with Sarah. Finally there was a lull, and he rose, pulling her up with him. "Come on, Sarah Anne. Let's dance."

Sarah tightened her fingers around his, experiencing another flutter of uncertainty. It had been so long since she'd danced that she wasn't even sure if she remembered how, and the thought of getting out on that floor in front of all those people made her heart pound. But more than anything, she wanted to dance with Nat. She took a deep breath, her voice uneven. "I'm a little out of practice," she whispered.

He touched her hair, a warm smile lighting his eyes. "I couldn't care less if you have two left feet," he said softly. "I just want a legitimate reason to hold you."

She stared up at him, a wild flutter unfolding in her chest. Taking another unsteady breath, she tightened her fingers around his, knowing she couldn't have answered him if her life depended on it. He tucked the tendril of hair back, the warmth in his eyes intensifying as his smile deepened. He didn't say anything. With that smile, he didn't have to. He gazed down at her an instant longer; then he turned and led her onto the dance floor. The band was playing one of those songs about dark nights and loneliness, one that was made for slow dancing, one that pulsed with sensuality. Nat released her; then, sliding his hand up her back, he pulled her into a snug embrace. Sarah had never known anything could feel so wonderful. Her throat contracting from the fullness in her chest, she slid her arm across his shoulder, feeling weak all over. As if sensing what was happening to her, he tightened his arm around her waist, drawing her even closer, and Sarah closed her eyes, slipping her hand up the back of his neck. Wonderful? God help her, this went beyond wonderful. This was sheer heaven.

By the time they finished the set, she was enveloped by warm, rich sensations that made her feel almost weightless. A kind of quiet, effervescent joy filled her, and she felt lighter, happier, than she could ever remember feeling. And she didn't even want to think about what those feelings meant.

Nat didn't lead her back to the table. Instead they wandered through the crowd on the floor, secluded in their own little piece of privacy. The music started up again with a 1960s hit that was pure rock and roll, and Nat looked down at her, a dangerous sparkle appearing in his eyes. Giving her a bad-boy grin, he picked up the beat, moving his whole body to the rhythm, and she *knew* this boy could dance. Catching her up in a classic jive position, he rocked her to the beat, that sparkle in his eyes daring her to follow him. She couldn't resist—not him, not the dare, and certainly not the effervescent high that made her feel lighter than air. If he wanted her to let loose and have some fun, then, damn it, she was going to do exactly that. Nathan Cassidy was going to teach her how to fly.

It was the most fantastic experience of her entire life. It was as though some door had been thrown wide open, liberating her from every inhibition she'd ever had. He kept her on the dance floor until her lungs were ready to collapse and her whole body was damp with perspiration, then he dragged her back to the table, laughing at her as she tried to catch her breath. He teased her and kept making her laugh, but what made her insides go all soft and fluttery was the way he maintained almost constant physical contact. It was almost unthinking, the way he rested his arm across the back of her chair, then idly caressed her upper arm as he talked to Vic, or the way he would turn her against him if they were caught in a crush of people. Without saying a word, he let her know that he wanted her close beside him, and even with the most casual touch, he made her feel special. Sometimes it was all she could do to keep from turning in his embrace and burying her face against his neck.

Vic took the boys home around eleven, but the adults stayed until the last song was sung. Much to Sarah's relief, Nat declined Joyce's offer for a ride home and coffee, saying they were going to walk. The intermingling part of the evening was over, and she didn't think she could manage even five more minutes of conversation, let alone another half hour over coffee. She just wanted to go home alone with Nat and shut out the rest of the world.

The minute they turned up her front walk and were secluded between her house and Mr. McGregor's, Nat hooked his arm around her neck, drawing her against him, then covered her mouth in a softly searching kiss.

Her heart went dead still and her breath caught, a heady weakness making her knees want to buckle. Lord, but she wanted this, the moistness of his mouth moving against hers, the warmth of his body so temptingly close, so tormentingly far away. With lazy thoroughness he deepened the kiss, and she swayed toward him, the sudden clamor in her chest robbing her of her remaining strength. Widening his stance, he turned her and caught her around the hips, pulling her up against him in a tight, intimate embrace that dragged a low sound out of her. A thick, throbbing heaviness blossomed in her, and she sobbed against his mouth, locking her arms around his neck, wishing he could drag her right inside his body. She could feel the tension in him, the hard, thick ridge of his arousal pressed against her, and her mouth went slack beneath his, the clamor turning into a desperate need.

With a low groan, Nat dragged his mouth away and forced her head against the curve of his neck, his chest heaving and his heart hammering against her. Tightening his arms around her, he dragged in a lungful of air and tucked his face against hers, his voice labored as he whispered huskily, "Lord, but I've wanted to do that all night."

Struggling against her own labored breathing, Sarah pressed her face deeper into the curve of his neck, her voice catching as she whispered, "Let's go inside."

He dragged his hand across her back and pressed a kiss against her hair, then spoke, his tone husky with regret. "If I go in, it's going to be too damned hard to leave."

Knowing any other answer was unthinkable, she caressed the back of his neck. "I don't want you to leave, Nathan."

Easing his hold, he tipped her face up. The illumination from the streetlight in front of the house cast his face in a mix of light and shadows, his expression solemn and intense as he slowly caressed her bottom lip with his thumb. "Be very certain that's what you want," he counseled gruffly. "I don't want you to ever have any regrets, Sarah."

Transfixed by the warmth of his touch, she gazed up at him, her tone certain when she whispered, "It's what I want."

He stared down at her for an instant; then, murmuring her name, he hauled her into a fierce embrace, his breath hot against her neck, the barest hint of humor in his voice. "God, you don't know how much I was hoping you'd say that." Without giving her a chance to react, he turned, pulling her with him as he started toward the back door.

They got as far as the hallway leading to her bedroom before the reality of what was about to happen set in, resurrecting the other reality that went with it. At the bathroom door she paused and eased out of his hold, then clasped her hands together. She didn't know how to handle this. How did she tell him that she was physically at risk right now? That she was going to have to slip into the bathroom? It was just so awkward.

Gripping her by the shoulders, Nat turned her so she faced him, then he hooked her under the chin, urging her to look at him. "What?" he asked softly.

Feeling totally inept, she glanced at the bathroom door, hating the heat that crept into her cheeks. "I—there's something I have to do."

A warm, comprehending look lightened his eyes, and with infinite gentleness, he took her face in his hands. "Do you trust me, Sarah?" he asked softly.

Meeting his gaze, she nodded. "Yes."

"Will you trust me to take care of it?"

He was watching her with such tenderness that, without warning, her eyes filled. God, how she loved him. Swallowing hard, she whispered her answer. "Yes."

Reaching behind him, Nat switched off the hall light, then drew her against him in an enveloping embrace. He simply held her for a few seconds, then tucked his head down against hers. "Are you okay?"

Feeling more sure than ever before, she shifted her head, brushing her mouth against his. "Oh, yes."

She felt his chest expand sharply beneath her hand, but he remained motionless, taking only what she offered, returning her light caress with immeasurable gentleness. His restraint, his gentleness, completely unraveled her, and she clasped the front of his shirt, not sure her legs would hold her. That was all it took, that one small movement, and Nat responded. Cupping her bottom, he lifted her up against him, guiding her legs around his hips as he turned toward the bedroom.

The faint light from the streetlight outside filtered in through the lace curtains on the windows, the pattern of the fabric mottling the bed in shadows. Tipping his head, Nat gave her another softly searching kiss; then, with an unsteady sigh, he slowly eased back, running his hand up her thigh. "I don't know how long I can handle this, Sarah," he said, his voice gruff with strain.

Taking his face in her hands, she leaned down, her lips brushing against his when she whispered, "I won't break, Nathan." She tightened her legs around him, her voice catching. "And I don't want you to try to handle anything."

The instant she tightened her legs, Nat shuddered and clutched her tighter, all hell breaking loose in him. She was hot and yielding against him, the heat of her like a brand against his arousal, and he groaned, unable to stop from thrusting his hips against hers. Emitting a low sound against his mouth, she flexed her pelvis, moving against the hard ridge of his swollen flesh. Dragging his mouth away from hers, he splayed his hand against the back of her head, his face contorting with a nearly unbearable need. He clenched his jaw against the agony of pleasure, moving in restrained counterpoint to her slow, tortuous rhythm, a film of perspiration breaking out on his body. His control eroding with each thrust of her body, he crushed her against him, his fingers tangling in her hair as he fought to contain the pulsating need that continued to build. He didn't know how long he could keep this up without exploding, yet he didn't know how he could find the strength to stop.

Tightening her hold on him, she pulled herself up against him one more time, a fierce tremor coursing through her, her voice ragged with urgency when she sobbed out his name.

Hauling in a harsh breath, he gritted his teeth, steeling himself against the agony of separation. Grasping her behind one knee, he pressed his cheek against hers, his voice guttural and hoarse with strain when he whispered against her ear, "Easy, sweetheart. Easy. Let's get into bed." Securing her in a firm grip around her torso, he gently disengaged her leg, shuddering when she loosened her hold, her body slipping down his.

Not sure how he was going to maintain enough control to get their clothes off, Nat steadied her as he slid his hand up the back of her thigh, pulling the skirt of her dress up as he went. Trembling and unsteady, Sarah made a ragged sound and dropped her forehead against his shoulder, her movements faltering as she slid her fingers under the waistband of his slacks. Nat felt as if he'd been hit by a thunderbolt, and he went rigid. Hot, driving sensations piled in on him, pushing him to the very brink and nearly decimating his control, and he inhaled sharply through clenched teeth, sweat prickling his back. Just when he thought he had it licked, she undid his zipper, the backs of her fingers riding against his hot, swollen flesh. Unable to hold back a hoarse groan, he gripped her wrist and snatched her hand away, unable to handle even the lightest touch. Fighting to regain some element of control, he unbuttoned his shirt and pressed her hand against his naked chest, then shut his eyes and rested his forehead against hers, aware of how badly his legs were shaking. He remained like that for a moment, collecting what little reserve he had left; then he slid his hand along her jaw, thrusting his fingers into the silky mass of her hair as he angled her face up.

He gave her a light, gentling kiss, then let his breath go in an uneven sigh, his touch feather-soft as he stroked her cheeks with his thumb. "Come to bed, Sarah," he whispered.

Her hand closed around his wrist, and he felt her take a deep, steadying breath, the pulse in her neck wild and erratic. Finally she eased away and looked up at him, her eyes dark and mesmerizing in the faint light. Bracing himself for the endurance test ahead of him, he dropped his hand and started undoing the tiny pearl buttons down the front of her dress.

By the time he had removed both his clothes and hers, his hands were shaking so badly he had trouble tearing open the small foil package he had taken from his slacks. What little control he had dissipated instantly when she took the contents out of his hand; then, with her hair brushing against his naked chest, she sheathed him, her touch cool and gentle against his heated flesh, her tormenting ministration making all the muscles in his abdomen contract. Certain he was going to come apart in her hands, he carried her down onto the bed, unable to contain a harsh groan when his body connected with hers. Sarah choked out his name;

then, with another low cry, she brought her knees up alongside his hips, lifting her pelvis against his.

Sliding his arms beneath her back, he cradled her head tightly against him, his face twisting in an agony of need as she thrust her hand between them, guiding him into her.

A ragged, guttural sound was wrenched from him, his whole body convulsing as he thrust home, her body hot and tight around him. On the edge—on the absolute edge—of losing it, Nat went rigid, trying to hold on, trying to hold back. But she moved, and he knew there wasn't a chance. Not a chance in hell.

Driven by a need so raw, so all-encompassing, that he had no control over it, he started to move deep inside her, the pressure building and building until he didn't think he could survive the outcome. The only things he was conscious of were Sarah and the frenzy of need that possessed him.

His voice thick with strain, he urged her on, holding her with every ounce of strength he had. Thrusting his hand beneath her, he lifted her hips hard against him, the tension in her making her movements wild and incoherent. Then, giving a choked cry, she arched against him, her whole body going rigid as she convulsed around him, the heavy contractions of her body sending him over the edge. Crushing her against him, Nat let go, his wrenching release sending violent tremors through him, leaving him spent and shaking. Never in his entire life had he experienced anything like it. Total and complete, it was as if two halves had been welded into one glorious whole. And he loved her—oh, God, how he loved her.

Reality filtered in piece by piece, and he realized she was clinging to him with the same desperate strength as he was holding her. Taking a deep, unsteady breath, he tucked her face more securely against his neck, a great, huge tenderness blossoming in his chest. His throat cramping from the fullness around his heart, he nestled her closer and pressed a soft kiss against her neck, aware for the first time that tears were slipping down her temples. With infinite gentleness he wiped away one trail with his thumb.

He held her like that for a long time, until she stopped trembling and his heart rate settled. Then, brushing her hair behind her ear, he gathered his strength and raised his head, cupping his palm against her jaw as he kissed her softly, soothingly, with immeasurable care. Releasing his breath on a long sigh, he finally lifted his head and looked down at her, grateful for the faint light infiltrating the room.

Her eyes shimmering with tears, Sarah gazed up at him, her fingers trembling as she covered his hand; then, with a shaky sigh, she turned and kissed the inside of his wrist. There was so much feeling, such unspoken communication, in that one small gesture that Nat felt almost raw inside. He wanted to tell her that he loved her, but he couldn't lay that on her. Not now. Not when he could offer her nothing but his coming absence. Brushing his fingers against her ear, he turned her head, angling his mouth against hers in a light, lingering kiss.

His chest expanding with all the feelings inside him, he slowly raised his head and gazed down at her, a soft smile settling around his mouth. Wiping the moisture off her bottom lip with his thumb, he spoke, his voice roughened with emotion, his tone a mixture of praise and amusement. "Well, well, Sarah Anne. Now I know what a nuclear meltdown feels like."

She gave a husky little laugh and hugged him, her hair feathering across his arm. Feeling more content than he could ever have imagined, he fulfilled his own personal fantasy and began running his hand through the thick, copper mass, reveling in how the silky strands curled around his fingers. He knew he was too heavy for her, but he could not bring himself to move away. At least, not yet. Shifting his head, he found her mouth, savoring the pure enjoyment of a long, softly searching kiss. Lord, but she was sweet.

Sighing with pure satisfaction, he lifted his head and gazed down at her, smiling into her eyes. "Do you have any house rules about second helpings?"

She grinned at him. "Not if it's the main course."

He laughed, gave her a hard hug and kissed her soundly. Collecting his strength, he braced himself to make the move, wishing he could hold her like this all night, knowing he couldn't. Sucking in his breath through clenched teeth, he abruptly withdrew, his flesh so sensitized it was almost tender. Sarah convulsed beneath him, and he held her tightly against him, giving her time to adjust before rolling onto his back. Shifting his hold, he nestled her head on his shoulder, then snuggled down in the pillows as he drew her leg across his thighs. It was almost as good as making love.

Tucking her hair back, he rested his cheek against the top of her head and stared into the darkness, idly stroking her shoulder. This was nice—terrific, in fact—just being able to hold her like this. He ran his hand up her arm, cuddling her closer. "Sarah?"

"Hmm?"

"What happened to Davy's father?"

She stirred and shifted her head against his jaw, and he felt the brush of her eyelashes as she opened her eyes. Her voice was quiet when she finally answered. "It's a long story."

He tucked his head against hers and stroked her jaw with the heel of his hand, trying to reassure her. "I'd like to hear it," he said softly.

She sighed heavily, then spoke. "I took a course in banking at the community college in Millard when I got out of high school. I met Jeff the last semester and we started dating. He wasn't from around here—he played semi-pro hockey with the Millard Devils. Anyway, we got married two months after I graduated, and I worked for a year, then got pregnant with Davy." She paused, and Nat knew she was staring off into the darkness, caught in her recollections. Finally she continued, her tone somber. "We were both twenty-one when he was born, and in the beginning Jeff got really caught up in being a father. But once the novelty wore off, he started to resent the responsibility. It was pretty obvious by then that his hockey career was going nowhere, and he was bitter about that. It was just a couple of weeks after Davy's second birthday that he pulled out. I came home from work, and he was gone. I haven't seen him since.''

''What did you do?''

''We'd been living in Millard, so I moved back here. There was a position open at the bank, and Joyce offered to look after Davy. And Dad was here. It seemed like it was the best place for Davy to grow up.''

Sobered by what she'd told him, Nat continued to absently caress her shoulder, considering the situation. She'd revealed more than she realized. She'd settled here because of Davy, because of the stability a place like Alton offered. But what disturbed him most was that she'd been abandoned by Davy's father. And soon she would be abandoned again—only this time by him.

''I have to leave the first of July, Sarah,'' he said quietly.

''I know,'' came her husky reply. She kissed him on the neck, then levered herself up on one arm, her hair a wild tangle around her face. She gave him a reassuring smile, her touch light and tormenting as she caressed his ear. ''It doesn't matter, Nathan,'' she said softly. She leaned down, her hand tightening against his face as she kissed him. ''You've already given me more than I ever hoped to have.''

Sliding his hand up the back of her neck, Nat drew her head down. It wasn't enough. Not the light brush of her lips against his, not the soft fullness of her breasts pressed against his chest. And not the short space of time they had left together. Not nearly enough.

Chapter Seven

Friday, June 23

Nat stood by the fender of the company truck, the steady rain rattling against the hood of the vehicle and sluicing across the new roadbed, cutting channels in the sandy soil. Water trickled down the collar of his slicker as he stared at the quagmire before him, the huge shapes of the parked equipment looming through the heavy drizzle. Damn it all to hell, couldn't anything go right? It had rained on and off for nearly two weeks, and the days when they *had* been able to work, he'd nearly gone nuts trying to stay halfway on schedule. Shaking his head in disgust, he turned and yanked open the cab door, scraping off the worst of the mud on the running board before he climbed in, his frustration at a dangerous level. His jaw set in angry lines, he switched on the ignition and jammed the vehicle into reverse, the motor revving to a heavy whine as he backed up through the thick gumbo. Right then he didn't give a tinker's damn if he blew the engine to smithereens.

Muck flew against the mud flaps when he pulled onto the highway, the steady whip-whap of the windshield wipers slicing through the grim silence. It wasn't just the damned weather that had him ticked off. It was everything. They were behind schedule, there had been several breakdowns, and he'd had problems with some of the crew. It was enough to drive him crazy.

Expelling some of his frustration in a heavy sigh, Nat reached over and switched on the radio. Finding nothing but talk shows, he switched it off again. That was one aggravation he could do without right now. Stretching, he rested his elbow on the window ledge, his mood growing somber. It wasn't just the damned job that was getting to him. In fact, it wasn't the job at all. It was this thing with Sarah.

He'd been walking an emotional tightrope ever since the night of the dance, and he didn't know what in hell to do. The only way he could get out of the contract in South America was to drop dead, so that wasn't even an option. Yeah, he could talk to Sarah about the future, but three years was a long time, and that kind of separation was tough on any relationship. Especially when she'd already had to deal with a truckload of crap once in her life. The only other alternative was to take her and Davy with him, but that was hardly an option at least from her point of view. Granted, on a job that size, accommodations would be provided for families, but that would mean uprooting Davy and leaving everything familiar behind. She'd moved back to Alton to provide a stable, safe environment for her kid to grow up in. He understood that; he would want that for his own kids if he ever had any. And he knew if he asked her to go with him, she'd feel she had to make a choice between him and Davy, and he couldn't lay that on her.

A painful tightness formed in Nat's throat, and he tried to will it away, but the effort only made it worse. He didn't know how he was going to do it, leaving them both behind when it came time for him to pull out. Lord, but he dreaded it. He dreaded it during the day. He dreaded it at night. The only time the hollow feeling eased up was when he was with them, then he could pretend nothing was wrong. Except it was; his whole damned life was wrong. And there wasn't any way to fix it.

And on top of everything, there was the kid. Two nights before, Davy had made some comment at the supper table about how maybe Nat could help coach when hockey season started, and both Nat and Sarah had gone dead silent. Sarah had abruptly left the table, her expression so stark that Nat had had to look away, a sick sensation churning in his gut. Feeling like a total bastard, he had explained to the boy that he would be leaving by the first of July, and why. Davy had stared at him, his eyes stark with alarm, then he, too, had bolted from the table. Nat had found him outside, huddled against the fence by the garage, his face buried in Scout's fur, crying his heart out.

A small smile appeared as Nat recalled the episode. Davy had let Nat know in very specific terms what a rotten deal he thought it was. Nat found it easier to level with Davy than with his mother. But then, Sarah never gave him a chance to level with her. Every time he tried, she either changed the subject or left the room. And even if she would have discussed it, what could he say to her? That three years wasn't that long?

That he'd come back when he could wangle some vacation time? That he'd write? Those kinds of assurances didn't mean squat under the circumstances. He was going to have to leave in a few days, and there wasn't a damn thing he could do about it.

His mood getting darker by the minute, Nat reached out and turned the radio back on. The aggravation of a talk show was preferable to the way his thoughts were going.

Friday, June 30

Sarah stood at the kitchen window, her arms tightly folded in front of her, the awful ache in her chest not unlike the grief she'd experienced when her father died.

Hours. There were only hours left. Weeks had dwindled into days, and now only a few hours remained. Nat should have left two days ago, but he had cut his planned time in Edmonton with his family down to less than a day. He had stretched his time in Alton for as long as he could, but tomorrow morning he would have to leave, and she didn't know how she was ever going to make it through the few remaining hours. The thought of having to say goodbye created such a wrenching sense of loss, such an aching emptiness, that she hadn't slept the night before.

Swallowing hard, she wiped away the tears that kept spilling over, the cramp in her throat nearly suffocating her. Unable to turn away, she watched Nat and Davy as Nat fixed her son's bike, their heads only inches apart. Her eyes brimmed again when she thought of all the repairs Nat had done around the house, of the work he'd done on her car, and now Davy's bike. It nearly killed her, knowing what he was doing. It was his way of taking care of her and Davy, of making sure they wouldn't be left to cope with a bunch of problems after he left.

The pressure in her chest becoming nearly unbearable, she tried to ease a breath past the awful constriction in her throat, a fresh swell of tears blinding her. It wrung her heart to watch the two of them out there, knowing how little time was left. And she wasn't the only one who was going to feel the wrenching loss. Davy was going to miss him, too. He had crept into her bedroom the night before, clutching the quilt off his bed around his shoulders, his voice wobbling when he whispered into the dark, wanting to know if she were asleep.

When she'd wanted to know what was wrong, he hadn't answered right away but had stood huddled in the doorway, his head bent. His small voice thick with misery, he had wanted to know if there wasn't something they could do to get Nat to change his mind. Fighting her own tears, she had tried to explain why Nat had to go. Huddled on her bed, Davy had listened, then he'd looked up at her, his eyes bleak with sorrow when he wanted to know if she thought Scout was going to feel bad, if he was going to miss him. It had taken everything she had to keep herself together in front of her son, to reassure him, because right then she would have sold her soul if she could have curled up in Nat's arms and wept.

And Nat. God, but it nearly killed her to see what this was doing to him. And she was partly to blame. He had tried on several occasions to discuss the situation, but she had refused to give him a chance. She knew that if they ever did, she would fall totally apart, and she didn't want to do that to him. He had to go; she knew that. She'd known that right from the beginning; and even knowing what she was going to have to cope with in the months to come, she wouldn't have changed one minute of their time together. Not one, wonderful minute.

Blinking furiously, she fished a damp tissue out of her pocket and blew her nose. She had to stop this. She did not want to spend their last few hours together in tears. And she did not want Nat to know she'd been crying.

She had nearly convinced herself that she had things under control, until Nat drew Davy beside him and showed the boy something on the bike. Then she totally lost it. Barely able to see, she headed for the bathroom, all her determination and self-talk not worth spit. What she needed was a good cry.

By the time Nat and Davy came in, she had used enough cold compresses to get rid of most of the evidence of her bathroom breakdown, but she wasn't taking any chances, so she deliberately busied herself with supper. She heard Nat tell her son that he'd better wash his hands because he had grease from the chain on them; then he came over to the kitchen sink, rolled back his sleeves and began washing his own hands. Sarah began dicing an onion for the gravy, not because she liked onions in the gravy, but because it seemed like a good excuse for the puffiness under her eyes.

Nat reached across her for the towel lying on the counter, then leaned back against the cupboard and began drying his hands. His voice was quiet when he finally spoke. "Sarah?"

Feeling a new surge of tears, she whacked off another thick slice of onion. "Hmm?"

"I'd like to leave Scout with Davy if you don't mind."

Slapping the knife down on the cutting board, she closed her eyes, trying to clear away the sudden thickness in her throat. It took her a minute before she could answer. "You don't have to do that," she said, her voice dangerously uneven.

His own tone was gruff when he responded. "I'd like to, but I don't want to stick you with a big hassle."

Unable to see a damn thing, she swallowed hard and tried to ease a breath past the tight ache in her chest. "He won't be a hassle—and Davy would be thrilled."

Tossing the towel back on the counter, Nat caught her by the shoulders and turned her to face him, forcing her to look at him. His gaze was somber as he gazed down at her, lines of tension bracketing his mouth. "I'm sorry, babe," he said, his voice strained.

Her eyes brimming, she gazed up at him, trying her darnedest to smile. "You don't have anything to be sorry for, Nathan," she whispered, meaning every word.

His expression strained, he drew a deep, uneven breath, about to speak. Hanging on to her smile for dear life, she shook her head and pressed her fingers against his mouth. "Don't," she whispered, her voice breaking a little. "Don't be sorry, Nathan. I don't have any regrets. Not one."

Closing his eyes against his own internal struggle, he pressed a rough kiss against her palm. Somehow strengthened by the torment she sensed in him, she slipped her arms around him and pressed his head against the curve of her neck, her touch comforting as she stroked his hair. Drawing a deep, uneven breath, she shifted her head and kissed him on the neck. "Spend the night," she pleaded unsteadily.

Nat tightened his arms around her, burying his face against her neck, his body riddled with tension. He didn't say anything; he just held her, his hold both fierce and gentle, protective and desperate. Smoothing down her hair, he gave her one final hug, then began rubbing her back, his touch slow and soothing. He finally spoke, his voice low. "I don't want Davy getting up in the morning and finding me still here, Sarah," he said, his tone gruff. "It's not fair to him, and it's not fair to you." Running his hand up her spine, he pressed her closer as he brushed a kiss against the curve of her neck. "But," he murmured, his tone lightening a little, "that doesn't mean we can't work something out after he goes to bed."

Buoyed by the trace of humor in his voice, she hugged him hard. He had been adamant about that all along, that he would never be there in the morning when Davy woke up. And he never had, but he had stayed late—very late—on numerous occasions, and those late-night encounters had been sexual revelations for her. He was not a silent lover, nor was he a reticent one. He had obliterated every inhibition she'd ever had, he had made love to her in ways she'd only read about, and he had lifted her to heights she hadn't even known existed. And through it all, he had always, always made her feel protected, appreciated and so very cherished.

Not wanting to dwell on either the past or the future, Sarah concentrated on that tiny hint of amusement she'd heard in his voice. She wanted his laughter. She didn't want him thinking about tomorrow. *She* didn't want to think about tomorrow. They still had tonight, and she was going to do everything in her power to keep it light.

Running her hands up his neck, Sarah stretched up on tiptoe, brushing a light, tormenting kiss against his mouth. "Figure it out, Nathan?" she murmured provocatively. "That sounds like work."

Laughing against the teasing lightness of her kiss, he caught her wrists, pulling her arms from around his neck. "You keep this up and I'm going to stuff you in the hall closet and lock the door."

Grinning up at him, she slipped her hands into his, caressing his palms with her thumbs. "No you won't."

He gripped her hands, stilling her tormenting movements, the sparkle of amusement intensifying in his eyes. When he spoke, his tone was eloquent with innuendo. "Your timing stinks, Sarah Anne."

Giving his hands a firm squeeze, Sarah laughed up at him, loving the glint in his eyes, loving the lazy, intimate half smile of his that always made her pulse flutter. "Yes, it does," she agreed. "You'll have to *work* on that later."

Determined not to let the dread of tomorrow cast a pall over their remaining time together, Sarah did everything she could to keep the mood light and nonsensical. She even managed to distract Davy, who trotted off to bed at ten o'clock, pleased as punch because she let him take Scout with him. Her determination nearly faltered when she returned to the living room after tucking Davy in and found Nat staring out the window, a bleakness in his expression that made her heart shrivel. Just for an instant her resolve wavered, the constriction in her chest nearly overwhelming her. But she somehow managed to will away the feeling and face him with a smile.

She teased him until she made him laugh, and it wasn't until later, until they were behind the locked door of her bedroom, that the mood changed. Their lovemaking took on a new intensity that night—silent, almost desperate, and underscored with a sense of finality—as if each moment would be their last. But somehow, through the long and solitary night, Sarah held back the tears. There would be time for that tomorrow—and all the long, empty days that followed.

When she awoke at the first light of dawn, Nat was gone. Panic welled up in her, and she got dressed, her hands shaking so badly she could barely manage the task. She kept telling herself that he'd be back, that he wouldn't leave without saying goodbye. With a chilling feeling in the pit of her stomach, she stood at the living room window, waiting for his truck to pull up outside. But as the sun edged over the horizon, turning the cloudy sky to a vibrant mix of red and orange, the panic turned into a cold, hollow dread. Driven by an urgent need to see him one more time, she snatched up her sweater and headed toward the back door, her chest so constricted with panic she could barely breathe. She could not let him leave without telling him how much she loved him.

But the instant she entered the kitchen, her world came crashing down. A huge arrangement of creamy white roses stood on the kitchen table, a long white envelope propped against the crystal vase, and she knew. She knew. A wrenching pain hit her with a devastating force, overwhelming her with an unbearable sense of loss. He was gone. And he wouldn't be coming back.

His eyes so gritty he could barely see, Nat stared at the gray ribbon of highway stretching out before him, the first light of dawn casting the landscape in various shades of gray. He hadn't slept at all the night before. And he hadn't slept much the night before that—or the night before *that*.

Propping his elbow on the armrest, he leaned back in the seat, trying to block out the churning in his gut. He couldn't stop thinking about those last few hours with Sarah. After she had fallen asleep, he had held her until the tightness in his chest got so bad he couldn't take it anymore. His insides heavy with dread, he'd gotten up with the intention of sitting it out, but as dawn got closer and closer, he knew he could not get through that final goodbye in the state he was in. He had picked up the flowers in Millard the day before and planned on taking them to her in the morning, after he'd cleared out his gear from Kenner's trailer. He'd gone back to the trailer just before four in the morning, and it was then, when he was setting the bouquet in the cab, that he knew he could not say that final, gut-twisting goodbye. So he'd written her a letter instead, then taken the flowers and the letter back to her house, feeling as if he were abandoning her when he closed the door behind him for the final time. He'd been so torn up, he'd driven the first fifty miles in a daze of emptiness, the ache in his chest nearly blinding him. It had been a hell of a trip.

His throat closing up on him, he rubbed the sting out of his eyes, disgusted at the moisture that collected on his eyelashes. It was better this way. It had to be better. Swallowing hard, he set his jaw against the unrelenting ache. But then, it couldn't get much worse. And he'd only been gone an hour and a half. Another hour and a half to go and he would be at Edmonton city limits. Half an hour after that he would be pulling up in front of his brother's apartment. Two hours total. Maybe he could get it together in two hours.

By the time he parked in front of the high-rise overlooking the river valley, Nat had such a splitting headache, he didn't know if he had himself together or not. All he knew for certain was that he felt like hell and he was looking for a fight. A wry smile appeared. He wondered if Adam, who was four years younger, would oblige him.

His body aching from the long-term effects of tension and too little sleep, he climbed out of the truck and slammed the door, the sound echoing in the stillness. He glanced at his watch, a flicker of dark humor tugging at his mouth. He might not have to pick a fight with Adam after all. His brother, who had a notorious reputation as a swinger, was not going to appreciate being hauled out of bed at eight o'clock on a Saturday morning. Pocketing his keys, Nat started toward the front door of the building, then paused, remembering he had left the key to Adam's apartment in his jacket pocket. Swearing under his breath, he returned to the Bronco. When he'd left the trailer that morning, he'd thrown his luggage into the back seat and vaguely recalled tossing his jacket in after it, but it wasn't there. Fishing his keys out of his jeans, he heaved a disgusted sigh and went around to the back. If it wasn't in the back storage compartment, he was going to be damned ticked off. He liked that jacket. Unlocking the door, he yanked down on the handle and pulled the hatch open.

His jacket was there all right. But so was a dark brown sleeping bag—a dark brown *unfamiliar* sleeping bag. Feeling as if he'd just been sucker-punched, Nat snatched up the jacket, uncovering a blond thatch of hair. His headache suddenly a hundred times worse, he dropped his head and wearily massaged his eyes with thumb and forefinger, swearing some more. Damn it, what was the kid doing in the back of his truck? And how in hell was he going to handle *this?*

Releasing his breath in a heavy sigh, he dropped his hand to his hip and and stared at Davy Jefferies. The kid was either a Class One faker or he was dead to the world. A tiny flicker of amusement surfaced. So much for making a clean getaway.

Experiencing a new tightness in his chest, Nat placed his hand on the buried form. "Davy. Wake up, sport."

The only response he got was a small sound of protest. Nat's expression softened. Folding back the flap of the sleeping bag, he gripped the boy's shoulder. "Come on, Davy. Rise and shine."

Davy's eyelids fluttered, then he murmured something and slowly opened his eyes. He gave Nat a sleepy smile. "Hi."

Bracing his arm on the back bumper, Nat bent over him, giving him a wry smile. "Hi, yourself. Do you mind telling me what you're doing here?"

Davy stared up at him, confused by Nat's question, then his eyes widened and his gaze swiveled to the street outside. His eyes widened even more. "Oh-oh."

Nat almost smiled. It was obvious that ending up in the city hadn't been part of the kid's plan. He stared at him, a no-nonsense tone in his voice when he asked, "Davy?"

His face paling, Davy looked up at him, a dumbfounded look in his eyes. "Where are we?"

"We're in the city—at my brother's place. Now I think you'd better tell me what's going on here, sport."

Davy scrambled up, his face stark with alarm. "Oh, boy. Mom's going to kill me."

Nat stared down at him, considering the kid's response. Mom probably *was* going to kill him. He exhaled carefully. "Your mother doesn't know where you are." It wasn't really a question. Jamming both his hands on his hips, he stared off into the distance, trying to sort through this mess. Finally he looked back at Davy, his expression easing when he saw the look of remorse on Davy's face. Draping his jacket over his shoulder, he reached for the boy, his voice quiet when he spoke. "Come on. We'd better go call her and tell her where you are. She's going to be worried silly if she wakes up and finds you gone." He helped Davy out, then started toward the apartment complex.

Out of the corner of his eye, he saw Davy drag his sleeve across his eyes, and Nat experienced a gut-twisting response. Damn it, but he loved this kid. Waiting for the lump in his throat to ease, he stopped, then crouched down and turned Davy to face him. "Want to talk about it?"

Misery written in every line of his face, Davy looked down and gave a woeful little shrug. Understanding the kid's non-answer, Nat gave him a lopsided smile and ruffled his hair. "Don't worry, sport," he said, his tone quiet and reassuring. "She's going to be upset, but she loves you, you know."

Davy's mouth trembled. "I know," he whispered.

Knowing he was going to end up in big trouble if he pursued this now, Nat rose. "Let's go make that phone call."

As Nat had expected, Adam's apartment was dark and still. Resting his hand on Davy's shoulder, he guided the boy inside and closed the door, tossing his jacket on the old steamer trunk in the hallway. Finding the gloominess almost oppressive, he went directly to the row of windows and drew back the drapes, then opened the patio door. Resting his hand on the door frame, he stood staring out. He felt as if he'd been run over by a truck.

"Nat?"

Exhaling heavily, he turned and looked at Davy, his expression easing when he saw the anxious expression on the kid's face.

Davy looked up at him, his eyes dark with worry. "Are you going to phone my mom?"

Nat stared down at him, contemplating the question. Lord, but he did not want to phone Sarah. If he'd thought saying goodbye to her was going to be rough, this was going to be even worse. He released his breath in another heavy sigh, then answered, his voice quiet. "Yeah, I'll call her."

Unearthing the phone from under a stack of clothes and newspapers, he picked it up, holding the receiver in his hand as he punched in the numbers. Still holding the phone, he turned and went over to the window, a familiar weight settling in his belly. What in hell was he going to say to her?

He let the phone ring several times, but there was no answer. Pressing the disconnect button, he turned and looked at Davy, the strain of the last few moments making his voice gruff. "Your mom's not at home, sport. What's the Mansons' number?"

That call was answered on the first ring. Nat knew by the tone of Joyce's voice that she knew Davy was gone. When he told her where the kid was, all she said was, "Oh, my God." It took him a while to get her on track, but she finally told him that Sarah had only just discovered Davy was missing, and she'd gone over to the road camp to see if he were there. Nat knew there wasn't a hell of a lot he could do about the kid. His plane left at six that evening, it would take six hours to get to Alton and back, and he was so damned tired, he wasn't fit to be behind a wheel. Nor could he bring himself to stick the kid on a bus and send him home. And he did not want Sarah on the road in the state she'd be in. That left Adam.

Closing his eyes, he tried to think it through, looking for alternatives, not even listening to Joyce's explanation. Adam. It had to be Adam.

Straightening, he shot a glance at the boy. "Joyce? Tell Sarah that Davy's just fine, and that my brother will be driving him home sometime this afternoon."

He made her repeat the message, then hung up the phone, a spurt of irrational anger reviving him. Damn it, this shouldn't be happening.

Slamming the phone back down on the table with more force than necessary, Nat looked up and found Adam lounging against the archway to the kitchen, his arms folded, watching him with a knowing smirk. He tipped his chin toward Davy, who was hanging on the balcony rail, totally absorbed by the view. "Yours?"

Nat snapped back. "Don't push it, Adam. This isn't some damned joke."

His brother's expression altered, his eyes narrowing in a thoughtful look. "No," he said quietly. "I can see that it isn't."

As briefly as he could, Nat told him what had happened, his eyes so gritty he could barely see. He was running on empty, and if he didn't get some sleep soon, he was going to plant his face in the floor.

Adam got a jug of orange juice out of the fridge, then raised it in a questioning gesture. Nat shook his head. If he dumped any more acid in his stomach, he would go blind. Adam slopped some into a glass. "So, what's the scoop on the kid? How come he stowed away?"

Leaning back against the counter, Nat closed his eyes and rubbed at them, his voice weary when he answered. "I'm afraid to ask." Exhaling heavily, he raised his head and met Adam's gaze. "I need a favor, Bro."

Adam studied him, his expression sober. "I take it this move to Bolivia has turned sour."

"Yeah," he responded softly. "It sure as hell has."

Adam gave him a wry smile. "I heard. Yeah, I'll take him home." He folded his arms again, then tipped his head to one side. "Tell you what. Why don't you crash for a couple of hours, and I'll take him out for breakfast. Then we'll figure out a plan."

Nat almost smiled. Adam always had a plan. A bone-deep weariness pulling at him, he shoved himself away from the counter. "I'll tell Davy."

Nat decided there was something to be said for being dead-in-your-tracks tired, nothing got through the clog of gray fuzz in his mind—not memories, not disturbing stray thoughts, not even the tight ache in the region of his heart. Excluding his throbbing head, he felt completely dead. Stripping off his shirt and boots, he sprawled facedown on Adam's rumpled bed, his last conscious thought that he was damned glad it was empty.

He was still in the same position two hours later when the sound of the apartment door slamming penetrated the heavy blackness of sleep. Feeling a little like road-kill, he buried his head under the pillow, his heavy beard scraping against the sheet beneath him. Hell, he felt *worse* than road-kill; he felt as if he were hung over from a three-day drunk.

He heard the bedroom door edge open; then an uncertain, slightly cautious voice whispered, "We brought you some breakfast, Nat."

Trying to shake the hung-over feeling, he shoved the pillow away and rolled over, squinting at Davy.

The boy managed a wobbly smile, then gave a discomfited shrug, his gaze sliding away. He finally approached the bed, a white bag clutched in his hands. "We brought you some coffee, too."

Stuffing the pillows behind him, Nat leaned back against the headboard, his expression growing solemn as he watched Davy approach. It was pretty obvious that the kid was an inch away from tears. Sobered by what he saw, he took the bag, secured it beside the pillows, then grasped Davy's arm. "Come up here, sport," he said, his voice still rough with sleep. "I think maybe we need to have a talk."

Davy resisted for an instant, then scrambled up on the bed, a choked sob breaking loose as he flung himself into Nat's arms. Closing his eyes against the raw burning sensation behind his lids, Nat gathered Davy up in a hard embrace, his jaw clenched against the fierce ache that clamped around his throat. Damn it, but he wanted this kid.

He let Davy cry it out, his own eyelashes matting wetly. Three years. Davy would be so grown-up in three years. And he would miss watching it happen. Tucking Davy's head against his shoulder, he eased a breath past the lump in his throat, his jaws aching from the effort. He opened his eyes, a jolt of awareness shooting through him when he saw Adam standing in the doorway, his shoulder braced against the door frame, his hands stuffed in the pockets of his jeans. His brother gave him a small smile. "That's one hell of a kid, big brother. And I hope you know how lucky you are." Without giving Nat a chance to respond, he pushed himself erect, then quietly closed the door. Nat wanted to punch him.

It took some doing, but he finally got Davy to settle down. Finding a T-shirt among the bedding, he wiped the boy's eyes, his gaze somber as he studied his white, ravaged face. "I need you to talk to me, Davy," his said gently.

Davy met his solemn gaze, so much misery in his wide gray eyes that Nat's stomach knotted. "I didn't want you to go," he whispered, his voice catching on the remnants of a sob. "I woke up, and I knew I couldn't talk to you when Mom was there, so I got dressed and took my sleeping bag and snuck out to the truck. I thought I'd wake up when you went back to the trailer."

Watching the kid, Nat experienced a tiny flicker of amusement. Trust Davy to take the bull by the horns. His expression sobering, he wiped away the moisture caught on Davy's eyelashes. "I don't want to go either, sport," he said, his tone quiet. "But I have to. I signed a contract, and I'm responsible for the project. As much as I don't want to, I have to go."

Taking a swipe at his runny nose, Davy stared up at him, a hint of stubbornness glinting in his eyes. "Why couldn't we go with you?"

Nat sighed. "It's not that simple."

The glint intensified. "Why not?"

Nat found himself almost smiling again. "For a lot of reasons. You'd have to leave all your friends, the camps aren't always a nice place to live, and I don't think it would be fair to your mom.''

Davy abruptly struggled into a sitting position, his expression altering dramatically. The glint of stubbornness was gone, replaced by a flash of hope. "She'd like it, Nat. Honest she would. She's always reading about other countries. It would kinda' be like an adventure, and she'd like to go on an adventure. Honest she would. We sometimes talk, you know— about the things we want to do. Like go on a safari in Africa or go see those ruin things in Greece, and those triangle things—you know, the pyramids, in Egypt. I wanted to go on the safari, and the pyramids would be neat because we could get to ride a camel, but I thought the ruin things might be kinda' boring. But we both wanted to go to China to see the Great Wall and real pandas, so going to South America would be that kind of adventure. I know she'd go if you asked her.''

His hung-over feeling suddenly dissipating, Nat stared at the kid, trying not to get sucked in by Davy's enthusiastic sales pitch. He couldn't get sucked into it. There was just too much at stake. Taking a deep breath, he spoke, his tone uncompromising. "What about you? How would you feel about leaving all your friends—your ball team, your hockey? There won't be any of that in South America, Davy.''

Davy stared at him, then looked down, his expression grave as he twisted the tail of the T-shirt into a tight wad. Finally he looked up at Nat, his gaze somber and oddly mature. "Would we go back to Alton sometimes?"

Nat shrugged. "Sure. We could go back for vacations."

"Would we have to sell our house?"

The strangest feeling began to blossom in Nat, and his pulse rate accelerated. "No."

Mulling over Nat's response, Davy stared up at him, his expression thoughtful. Finally he answered. "Then it would be okay."

Feeling as though his whole life was balanced on some precarious edge, Nat studied the boy, one last question to be answered. His voice wasn't quite steady when he spoke. "Why did you want me to stay, Davy?"

His gaze level and unwavering, Davy looked up at him, his small face drawn and pale. Then he took a deep quavering breath, his eyes filling with tears. "Because I want you to be my dad," he whispered brokenly.

Sarah paced back and forth in the kitchen, trying her level best to stop crying, ready to climb the walls. For the hundredth time she checked her watch, her insides churning. Nat's brother had phoned over two hours ago, saying that he would have Davy home by four. Unable to stay still, she'd been pacing ever since, the minutes dragging by with agonizing slowness. It was half past three. Another half hour and he would be home—just another half hour. She hugged her sweater around her, her eyes filling up again when she saw the bouquet of roses on the table. She had nearly pitched them into the backyard when she'd realized what he'd done. But that burst of temper had lasted only as long as it took to read the letter. He had told her very specifically why he'd left the way he had, why he simply could not say goodbye.

Sarah pressed the heels of her hands against her eyes, trying to swallow the unshed tears caught in her throat. She'd been bawling her eyes out off and on ever since. But she had to stop. She was going to stop *now*. Nat's brother was going to think she was some kind of manic-depressive if he saw her like this. Straightening her spine, she took a deep, cleansing breath, then turned toward the hallway. She would go make the beds and clean up the bathroom. Scouring out the toilet seemed somehow appropriate.

She deliberately bypassed Davy's room and headed straight to the bathroom. The main reason for bypassing his room was obvious, the second was more practical. She couldn't make the bed when Scout was sleeping on it. A tiny smile appeared. She had nearly driven the poor beast to distraction. He'd followed her around all day, a worried look in his eyes, and every time she sat down, he'd put his head in her lap and looked up at her with such soulful eyes that she'd started crying all over again. In an act of contrition, she'd fed him the whole steak she'd had defrosting in the fridge, then given him one of her old shoes to chew.

Fishing the glass cleaner and paper towel out from under the sink, she straightened, prepared to polish the mirror and taps. She took one look at herself and junked that idea. Her eyes were so bloodshot and her face so puffy and blotchy that she looked as if she were having an allergy attack. She tossed the paper towel back in the vanity under the sink and reached for the toilet cleaner.

The first thing that penetrated the clog in her head was Scout bounding from the bed, the second was the scrabble of his nails against the hardwood floor in the hall. His excited barking brought her fully out of her numb trance, and her heart lurched crazily in her chest. Davy. It had to be Davy.

Dropping the cloth she'd been using to polish the tub, she sprinted for the kitchen. It was just as she was rounding the corner that she realized she had her sweatshirt on inside out. Adam Cassidy was going to think she really had a screw loose.

She looked up, her heart dropping to her shoes, her mind going completely blank. No. Her heart lurched back into her chest, suddenly racing with dizzying frenzy when reality hit. She stared at Nat Cassidy, her knees wanting desperately to buckle beneath her.

Nat watched her, his expression drawn and solemn, his gaze intense. Without taking his eyes off her, he spoke to her son. "Why don't you take Scout out for a run, sport? Your mom and I need to have a talk."

Leaning against the wall to keep her legs from collapsing, Sarah stared at him, so many emotions churning inside her that she felt as if there were a war going on in her chest. The sound of the door slamming reverberated in the charged silence, and she was sure she was going to faint.

Nat didn't give her time to. His gaze riveted on her, he started to speak, his voice clipped. "I've got nine days, that's it. There are accommodations on-site—I can get a new double-wide trailer and an extra vehicle. The company's bringing in teachers and medical staff, but it's still a camp stuck out in the middle of nowhere. I get six weeks' vacation a year, and the company provides regular flights in and out from the dam site. But it's still going to be three years of tropical living. It won't be a picnic."

A crazy flutter took off in her chest, and she stared at him, hope getting mixed up with uncertainty, joy wrestling with the fear of misunderstanding. Hauling in a shaky breath, she spoke, afraid of the answer, yet desperate to know. Her voice shook so badly she could barely get the words out. "What are you saying, Nathan?"

He moved closer, his eyes never leaving hers, his face carved with tension. "Come with me. Marry me and come with me."

Joy burst free, and she started crying and laughing, not one single doubt in her mind as she flung herself into his arms. "Yes! Oh, God—yes!"

His face ravaged by emotion, Nat caught her up in a crushing embrace, his hold so fierce she could barely breathe. But she didn't care. She didn't care. He was back, and that was all that mattered.

Slipping his hand into her hair, he roughly tucked her head against his shoulder, his voice thick with emotion when he whispered, "God, but I love you, Sarah."

Tightening her arms around his neck, Sarah dried her face against his shirt. She was so happy—so very happy. Her breath catching on a sob, she drew his head closer. "I love you, too, Nathan," she whispered unevenly. "So damned much."

Nat dragged his hand up her back, molding her even tighter against him. Finally he exhaled raggedly and eased his hold, his tone gruff with concern. "It's not going to be easy, sweetheart. Camp life can be rough."

Taking his face between her hands, she gazed up at him, her smile tremulous. "I don't care, love. We'll work it out."

He stared at her, then a twinkle appeared in his eyes. "Are we back to working it out?"

She laughed softly, rubbing her thumbs along his jaw. Lord, but she loved that slow, lazy grin of his. A surge of emotion wedged in her throat, she gazed up at him, her expression sobering. "How come you came back?" she asked huskily.

His smile softened. "Your son and I had a long talk."

Sliding his hand deeper into her hair, he lowered his head, covering her mouth with a sweet, searching kiss. "Just be sure, Sarah Anne," he murmured against her lips.

Settling deeper into his embrace, she ran her hand up the back of his head. "I'm sure, Nathan. Very, very sure."

Monday, July 3

Davy sat on the back doorstep, Scout watching with interest as the boy opened a spiral notebook, then picked up the pencil he'd brought outside with him. He was so excited he felt he had a fat balloon inside him. He couldn't wait to tell Grandpa the news. Placing the pad on his knees, he hunched over his task.

Dear Grandpa,
Oh, boy, Grandpa, do I have something IM-PORTANT to tell you. Mom and Nat are getting married the day after tomorrow. It's going to be so neat. We're going to go to South America and live with him while he builds a big dam, and he says we're going to do all kinds of neat things, and maybe we'll even go on a safari in Africa for

one of our holidays, and if we do that, he says we might as well go to Egypt to see the pyramids. Do you think we'll get Mom on a camel, Grandpa? I think so—so does Nat. He says Mom's a gutsy lady.

Just so you know, I'm really happy, Grandpa. So is Mom. I told her that you'd really like Nat. She gave me one of those big, hard hugs. I hate big hard hugs, Grandpa—well, sometimes they're okay, I guess. Anyhow, she gave me one of those dumb hugs and said, yes, she knew you would. And you would, Grandpa. He makes Mom laugh and he kinda takes care of her—like I was going to do when I got big.

Anyhow, now I've got my dog—Nat says Scout is mine—and now I'm getting a dad. Now if I can just figure out how to get Wayne Gretzky's autograph.

I got to go now, because Nat's taking us to Millard so we can get some different clothes to take with us, and they need to pick up some stuff for the wedding. I'll write you real soon, Grandpa. Then I'll tell you all about the wedding and stuff. Nat's whole family is coming. He has three brothers and two sisters and a whole bunch of nieces and nephews. I'm going to be the best man. What does a best man do, Grandpa? I hope I don't have to kiss anybody.

Nat knows I write you letters—well, he kinda asked me, and I told him. He didn't laugh or anything and he said not to worry, that it doesn't matter where I write you from, that you'll still know. He's going to be the best dad, Grandpa. I just know it. This summer has been better than Christmas.

Mom just called me again, so I HAVE to go. I promise I'll write real soon.

Love,
Your grandson, Davy

Judith Duncan

I'd rather have a root canal than write a biography, probably because there isn't much to tell. My early childhood was spent on a farm in eastern Alberta, where I had the rare privilege of attending a one-room school where all the kids either walked or rode horses to class. It was a great environment for a tomboy who thought horses had four legs so they could run twice as fast. I wanted to be either Dale Evans or Annie Oakley.

I spent a lot of my younger years talking to myself in the mirror, or to people who weren't really there. My elementary school teacher said it was because I had such a wild, unmanageable imagination; I suspect she was just being kind. I spent my adolescence and teenage years in the very small town of Kitscoty, where I put down roots that still tug at me now and again. Nothing is more grounding than going back and visiting old neighbors who saw you through skinned knees, music recitals, acne and the senior prom. That kind of continuation gives life a very enriching foundation.

I wanted to write ever since I can remember, but I stuffed that fantasy away with my prom dress. Girls were either nurses, teachers or secretaries. Secretly I wanted to be L. M. Montgomery, Mary Stewart or Gene Stratton Porter.

My secret dream of writing would have remained wadded up with my prom dress if my husband, Tom, hadn't literally shoved me out of the closet. He didn't buy my excuses about not having a degree in English, or not having passed through the portals of forty-three creative-writing courses. He said, "Do it, damn it! You won't know until you try." There are times I both bless him and curse him for giving me that shove. I love having written, but I get panic attacks the size of Montana when I sit down to start a new book. The process terrifies me.

My family puts up with my little idiosyncrasies and my wringing of hands. I have five kids who accept the fact that their mother spends most of her time with people who don't even exist, and that chocolate-chip cookies don't happen at home. They do power cleans when things get really unbearable and go grocery shopping when the fridge yields nothing but a bunch of wilted celery, an empty bottle of catsup and a withered corsage. And for the sake of highway safety and all those other drivers on the road, they take my car keys away from me when I get that glazed, I'm-somewhere-else look in my eyes.